Lilif

A Supernatural Thriller

R.P. FALCONER

ISBN: 978-0-9928498-1-8 paperback

Published by Silverstone Publishers

Paperback Edition

This book is a work of fiction. Incidents, names, characters, and places are products of the author's imagination and used fictitiously. Resemblances to locations, events or persons living or dead are coincidental.

FOREWORD

Lilif is the first of my many manuscripts to wander into the realms of novel-hood.

A lot of early mornings, late nights, love and doubt have gone into what you are about to read. I hope you enjoy reading this book as much as I did writing it; I hope you cheer every success and sympathise with every fall of my characters. Without further ado, I present to you: ***Lilif***.

This book is dedicated to my wonderful family for their continuing love and support, and to everyone who has taken the time to read it.
Thank you.

Contents

Prius

"I don't care!"

"Bu-but it's front page, shouldn't we ca—"

"Enough!!!"

Valda slammed down the phone and stood hovering over it, her hands on either side as if she were a lioness protecting the takings of a kill. Her hazel eyes searched for approval from Ricardo Braga. The skinning of his pristine bleached teeth gave it. Valda's strawberry-blonde hair is pulled back into a tight clinical ponytail, pulling her face taut, stretched and shiny, resembling melted plastic. At size 10, her waist is small and her breasts are petite.

"You're one tough bitch," Braga commented.

Valda lowered herself into her chair, smiling. Her large black marble desk made midgets of them both, Ricardo's white teeth shone, outstanding in its reflection.

"I hope this won't impede upon things?" Valda asked.

Braga leaned back in his chair and flung one leg over the other with a flamboyance that dispelled any notion of heterosexuality. He brought both hands together to clasp his knee.

"Do you think I would be where I am today if I gave a shit about what the press or people say? If breeders allow their daughters to wear lingerie, that's their problem, not yours, and certainly not mine."

At forty, Valda Payne was founder and full owner of BBL (Bad Bitch Lingerie). With a gross turnover of £500 million in 2012, it was safe to say her company sat firmly at the top of the lingerie totem pole, looking down.

She had begun her ascent to the top as a lowly shop assistant. Who praised, flattered and fucked her way to the summit of former lingerie giant Ellen's Brassieres.

"From a twenty-nine-year-old customer service assistant to CEO of Ellen's in less than five years," the *Financial Herald* wrote. The parts it missed out were how she manipulated, gained the trust of and destroyed rich and influential people within the company, separating powerful men from their friends and families, as a pride of lions would separate an elephant calf from its mother in order to kill without resistance or reprisal.

Their secrets held them hostage, and the threat of exposure gave her enough leverage to obtain what she really wanted from the company: its ultimate and absolute destruction.

She ensured they sold high when it was best to sell low; she advised they brand towards a younger market, knowing outrage would follow. Old successful blueprints went out the window, along with centurions who dared to oppose her, making way for ideas and plans that would spell the beginning of the end of Ellen's.

By 2005 Ellen's Brassieres had gone from a company turning over £200 million a year, to a company forced to close all its stores globally, trading exclusively online, barely making £500,000 a year.

Heads rolled when the financial reports came in. It was said in one day Valda had fired five members of staff, simply for executing plans she had crafted. Valda had a way of burying her ideas in the throats of others, deflecting all attention away from the real source.

When enough damage had been done and Ellen's was all but dead, she summoned the cream of the crop from the company into an emergency meeting, under the radar of shareholders. She painted a bleak picture of those above her, as old dragons set in their ways unable to cope with the ever-changing world of fashion and lingerie. She assured them the ship was sinking, and it was best they bail out while they could.

It was at this meeting that she pitched the idea of Bad Bitch, her own company. She offered great salaries and superb packages to lure the staff who had made Ellen's a formidable company for many years. Staff left and joined her, signalling the end for Ellen's and the birth of BBL.

Among aspiring businesswomen, her exploits were seen as legendary, beyond anyone or anything the world of business had seen in a while. For years after, business owners unofficially refused to promote women any higher than managers for fear of another Valda situation.

Valda stood and walked around the table towards her drinks cabinet, opened only for guests of Braga's importance. She poured two drinks, a brandy for him, coloured water for her, giving the illusion of the same beverage. She wanted him merry. Her sexuality held no weight with this man, but alcohol, drugs and enough flattery could make up for that.

Ricardo Braga more or less owned sex in Brazil and South America. Escorts, sex shops, porn films – the lot: dicks never entered vaginas, asses or mouths without Braga making money somewhere.

Valda wanted access to those territories. Access to even one-fifth of the income stream generated there would send BBL into a whole new financial space, doubling its income from £500 million a year to £1 billion easily.

Valda brought nothing to Braga's plate, financially or otherwise. He was there because he loved her legendary status. A self-proclaimed megalomaniac, he liked to collect exceptional people like stamps. He obsessed about power circles and the creation of economically dominant groups made up of people who made world-changing moves by any means necessary.

He knew her aim was to suck as much money and energy as she could out of their situation. This didn't bother him in the least: he loved the idea of taming such a feared and ferocious creature, accommodating every little request he could envision.

Valda gave him his drink and made her way back to her seat.

"Do you know why Bad Bitch has done so well?" She questioned.

Braga took a sip of his brandy, paused then spoke.

"Enlighten me."

"Fear!"

"Fear?"

"Absolutely. We are living in times of austerity; women are more reliant on their pussies than they've been in years – from housewives in homes, to prostitutes in the streets and brothels."

Braga smiled. The orange skin around his trout pout cracked, revealing pink skin in its indentations where the spray tan hadn't reached. He leaned forward.

"Fascinating concept. Elaborate."

"Well, in the current financial climate, housewives and girlfriends have to rely on income from their husbands and boyfriends more than ever. They can't risk their partners squandering all their pocket money on other women, so they have to make sure the bedroom's rocking and cocking. They have to out-spice his secretary, out-spice the little bitch at the gym – and that's where we come in. Affordable, cheap man control in a box."

Braga's eyes glistened.

"And the hookers?"

Valda leaned towards him.

"They need to make sure they're making that sale. Guys are getting harder to separate from their pounds and if he has to choose between two beautiful hoes he'll go with the clothes …"

"And that's where you come in!" he added.

Valda smiled.

"Well … you seem to have grasped what we're about," she replied.

Braga nodded and necked the rest of his brandy. He uncrossed his legs and stood.

"I'll get my people to talk to your people come Monday, and we'll get the ball rolling," Braga said, wrapping his scarf around his neck.

Valda rose and walked around the table to see Braga out.

"Fantastic! So we have a deal?"

"I don't see why not. Your numbers are impressive and you remind me of an early me."

His statement hardly flattered, but she forced out one last exhausting smile for the night and signalled the end of their interaction; as come Monday, Valda would have entered into a deal she had no control over – a deal that would rip apart her world and the very little she held dear.

~

The night shed the day's clouds, giving stars free rein over London's dark city sky. Stars fattened and thinned as if they were seconds away from rupture, the rest glowed constant and consistently.

Valda walked out of the lift, past empty offices, evacuated hours earlier by staff, desperate to start their weekend, grateful they had made it through another 24 hours unscathed and still in employment. No matter how impossible to please and oppressive the regime they worked under, anything was better than life on the dole, forced to fight for cleaning jobs, competing with people who would accept – and appreciate – a meagre hourly working rate of £5 per hour.

Word had got round that Braga had agreed to help BBL expand into the Americas, and staff drank to that, hopeful and optimistic about their futures, unable to fathom what the following year would bring.

Valda stopped at reception. Mercy was bent, anxiously rummaging around behind the pod, unaware she was being watched. Valda coughed to get her attention. Mercy stopped, looked up and almost jumped out of her chair, bringing her hand to her chest.

"Valda!"

Valda scanned her from head to waist, pressed up against the pod she stood behind. She held a gold envelope in one hand and used the other for expression.

"You're still here," Valda commented.

"So sorry. I was given a letter earlier to hand-deliver to you personally."

Valda squinted and homed in on it.

"And you couldn't deliver this earlier because?"

Mercy nibbled her lip with nerves, terrified either the right or wrong answer wouldn't suffice.

"You know, with Braga being here, t-t-t-then you didn't come down and I-I-I-I thought maybe you didn't want to be disturbed."

Valda exhaled and held out her hand. Mercy swallowed and gave her the letter. Valda snatched it and placed it in her bag and looked at her name badge: *Mercy.*

"Do you have children, Mercy?"

"Yes."

"How old?"

"Ah, sixteen and twelve."

"And you stayed three hours behind to give me a letter when they needed you?"

"Well, legally Sally can look after Thomas."

Valda shook her head in disgust.

"You're irresponsible Mercy, and I don't want irresponsible round here."

"Excuse me?"

"Don't bother coming back on Monday."

"But Valda… I-I-I need this job. Please!"

Tears gathered in Mercy's eyes. Valda smiled, spun round and headed towards the exit, shouting as she moved towards the security pod.

"Get your things together! Security will see you out."

Gestum

In this part of the world Patrick was considered more a simpleton than a sage. A big man who lived a small life, driving for people who spent more in an hour than he earned in two months. Many took his silence for ignorance.

He stood an impressive six feet two inches tall. The dark-brown skin pulled taut around flesh and muscles gave him the appearance of an embalmed pharaoh. His shirt and belt had never been troubled by a protruding belly filled with beer, fast food and neglect. His hands were steady, his eyesight 20/20, despite his advanced age.

Patrick stood by the back passenger door. The interior light glowed with warmth and welcomed Valda back. The pair stared at each other as she approached; neither said a word as she bent down and slid across the Bentley's caramel seat. He closed her door, assumed his position in the front and commenced driving.

The West End lights had drawn people to the road like moths to flame, phantoms obsessed with celebrity, their opulence and self-importance. Miniature clones of Kim Kardashian, Katie Price and Kanye West spilled out into London's roads, their vices fuelled by the alcohol, youthful optimism, ecstasy, coke and LSD that surged through their veins.

Valda stared out of the window as they drove past hordes of youths waiting to get into nightclubs, eager to dance repetitious lives away, the females unaware that they possessed a God-given ability Valda Payne could neither train nor, apparently, pay for.

Valda exhaled with remarkable exaggeration. Patrick looked up into the rear-view mirror as expected and met her gaze there. Patrick awaited elaboration.

"Do you believe in God, or Jesus, or whatever?" Valda asked.

Patrick squinted, thrown by the question but, unlike Mercy, unconcerned about the condition or angle of his reply. He held a position in Valda's life that exceeded his physical role of chauffeur.

"I'd say yes and no," Patrick replied.

"How is that possible?"

Patrick made a sharp left to avoid traffic.

"Where I come from, Christianity is popular, but I'm more … let's say spiritual."

Her silence drew Patrick's gaze back to the rear-view mirror where he met her again, her face fashioned with thought.

"Hmm, I don't believe in any of that shit."

Valda pointed out of the window, her reflection pointing back.

"Some of these people are living far cleaner lives than me and a majority of my associates, yet they struggle, day in, day out, while money swells in our pockets. What kind of fucking God would allow that?"

Patrick looked for sensationalism in her stare but she offered none. He exhaled.

"Ebry dyay debble help teef; wan dyah Gad wi help watchman," he said.

"In English," she replied.

"Every day the devil helps the thief; one day God will help the watchman."

She stared blankly then spoke.

"That's cute; next you'll be telling me money isn't everything."

Patrick looked away from the rear-view mirror without reply. Valda didn't expect it. She always talked to him about general subjects or personal matters that she wouldn't have dared discuss with any business colleagues or social associates. She couldn't trust anyone birthed from the same embers as her; opportunists, with a voracious thirst for everything.

Non-business or political convo of any sort could be viewed as a chink in her armour, a sign of human frailty among business gods and titans.

Patrick offered her an outlet to vent, confess and debate anything she wanted. He wanted for none of the things she pursued. He rubbed shoulders with none of the people she was anxious about. The people who really kept BBL running, people who could make life difficult for her, if only they'd stop looking at the black-and-white stripes merging to see how weak she really was without them.

The Bentley turned into Kensington, heading for Madia Vale. The pair sat in a silence, broken by her voice, so brittle and delicate he almost thought someone else had spoke.

"Your God won't give me a child."

Patrick looked up once more and met her in the slice of mirror. Her eyes had a film of red stretched across them, crow's feet radiated from their corners, tears gathered sparsely and dribbled down her pale cheeks. She looked vulnerable and childlike; he had never seen her in that condition before. His response was quick.

"God has a plan for us all, Valda … What is for you, is for you."

She didn't reply and he was grateful for it. His comment was neither a lie or contrived. In fact, it was right on the money, lacking enough personal detail that the non-spiritual narcissistic money-worshippers of the world would think it meant good things were on the horizon, when in actual fact the implication stood closer to "you reap what you sow".

They pulled up in Valda's driveway. With a sniff she drew her arm across her face and wiped away droplets of humanity. Patrick turned around, a pack of tissues in hand, and held it out for her to take. She snatched a handful of paper, blew her nose, wiped her face and let out a sigh.

"I don't need your pity; you're not paid for that."

Patrick sighed.

"You're right … Will you need me this weekend?"

"No," she said through a sniffle.

Patrick shook his head, got out, walked around to her door and opened it. She gathered her things and slid out onto her gravelled driveway. The pair stood for a second staring at each other, both quietly embarrassed for her.

"I'm sure I don't need to tell you to keep this to yourself …"

Patrick paused.

"I have no idea what you're talking about."

She began to turn, stones cracking beneath her heels.

"Good."

Patrick closed her door and got back in the car, unaware that he would be seeing her a lot sooner than they had both anticipated.

Domus

Valda's house was visually a carbon copy of her office. A shiny white marble floor carried you straight into a massive open-plan living area. Large black leather sofas circled a gigantic flat-screen television that was screwed to the wall. A platinum and crystal chandelier hung in the centre, while various Ancient Greek- and Roman-themed statues occupied various spots on the floor, each white marble with real gold trimmings. She had huge exotic plants on both sides of the TV and in various crannies.

Just before reaching the main living area, two staircases ascended, one on either side, meeting in the same space above, like lungs joined by a trachea. The kitchen went off to the left of the living room. A spare shower and toilet cubicle occupied the right-hand side.

Valda closed the doors behind her, dropped her bags to the floor and began to take off her coat and shoes. From her right, Alex trudged down the stairs, a newspaper, open at the front page, held outstretched in front of his face.

The headline read:

"Bad B%&ch's lingerie pitch to kids! Deemed disgraceful by MPs."

Valda froze on the second button of her coat, one shoe on, the other already slung half way across the room. Alex reached the final step and stopped as if he were too ashamed to share the same floor space as his girlfriend. He lowered the paper and folded it up. They both stood on pause.

"Tell me you knew nothing about this."

Valda continued to undo her coat, ignoring his question. Alex walked down and stood in front of her. Valda walked around him towards the sofas. Alex paused, tracing her movements.

"Valda!"

She turned and faced him, leaning against her sofa.

"What's your problem?" she questioned.

Alex looked at her, perplexed, shaking his head.

"Jesus Christ! You guys are advertising lingerie on teenage websites?"

"The website demographic is age fourteen to eighteen … Eighteen, Alex! Do you know what I was doing at that age?"

"I dunno; let's see, selling dildos to primary-school kids?"

"Get off your fucking high horse. You had no problem when I paid all your debt. How'd you think that money was made?"

Alex fell silent.

"Truth hurts, right? Want me to tell you where your chicken comes from, or who the fucking tooth fairy really is?"

Alex grinned with suppressed anger. "It's always about money, eh? Always about that money."

Valda leaned away from the sofa and walked towards him, stopping a few paces away. "Yes, Alex, it always is. Welcome to Planet Earth."

Alex threw the paper down, turned on his heel and jogged upstairs while Valda watched.

" Fuck this," he vented.

"Oh, you're leaving again? That's original. Don't spend too much of my wretched money."

Alex stopped on the landing and leaned over.

"Fuck you!"

Valda looked up at him and smiled, to annoy him.

"You can't even do that right. I'm not pregnant again, by the way."

"Thank the lord for that! You and children would be a fucking disaster." He hissed.

Valda paused, her face full of thunder.

"Truth hurts, right? Think I'll find someone my own age; ya know, start a family with a nice young girl. Someone with a heart and soul! Hope you and your money are happy together!"

Valda's tightened facial muscles relaxed, resulting in an ambiguous expression, unfit for their current interaction. They stared at each other in silence until she broke away and casually walked out of Alex's sight into the living room. She sat down, picked up the remote and turned the TV on, the sound low. Inside her, a whisper sat on the verge of a scream. Alex came downstairs a few minutes later and stood by the front door, watching her. He opened the door and stood.

"I'm sorry…"

She said nothing, her back to him, her face burning like white-hot coals, her breathing so shallow that she felt faint. Rage tore through every cell in her body. The type of rage during which you black out and come back to a dead loved one.

Alex bowed his head in remorse.

"I'll call you tomorrow, Valda."

He stepped out and closed the door, fading away, leaving bedlam.

Tears rumbled down her cheeks, taking black eyeliner with them. Her mouth shook as much as the Botox would allow. She bit into her bottom lip until her teeth were submerged in blood. Her legs and arms pulsated with fury. Her eternal whisper gave birth to audible speech, and speech became a scream that crawled up from her stomach and forced its way out.

She jumped up, clambered over the table and stuck her one high-heeled foot straight through the TV screen. Sliding her foot from her shoe, she left it hanging there. She grabbed for the nearest statue, a naked man with a discus, and pushed it to the floor with all her might, causing him to chip his face. Unsatisfied, she jumped over the sofa, bound for the kitchen like a lunatic, her eyes wide, blood drooling from her mouth, her eyeliner looking like war paint.

She pushed through the doors and went to the fridge. She grabbed a bottle of champagne and held it vertically to her lips, foam escaping from the corners of her mouth. She moved to a drawer and removed a large kitchen knife, an aid for more destruction. As she was leaving the kitchen, the window that looked out onto her garden gave her a glimpse of herself, bottle in one hand, knife in the other.

She stared at her reflection like a child would a distortion mirror at the fair. Her breathing eased and her arms lowered, dropping both items. Pain radiated from her bitten lip across her cosmetically deformed face. She placed her hand across her reflection, brought it back and struck the glass with her open palm several times, shrieking like a banshee.

She drew her arm across her eyes and wiped them. She turned and walked slowly back into the living room, where she fell onto the sofa.

She curled into a ball, closed her eyes and wept; Alex's words constricted around her mind, tightening their grip every time she tried to dispel them. He had achieved the unthinkable and found Valda's Achilles heel; a point of weakness, a way of making her lose composure and embrace the notion that she was human, just like he was, his words were as powerful as the sun and they burnt like hell.

There were tens of people who she had fucked over, shitted on and generally ruined, who would have paid handsomely to see her lose control – and even more for her to take the blade she held and pull it across both wrists.

~

She awoke to glorious sunlight ricocheting off her white walls and marble floor, giving her room the appearance of a creamy dream. The television slept in standby mode, her shoe still hanging from it. The statue still lay face-down.

During her moment of rage she had thrown her handbag over the table, and its contents lay scattered across it. Among her belongings was the gold envelope Mercy had waited three hours after her shift to ensure the sender's request had been fulfilled.

Valda exhaled and winced with pain from her bitten lip. She sat up slowly and stared for a short while, surveying the mess she had made. She stood and walked towards the TV, pulled the shoe out and threw it over her shoulder towards the front door.

She walked over to the Olympian statue and heaved him to his feet, his broken face as bad as hers. She swept the strewn contents back into her bag quickly, but slowed when she saw the gold envelope. She would have expected it to gleam in the presence of so much light. Instead, it seemed to absorb it.

She sat back down and pulled the lips of the envelope apart. As she were about to pull out the contents, a faint high-pitched sound seemed to emit from above, freezing her stiff. At first she thought it was the sound of a cat whining in suffering. She turned her head towards the staircase and listened. It came again, this time with greater clarity. It wasn't a cat at all – it was the sound of a baby crying.

Another sound followed, footsteps shuffling across the floor upstairs. She shot up immediately, as if royalty had entered the room.

She walked around the sofa and stood between the staircases, front door and living room area, the sound of the uninvited footsteps inducing fear, commanding caution, urging her to leave, but the baby's cry stroking her curiosity.

She took a deep breath of courage and turned towards the kitchen with her mind made up. She walked towards the sink, where the champagne bottle still lay on the floor, soaked in its own contents, the knife beside it. She knelt down, picked up the knife and made her way back out towards the stairs. She set foot on the first step and paused. The thought of calling the police entered her mind, as if she had forgotten it was an option. *What if you're imagining it?*

The fact she was in the public eye could mean the press getting wind that she had called the authorities to deal with a phantom and blow it out of proportion. She dismissed the option and proceeded.

At the top of the stairs, she looked down the hallway, across at the next set of stairs. Sunlight swelled in the passageway, melting into every crevice it could, making the white walls smudge. Every door on the landing was ajar – with the exception of one.

They had had a nursery built in anticipation of having a child, after their first bout of IVF. The nursery was ivory, from the cot to the walls and carpet. Life-sized polar bears sat in each corner of the room. Alex hated it; he thought it too sterile for a child and protested that it looked more like an expensive French hotel room than a nursery. His opinion had fallen on deaf ears.

Alex and Valda had met on the set of a TV show called *Beat The Boss.* Graduates were paired up with a company owner and set the task of changing any unethical practices the company may have indulged in, while maintaining profits.

Under pressure from PETA and various human-rights campaigners, the show was pulled after one season. Some bosses were found, threatened, terrorised and even attacked by people who didn't see the testing of cosmetics on rabbits or the child sweatshops of Cambodia as entertainment.

Alex had been paired with Valda; she gradually took a liking to him. He was tall, young, skinny, handsome and determined to change the world, which she thought was adorable. She was fascinated by his abundance of energy, fortitude and total lack of respect for power. He spoke out of turn, hounded and bullied her to navigate away from her company's practice and polices.

When the show was cancelled, he went his way, leaving a firm stamp on her heart, engulfed in the flames of attraction, so much so it stole sleep from her nights and hours from her day. She pulled in her resources, searched and eventually found him living in what could only be described as a squat.

She tainted him with opulence and poisoned him with objects a person his age could only dream of. Gradually, she replaced his charity-shop clothes with designer jeans and tops; his hair went from natural hippie chic to Vidal Sassoon standard. Everything that had made him who he was had been stripped and disposed of, until even he couldn't recognise himself.

Valda walked slowly towards the nursery. She pressed her ear against the door and listened. After a minute of silence she placed her hand on the handle, took a deep, silent breath and barged in. Particles of dust flew up into the atmosphere, mixing with concentrated sunlight, giving the effect of an enchanted forest. She stood in the doorway, staring in.

She stepped in slowly, waiting to be set upon by a deranged human-rights protester, carrying a baby around to show her how precious a child's life is: a lesson in moral enlightenment before he beat her head in with an eco-friendly cricket bat.

She crept in, hunched: the room ahead of her looked undisturbed. From her angle, the door's position concealed a small portion of room to her right, enough for a person to hide. She drew more courage, held the knife high and rushed to the opposite side of the room to view the room in its entirety.

Her back against the far wall, she scanned from left to right. Sunlight drowned the room, making it glow. Satisfied, with no sign of foul play, she lowered her weapon. The giant polar bears still sat guard in their corners, the chest of drawers was undisturbed and cupboards were closed.

She was almost sure she had heard a baby and footsteps up there, both sounds self-assured and bold as if they belonged there and she were the intruder. As she walked, she drew her finger across the top of the cot's frame, collecting a mound of pale dust on her index finger.

She had three thoughts. The first was how crazy she would've looked if Alex were to see her now, large knife in hand, strolling around the nursery, her face worse for wear. The second was: *maybe this house is haunted?* Sprits, hell-bent on tormenting her for all the wicked ways she had earned a penny, deliberately drawing her to the room to rub her face in the fact that, no matter how much money or power she had, God presides over everything and every man gets, or not, what they deserve.

Her third and final thought, which sat most comfortably with her, was stress. After last night's palaver, her strained mind could have turned the passing sound of a whining cat into a baby's cry, and a cat climbing up a fence as footsteps upstairs.

Valda stood by the door and took one last look at the nursery, still hoping one day the door would be ajar and in use like the others. She closed it, exhaled and checked the rest of the rooms, for peace of mind, before descending the stairs, back to the living room.

~

The gold envelope lay flat on the table. Valda picked it up, pressed the power button on the TV and proceeded to the kitchen. She placed the knife in the sink, and picked up the champagne bottle and placed it on the counter.

She opened the fridge and removed a chocolate mousse, grabbed a teaspoon and walked back into the living room, where she collapsed in front of the TV, switching to the business channel, surprised it still worked with its laceration.

One reporter and a media financial specialist debated on whether there was any truth that Hollywood was growing compliant with China's demands on the content of its releases relating to the country. Valda had little interest in the matter but turned up the sound, to give the house presence in the absence of others.

She exhaled, her cheeks puffed out gingerly, her lip tender and raw. She placed her hand into the envelope to withdraw the contents. At that point, her mobile phone rang in her bag. She leaned over and pulled it out. 'Alex.' She smiled and dropped it back in. She pulled out a small white card from the envelope. It read 'Lilif' and had a contact number beneath, both printed in gold ink. She turned it over between her fingers; the reverse was blank.

Noise from the TV seemed to drain from the room, her attention focused. She mostly received hate mail, business propositions, or letters from people begging for money, but this was original: this grabbed her attention and worked on that universal need to know. Who was Lilif? What did she want? Whoever she was, she had caught her with simplicity – there were no gimmicks or elaborate effort, just a name, number and wonder.

Valda placed it down on the table and reached into her bag for her phone. She laid it besides the card, contemplating whether she should call or not. She cycled through the hundreds of women she had met in her life and tried to place the name. She'd met several Lillys, Louises and Lisas but never a Lilif – she would definitely have remembered that.

She picked up the card once more and ran her thumb across the name.

"Lilif … Lilif," she whispered.

She placed it back down, picked up her mousse and began spooning it into her mouth carefully, avoiding her cut lip, her eyes fixated on the card. Making a call may seem like an easy thing for some, but they weren't public figures or owners of a multi-million pound company. When you occupied that space, every single move was much more important, requiring ten times as much thought and consideration.

Valda picked up her phone, scrolled through its options and turned on the private call setting. She had decided to feed her curiosity and call. If she didn't like the sound of the voice on the other end, she'd end it and get on with her day.

She muted the TV; the house fell soundless, with only the faint sounds of morning birds chirping in the garden. There was a pause of what seemed like minutes, and then the phone rang. Her heartbeat paced, her breaths deep and notable. She fondled the card slowly to calm herself, then there was a click.

She sat forward, her eyes narrowing to slits, her breathing silent, waiting to hear speech. The breathing on the other end was laborious, as if time and centuries of cigarette abuse had ravaged the person's lungs and voice box.

"Valda ... Valda Payne, is that you?"

Valda remained silent, searching her mind for a match for Lilif's raspy voice.

Lilif took a stretched rusty breath.

"I can help …"

Valda swallowed the saliva that had gathered in the back of her mouth.

With what? Valda thought, but dared not say.

"I can give you what your money can't, Valda …"

Both sat silent.

"I'm based on Lambert Road, just off Canal Street. I will be there from 3 pm until 4, number 18, today only."

The line fell silent, leaving behind a proposal and limits to ponder. Valda removed the phone from her ear. She leaned over and removed a pen from her bag, writing down the address on the blank side of the card, certain she wouldn't be going; sure it was a trap, devised by those who sought to humiliate her.

She picked up the remainder of her mousse, sat back and un-muted the TV. The debate show had ended, giving way to a business gossip show, the current topic Ricardo Braga's alleged meeting with BBL boss Valda Payne and the implications of expansion for BBL into the Americas. Typically, she would have been on the phone to James & Noble, making sure they watched for anything said that was actionable; but not now and not today, for her focus was fully on the clock in the corner of the screen, which showed 11 am.

Four hours until 3 pm, she thought.

Three hours and fifty-nine minutes until Lilif's session.

Lambert Road, Canal Street…

Valda stood and walked around the sofa, bound for her bedroom. Upon entry the lights faded in as programmed. She crawled onto her four-poster bed, draped in silk and satin ivory sheets. On her pillow lay a tablet she used to surf the net and read before sleep. She took a remote from the small cabinet on her side of the bed and opened the curtains and windows above. A bright morning breeze curled in, carrying the smell of nature from her garden below, designed to a fairytale illustration she loved. It had miniature waterfalls, stone structures, arches with vines twisted around them. Flowers of every colour of the rainbow made it a vibrant fairytale paradise.

She lay against her duck-feather pillows and Google mapped the address she had been given. She didn't expect anything to appear, yet it did. Number 18 Lambert Rd sat between two normal-looking shops. One sold confectionery, the other was a chemist. Number 18 looked newer than its neighbours: a large navy-blue door sat in a face of various coloured bricks, two frosted windows either side of it. Suspended above the door was a banner. Although she couldn't read the fine details, the name 'Lilif' stood out, with a slogan, "We'll make it happen" below.

She moved the image around to see if at any angle the subtext was legible, but no luck. She abandoned the task and sat back, submerged in her huge pillow. She closed her eyes, the warm breeze swirling around the sun-bleached room carrying the scent of the earth's finest fragrances.

"I can give you what your money can't," she whispered.

Curiosity killed the cat and satisfaction brought her back, she thought, her eyes closing, her bed too comfortable to resist its delicate embrace.

Valda fell asleep with questions, and awoke with them and the feeling someone had sat at the foot of her bed watching her. She sat up and stared at the space beyond her feet, her elbows angled for leverage. The tablet lay face-down on her stomach, as it did most mornings.

Clouds had gathered around the sun, the shade bringing definition back to walls and cabinets. A feeling of urgency washed over her from nowhere like a fighter floored in the twelfth round, certain of a points win, if he can rise and carry on for thirty more seconds.

She shuffled down the bed, sat on the edge and flipped the tablet round. The last page she had viewed was still there, but the time in the corner had changed, bringing the meeting closer than she liked. She jumped up without daring to think – in case her rationale mind made her ponder on what she was about to do and its many implications. She jogged downstairs, past the chipped Olympian, grabbed her phone and scrolled through her numbers until she got to Patrick's. It rang for a little while then he picked up, reggae music blaring, laughter and warmth vibrating through, his voice having to rise above the energy.

"Hello!"

"Patrick …"

"Ah, who dis?"

"Valda!"

Patrick paused.

"Sorry, let me go somewhere quiet."

The sound of the gathering began to fade until there was silence.

"Everything okay?" he questioned.

"I need you to drop me somewhere."

"With all due respect, you said you wouldn't need me this weekend."

"I know, but something's come up … Look, either you can or you can't."

Patrick could sense both desperation and frustration suppressed in her words. The "can or you can't" weren't real options, as the tone in which they were delivered pointed to an eventual ultimatum. Although they had an unusual relationship, he understood how good he had it – they both understood how good he had it: she paid him three times the going rate for a driver, whose only responsibilities were to pick her up on weekday mornings and evenings.

Patrick exhaled.

"What time do you need me?"

Valda looked at the time in the corner of the tablet.

"It's 1.45. Be here in half an hour."

"All right."

A burst of party lit up Patrick's end of the phone as someone exited the house he had been in.

"Patrick, I want you to use your personal car; don't bring the Bentley."

Patrick thought the request weird: She had never asked him to do this before. Her surprise request led him to the conclusion something serious was going on, something a simpleton wouldn't question but a sage could do well to at least query.

"If you don't mind, where are we going?"

"I'll explain when you get here."

"OKAY, I'll be there by 2.30."

"No, you'll be here at 2.15."

They listened to each other breathe.

"No problem."

Valda ended the call and sped into the ground-floor shower room, where she washed, brushed and groomed herself. She trotted upstairs, opened Alex's wardrobe and grabbed one of his hoodies and a baseball cap. She pulled on the jumper and tucked her hair underneath the hat, then went to the mirror to see if her disguise was adequate. She made a few adjustments, pulling the cap as far down as possible; then put up the hood for added stealth.

The doorbell rang. Valda ran downstairs, grabbing the card, tablet and bag off the table. She opened the door. Patrick had already turned, walking back to his car. Valda stepped out, closed the door behind her and walked across the gravelled driveway, haste in her stride. The sun had disappeared behind layers of hostile clouds, gun-grey and malevolent, waiting to weep.

Patrick stood by the back door of the car. Valda walked past him dipped low and slid across the cotton seats of the old Fiesta. Patrick closed the door and walked around to the driver's side. The car smelled of rum and Kouros. A faded Jamaican flag hung from the rear-view mirror as well as a knot of feathers and other bizarre trinkets. A satnav was attached to the windscreen, Patrick's finger touching its face, waiting for a postcode.

Patrick looked in the rear-view mirror.

"The address?"

"18 Lambert Road, WB1 6HN."

Patrick punched in the details and found it immediately. He reversed out of the drive way and set off.

Serpente

The clouds ruptured, spilling their load on London. The windscreen wipers whipped and lashed water from Patrick's screen. People in T-shirts ran with newspapers and bags over their heads, unprepared for the downfall.

Patrick looked up into the rear-view mirror, scanning Valda's face and attire; her cap pulled low and her lip.

"What happened?" he asked.

Valda looked up.

"To what?"

"Your mouth."

She sighed.

"It's a long story."

The light turned green and Patrick shifted his gaze back to the road. The satnav spoke, indicating they had ten minutes until they reached their destination. They came to a section of road controlled by temporary traffic lights, letting only a handful of cars through at a time.

Valda looked out of the window; the rain eased and sunshine breached the clouds in spots.

"I'm going to see a specialist; she claims she can help me with my issue."

She looked up, expecting to meet his gaze again, but he kept his head straight and his eyes on the traffic light. Judging by the state of her, Patrick wasn't quite sure what issue she was referring to. When he had dropped her off last night, there had only been one, and that was her inability to have children. Now her lip was mashed and she was wearing men's clothing, a millionaire demanding to be driven around in his clapped-out Fiesta.

"Someone delivered her business card to my building yesterday and I called her. She sounds genuine."

Another batch of traffic went through; they were due next.

Patrick looked up into the mirror and her gaze was already there.

"You think it's a bad move, don't you?" Valda questioned.

Patrick's eyes fell still.

"Well, I do. I think it is. I don't know who she is, or how she knows about me, but every fibre of my body says it's a bad move," she continued.

The traffic light flicked green and they passed through. The satnav said, "Five minutes until you reach your destination."

He remained silent.

"Patrick … didn't you hear me? I think you think it's a bad move."

"Sorry, I'm just listening."

"Do you think I should leave it or not?"

Patrick glanced between the rear-view mirror and road ahead.

"To be honest, I think it's a little weird that out of the blue a card just appears, and you haven't told anyone about your problem."

The satnav spoke again. "Take the third left and you have reached your destination."

"That's not true. The IVF doctors know – maybe it's one of their businesses or contacts. Maybe they didn't know how to suggest it to me while I was there, it would be against their code of conduct, right? Maybe they're just nice and they want to help for the sake of it." She said, her voice decorated with desperation.

Patrick passed the first left.

"Look, the turning's coming up now. If you're not sure, maybe you should rebook, so you've got time to research them properly and make your decision after that," Patrick replied.

Valda ran her finger across her broken lip. Rebooking wasn't an option: in fact, it was quite the opposite, a fact she didn't want Patrick to know about, as she knew he would smell what she smelled and strongly suggest she stay clear.

She wanted to be reassured, not assured it would be a terrible mistake if she went with it.

"I think I'll go... Look, at the end of the day, I've made hundreds of decisions that haven't seemed like the right ones at first, and I'm not doing too badly. If it's nonsense then I'll walk out, and if anything comes out about it I'll sue the shit out of her and crush her little business with legislation."

Patrick kept his head straight, unconvinced. They turned into Lambert Road and parked across from number 18. He unclipped his seatbelt and turned towards Valda.

Valda.

"Do you want me to come?"

"I'll be fine."

She pulled down the cap and hood.

"How do I look?"

"Like Alex."

"I mean, can you tell it's me?"

He squinted.

"I wouldn't say so."

"Good! If I'm not out within an hour, don't call the police – they'll leak it to the press. Call Alex, then you come and get me."

Patrick nodded and reached for his door handle. Valda reached over and laid her hand on his shoulder.

"Not here," she said.

Patrick froze, turned and looked at her.

"Too conspicuous."

"Oh." he replied letting go.

Valda got out. The rain had stopped, but the air remained damp. She moved across the road towards Lilif's building, making sure the hood stayed in place. The shops on either side were shut. The blue door was huge. A buzzer with a speaker was nailed to the wall besides the door. Valda pushed it, its buzz barely loud enough to hear. A voice came through almost immediately.

"I'm on my way down, please wait," the voice requested.

Patrick watched from inside the car. Valda met his stare until her attention was drawn by the unlocking of the door. Butterflies entered her abdomen; their wings flapped and tickled the muscles and organs within her. Suddenly she was aware of everything: a heightening of senses flushed over her. Nerves and self awareness ebbed away at her conscious mind, forcing her to question her reasons for being in such an odd situation. The door opened and the pair locked eyes.

Lilif had beautiful green irises that looked like they had been coloured in with crayons. The whites were clean and stress-free, her pupils greedy. Her face had perfect symmetry. Valda looked her up and down, her mature body wrapped modestly in a white fabric, her bodily proportions flawless, as if she were a grown cherub.

Patrick looked over. Even at his distance, Lilif's perfection stood out remarkably.

Valda stood in awe, almost forgetting why she had come. Lilif's voice had thrown a curve ball, creating an image of an old, hunched women, one leg longer than the other, commanding a compensating limp, her clothes stinking of cigarettes and stale cat's piss, black hairs growing above her lip and on her chin, her skin scaled and flaking. Instead, she exhumed mature elegance, and reminded Valda of Helen Mirren.

Lilif reached out and acquired Valda's hand gently, her skin felt tissue soft.

"Will you come in?"

Her voice didn't sound as rough as it had earlier, but it still didn't fit. Lilif tugged her hand to initiate movement, and turned to ascend the stairs, Valda looked over at Patrick – for what, she didn't know. Her mind seemed to have been wiped clean. She turned and followed Lilif, closing the door behind her, squeezing out daylight, replacing it with harsh neon light that shone from above.

At the top, they entered another door that opened out into a hallway, several rooms aligned either side. The walls were clinical white, with spotlights protruding from them. The fabric of Lilif's skirt hovered just above the black stone flooring, concealing her feet, giving the appearance of levitation. All the offices were numbered with roman numerals, the faint hum of conversation emitting from inside. The room they approached displayed VI. *6.*

Lilif slowed, placed her hand on the door knob, looked over her shoulder and released a small smile. She entered and stood, waiting for Valda to walk in.

Valda's mind began to run at a hundred miles per hour, a compendium of thoughts and feelings clambering over each other, trying to be prominent, trying to be heard, all saying Lilif's smile wasn't genuine, that this was a terrible decision, a choice born of desperation. Lilif's smile deepened and crow's feet cracked the skin around her eyes.

"I don't bite." Lilif whispered, her eyes glistening like polished jade marbles.

Valda ran her tongue over her bitten lip, the taste of iron faint on its tip. She almost turned and walked back the way she had come in. But the *"what if"* and *"if only"* factions of thought, would have plagued her childless life thereafter, she needed this more than she could've ever spoken in words.

Valda stepped in and Lilif released the door, closing it behind them. Valda noticed two things – the pictures on the wall and a smell of vanilla and various other spices she couldn't identify. The pictures were plenteous, all of various well-known celebrities. Valda slowly spun around, looking at them. Lilif took a seat at her desk and remained silent, leaving Valda to explore. Valda walked right up to one and stood looking at it, shocked, since she knew the woman: *Mariah Wray.*

"Believe it or not, everyone in the pictures has been treated here." Lilif said.

Valda turned and looked at her.

"All suffering the way you are, all that wealth and influence with nobody to inherit it …"

Lilif shook her head in pity, Valda turned slowly back to the pictures. Something unified them, something she couldn't put her finger on, a thread, linking these familiar faces. The answer felt obvious but her mind kept drawing a blank.

"Please take a seat. Time is of the essence. I have other appointments."

Valda walked over and slowly pulled the chair out, aghast at the ease with which she had taken the order; terrified by how badly she wanted what Lilif offered. Her personal limits seemed boundless, reminiscent of her rapid ascension in business.

Lilif's desk was black-matt. Valda observed a dark-red candle burning in one of its corners, rooted to a black saucer. Light rain bounced off the windows, playing the panes like instruments. The pair accommodated each other's gaze.

"Let's cut to the chase. You want a child and I can help."

Valda sighed. "Who told you that?"

"Does it matter?"

"Yes. I want to know who's been blurting out my personal business."

A smile cut Lilif's face.

"I'll never say. Let's drop it and get on with the session; time is ticking."

Lilif tapped an imaginary watch on her wrist. Valda smiled, uncomfortable with the trajectory of their interaction.

"Look, my dear, why should it matter who brought us together? Fate threw her dice and you got snake eyes. I can change that, right here, right now."

Lilif conducted her business like a rogue timeshare agent, constantly using time or the supposed lack of it as a tool to hasten customers' decisions, making them feel as if they were about to lose out on a deal that would never be offered again. Valda was fully aware this was a position she never occupied. People with her wealth had no sense of time: they commanded hours to slow, minutes to stop and killed seconds.

Valda exhaled.

"Fine! Let's get on with this. How does this work? How much will it cost?"

"Nothing."

"Excuse me?"

"Nothing. Not a penny."

"That's ridiculous. There has to be some form of incentive for you."

Lilif leaned forward in her chair, her hands clasped together as if she were about to pray. Her eyes widened, her pupils swollen, almost eclipsing her irises. In a low growl she spoke. "What would you give to have a child?"

Valda looked into her crayon-green eyes, the question melting through her Teflon-covered heart, attaching itself to feelings protected by ugly actions and outbursts, Valda's past trudged back in from the darkest corner of her brain. A childhood shrouded in rape, incest, murder and madness.

As a child, she had lived on the Church Road estate in Harlesden. A daughter to a once beautiful woman called Clover, who – over the years – had been weakened, tainted and dishevelled by a man both Valda and her brother Leon called father. A filthy hell-bound creature that smiled and projected wholesomeness. An ambassador for helpfulness in the community, Eric was an angel to most but little did they know that, at night, he crept into his baby's room like a creature born from nightmares.

Clover would cry in silence as her daughter whimpered, while he growled, thrusting himself in and upon her. His depraved actions grew bolder with time, having sex with both his wife and daughter in each other's presence, his son made to lie in his bed down the hallway, crying and praying for death.

One bright winter's day Valda waited for her brother at the school gate. When he didn't emerge, she made her way home. She found the front door open and was instantly glad she had found it that way, and not her father. She peeled off her coat and shoes and walked into the living room, where she found Leon hanging from the light fitting. He swayed so gently that it was disturbingly calming, his face blue, with an inappropriate look of bliss etched across it. He had found his release and in a strange way Valda was both happy for, and jealous of him. She kissed his hand still warm; switched on his favourite cartoon and turned it up loud enough so he could hear it, wherever he was, then she cried. When her mother got home and discovered him, she screamed and ran wild about the house, sense fleeing her, never to return.

Clover calmed herself and sat, her eyes, wide and vacant, looking into nothingness. Valda sat in the other mouldy brown sofa and watched her. Suddenly she stood upright and looked at Valda. "We need to clean up for Daddy." Valda thought it weird at a time like this to think of her father's approval, but neither questioned or refused. They went about the living room, passageway and kitchen, tidying where her mother had disturbed in her anguish. After they had finished, Clover told Valda to put her coat, gloves and boots on, as they were going to the shop. Once out, Valda looked at her mother striding along with intent. She seemed so calm, even stopping to talk to several neighbours, both on the way there and back.

Once back home, Clover dragged a chair from the kitchen, stood on it and untied her son. Valda watched from the door way as her mother rocked back and forth, kissing and stroking his crown, tears surging down her reddened cheeks. She turned to Valda and told her to prepare some rice. Valda stood, baffled. Her mother had never taught her to make anything; those lessons that are passed on from mother to daughter lost through years of torment and maternal neglect.

Her mother repeated herself, this time barking the order. Valda jumped and replied, "I don't know how." Clover began to cry harder, rocking faster, realising how much she had fucked up their lives with inaction. Clover looked up at the clock, calculating how long they had until his arrival. She stood with her son's limp body and propped him up on the sofa.

"Go and get me a blanket."

Valda met her mother's angry stare. "I said, go-get me ah blanket." She growled.

Valda paused then turned, bound for their bedroom. She came back down and handed the blanket to her mother. Clover spread it over Leon's body, pushing, pulling and contorting him, to make him look like life still flowed through his veins.

She kissed his mouse-brown crown and turned to Valda. "Right! You're going to learn today."

She walked past Valda and pulled her shoulder to initiate movement. Valda liked this version of Mum: strong, powerful, commanding, everything she should have been. They boiled some water, poured in the rice, then poured in the rat poison they had purchased from Hogan's wholesale store. Then her mother turned to her, her face serious.

"Never put rat poison in your food, Valda, it will kill you. This pot's for your father, and this one's for us."

It was at that point that Valda understood, at the tender age of eleven, that they were crafting the devil's last meal and, boy, did it feel like heaven. They hummed and sang with the radio in between bursts of tears and hurt, at times laughing like a mother and daughter should, as they seasoned chicken with sea salt, cracked black pepper and venom.

Valda took a second, paused and looked up at her mum. Within that glance she had finally understood how good her life should have been – could have been, had her mother had an opportunity to be mum.

"Right! Go and put on your best dress, the one your father likes. It's a day for treats."

They smiled at each other. Valda walked out and ran upstairs. When she returned, the table had been set for three. The rice steamed and the chicken was all but ready. Her mother stood still, looking out of the kitchen window; the humming, singing and happiness had stopped.

"Take a seat, Valda. Daddy's home." She murmured, her voice distant.

His key in the door normally initiated dread for both mother and daughter, and today was no exception. He came in with a huge smile, whistling like a good man. He slung off his huge work shoes by the front door. Clover walked out to meet him in the passage, in order to divert him to the kitchen.

"Hello, wife."

She smiled and kissed his cheek, as he had instructed her to do every time he entered his den. He looked in at Valda, sitting at the kitchen table.

"Ah, my lovely daughter."

He took off his coat and wrapped it round the back of his chair. He looked down at the table, the food steaming hot. He took a seat, as did Clover. Mother and daughter watched him as he made himself comfortable, loosening his top button and tie. He looked across at Leon's space, unfilled, and turned to Clover.

"Where's Leon?"

Clover paused aware, her next line would have to be Oscar-winning, or everything would be ruined.

"They sent him home from school early. He wasn't well; he has some kind of contagious disease."

Eric stared at her, his eyes wide; Valda kept her head low, looking at her plate.

"Disease? Where is he?"

"He's resting on the sofa."

Eric adjusted himself in his chair.

"Well, make sure he stays in his room after dinner. Valda will have to sleep with us tonight."

A wicked smile crept across his face.

"Anyway, let's eat up."

He stuck his spoon into his mound of white fluffy rice. Valda and Clover held their breath, looking at him out of the corners of their eyes. It was as if his spoon took a decade to travel from his plate to his face. With the first spoonful in his mouth, Valda expected him to jump from his chair in rage, demanding to know what they had done. Instead he spoke.

"Fucking 'ell, Clover, this rice is beautiful! You do something different?"

Clover smiled. "It's a day of treats."

Eric smiled back, then reached across the table and stroked Valda's little arm, running his fingers through the frills on her dress.

"It certainly is."

He put his spoon down, picked up the chicken leg and bit into it, humming.

"Mmm, you've really outdone yourself 'ere."

Clover looked over at him, licking his lips, his forked tongue running in between them. His stomach growled with acceptance. He put down the bone and picked up the spoon. Clover counted five heaped mouthfuls. *Still the fucker lives,* she thought.

"How was work?" Clover asked.

Eric spoke through chewing his rice and sizing up his next poultry piece.

"Ahhhh, the boss is on our—"

He stopped in mid-sentence and shook his head, his eyes closing his head jerked back. The girls almost rose out of their seats in anticipation. His nostrils flared and he sneezed.

"Shit!" he shouted.

He drew his arm across his nose.

"That fucker's given me his germs—"

Eric rose in anger, one hand beginning to undo his belt. Clover stood quickly and gently reached out to her husband's shoulder, the way you would calm a child having a tantrum.

"After, once you've finished your dinner, or it'll get cold!"

He paused, looked across them both, then sat slowly.

"You're right. Why should we let him ruin this lovely evening?"

A type of anger rose in Valda's stomach that a child shouldn't be accustomed to. Her hand tightened around her fork, visions of submerging it into his cheek and eyeballs playing over and over in her head. Her face had begun to betray her feelings; her mother rubbed her leg under the table softly and met her gaze with a calming stare that said, it will come, be patient.

Eric cleaned his plate then reloaded his rice and chicken. Forty-five minutes passed as if it were forty-five days. Clover and Valda were beginning to lose hope, beginning to feel as if this man had been sent to torment their lives, until each of them wrapped belts, ropes or cords around their necks, meeting the fate of both brother and son.

His plate was clean, both dishes and pots emptied. He sat back in his chair and loosened his belt. Clover didn't have a contingency plan: she had expected him to keel over the table after one helping, but still he lived, looking forward to beating Leon for passing on his germs, and abusing his daughter for pleasure. Clover knew his routine: the next step for him was to go to his chair in the living room, next to where Leon lay.

"Atif said you'd just been over there buying rat poison? When'd ya see one?"

Clover looked at him calmly.

"Rat poison? What on earth is that man talking about? Are you sure he meant me? I mean, half the time you can hardly understand what he's saying."

Eric began to lick his lips, swallow and slip his tongue in and out of his mouth. A thin line of sweat formed along his hairline. A mild look of discomfort crept across his face.

"I can understand him perfectly; he said you and Valda were there buying poi—"

His face and stomach squeezed in as if he were forcing out the biggest shit known to man. Eric's eyes widened. Valda looked at him and knew it had begun. He jumped up, knocking his chair on its back, ran for the sink, wrenched on the tap and placed his head under the running water. His belly made sounds neither Clover nor Valda had ever heard; he gulped water like a man who had been lost for days in the desert.

Clover stood and walked over to him. He pushed her away and looked up. His eyes and nose had begun to bleed. He made a loud donkey-type noise and lurched forward, grabbing Clover around the throat, his grip strong, his speech slurred.

"You flucking glitchhh … wud ya dun?"

He sneezed, blood splattering all over Clover's face. She held his wrists and smiled. He hung his head, his grip loosening, as if he were about to pass out. Somehow he found strength and stood straight, blood seeping out of every orifice, dripping out of the bottom of his trousers.

He let out a muddled cry.

Valda stood. Any other child would have screamed and cried, but his abuse had hardened her, making her a veteran of pain and suffering. She wanted him to suffer – she needed the devil to die. She walked forward and he slumped once more, his knees buckling.

Clover smiled and looked him dead in his blood soaked eyes, knowing both fear and rage consumed him; willing him to survive long enough to beat her one last time, a stern merciless trouncing, fit for her insolence.

Eric started to moan like a drunk man. Clover grabbed his weakened hands from around her throat, coupled them with her own and began to jig in jest, his kneecaps buckling as if he had a disease of the spine. She hummed, and his head slumped, vomit trawled down his chest, soaking his shirt with rice grains, chicken and blood. His feet began to buckle further. Valda didn't know so much liquid could come out of a man. She walked forward again until she was almost besides her mother.

Eric slumped on the floor, with Clover unable to hold his weight any longer. He moaned faintly and let out one last gasp, then was silent.

In the films, the mother and daughter would have turned and Eric would have jumped up for one final showdown, but this was no film, this was real life, and in real life poison does just that.

They stood over him in silence, a sense of release and redemption covering mother and child like a blanket. Valda pushed her small hand into her mother's. Clover took a deep breath and exhaled.

She looked down at her daughter, her smile as wide as a mile, her eyes as mad as a March hare's: that afternoon changed everything. "I told you, Valda … I told you it was a day for treats."

~

A tear dribbled down Valda's cheek, curling into the creases of her lips. She traced its movement, with her thumb mopping up its trail.

"You already know the answer to that," Valda said.

Lilif smiled, and lightning seemed to rumble in her eyes, the green growing darker.

"You're right," Lilif replied.

"Tell me what I have to do."

"Just say you want a child and it shall be done, but with one stipulation."

Valda stared, waiting for the rest. "Yes."

"I require one year of the child's life."

"One year?"

"Beginning or end," Lilif elaborated.

"What the fuck are you talking about?"

Valda rose from her seat. "I knew this was bullshit … I'm gonna have this shithole shut the fuck down."

Lilif laughed with authority, her rusty voice strained. "Calm down."

Valda walked around the chair and headed for the door. She placed her hand on the handle and pulled down.

Lilif raised her voice. "Oscar-winning Amanda Brace was unable to have children; she paid for the best fertility specialists from India to Russia. None of them could give her what she wanted – but I could. Grammy Award-winning Jane Heckle's cancer took away her ability to get pregnant, but she got it back after meeting me. Mariah Wray, heir to the

Chuggford Chocolate Company, found her answer here as well. The list goes on, Valda, hear me out!"

Valda opened the door a crack, turned and faced Lilif. The candle's smoke seemed connected to the ceiling; unbroken. Rain whipped the windows; the clouds were the colour of dying coal lit up from the inside with silver; the sound of thunder followed miles away then, close as if in the room.

"We operate on another level here; we work for higher forms. When I ask for one year of the child's life, I don't mean physically – I mean spiritually. We are an old creed trying to survive. I can give you what you want if you will expose the child for one year to our teachings."

The pair united in a stare.

"You don't believe I can help, do you?" Lilif questioned.

Valda stepped into the gap of the open door and looked back.

"You have two minutes left, Valda, two minutes to determine your destiny."

The rain outside became small hailstones crashing against the windows, thunder and lightning working together, with no gap, jumping out of ebony clouds.

"One minute and thirty seconds, Valda."

A feeling of loss crept into Valda's chest, her mind ran on. What if she's right and this is my last chance? And all I had to say was yes.

"One minute, Valda. Just say you want it and it's yours – a family of your own."

Her body and mind said leave – something didn't seem right here. It was as if Lilif wanted it more than she did. Why? Although logic said to flee, her heart glowed with the sound of children's laughter, and visions of beautiful British summers in her fairytale garden, Alex tending to a barbecue, while she played with their child – their own little unit, a unit of trust and true, uncompromising love. Her mind flashed forward to arguments and shopping trips with a daughter who looked just like her, with brown eyes and her father's brown-blond locks.

"Thirty seconds, Valda."

Valda took a deep breath. "Okay!"

"You have to say you want me to help you."

The intensity of the hailstones increased, crashing against the windows, threatening to shatter the panes, thunder and lightning exploding across the sky, as if God was at the peak of his wrath. Lilif continued to stare at her, unfazed.

"Ten seconds."

"Okay … I want you to help me have a child."

"Beginning or end?" Lilif questioned.

"Beginning!" Valda replied without thought.

Both paused. A smile crept across Lilif's face; her elegance seemed to fade, like that of a man who has achieved his objective and left a lady's quarters in the middle of the night, never to be seen again. Her soft face became hard, businesslike and robust. She went to her drawer and rummaged around.

"Come; take a seat. We have to run through a few things that you have to do to make sure we're successful."

Out of the drawer she produced a wooden bracelet and black bean, placing both on the table. The candle smoked away. Lilif looked up and waved her over.

"Hurry."

Valda let the door shut and walked back to her seat. The weather began to subside, the hail turning back to rain, the clouds calming. Lilif picked up the bracelet and bean and held them in her open palms.

"You must consummate our agreement tonight, or it will be ineffective. You must place the bean inside your vagina before intercourse and let it dissolve. The bracelet is to be worn the day the child is born, and for the whole of the year you agreed I could have. Any questions?"

Valda looked at the items in her palm and found herself, surprisingly, with few questions.

"What's the bean made out of? And why do I have to wear the bracelet?"

"The bean is a mixture of herbs and spices known in the old world to aid fertility. The rest – it's all ritual and far too long-winded to explain. I'm sure you have more important things to attend to, like consummation. You must not worry – it'll be all right, I promise."

Valda should have dug deeper, harder and pushed for more clarity, but Lilif was right – she wanted to get out of there ASAP; the meeting had exhausted her beyond all comprehension. The office felt like a tomb, with its walls closing in and air thinning. Lilif was an effortless negotiator; her obdurate ways should have been valued by Valda, who prided herself on being the same. Instead, she found herself loathing her for it.

Valda held out her palms and Lilif tipped the items into them. Valda looked at them briefly, then closed her hands into a ball and stood, pushing both into her hoodie's front pocket. Lilif rose, her hands behind her back.

"I would see you out, but I must prepare for my next client. You remember my instructions: the bean before sex, and the bracelet from the first day until our agreed year is up."

"Will I see you again?"

"Why would you? The instructions are easy enough, aren't they?"

"But how will the child get your teachings or learn about your religion? I have no literature or knowledge of it."

"Don't worry your head. If you do the things I've told you to, all will be fine."

"What if I don't follow through with wearing the bracelet after the child is born?"

Lilif paused, her small smile shrank, and the V above her brow deepened.

"Well. We all have free will but, being a businesswoman, you should know there are severe consequences to breaking a contractual agreement, whether written or verbal. I would advise you to stick to the script."

Valda had never been brought up with a faith. The little she learned about God from school or TV had been diluted the first time her father had laid his hands on her and stole her innocence. By the third, fifth or twentieth time, she had tired of praying for God to make his head explode without result, and with that, she had all but placed the God theory in a coffin, loaded it on to a boat, and burned it at sea.

This encounter made her call that boat in. If Lilif was a charlatan, she was a fine actress more than deserving of an Oscar, but if she wasn't and her religion, rituals or faith had the ability to make a barren women fertile, then there was a God. However, if there is a God, there must be the other: the father of creatures like Eric, the creator of poverty, greed, murder and lust. Valda didn't know which side Lilif played for, but had an awful feeling that she had made a fatal error; an inaccurate assessment of the risk and got involved with something beyond her comprehension.

Valda stood in the doorway. Lilif took her seat.

"One last thing. I would suggest you keep this to yourself until everything has been successful. People will only judge otherwise."

Valda nodded, turned and walked out into the hallway. The door closed behind her. The rooms she had passed earlier had fallen silent, the presence of anyone else undetectable. The hallway looked a lot longer now; remarkably longer and grey. A grey inhospitable hallway, with its rooms sealed shut on either side, holding god knows what. Valda moved with haste, walking so quickly anyone observing may have considered it a jog.

She looked back over her shoulder before descending the stairs, wishing a film crew would jump out of one of the rooms, screaming she had been set up, it was all a big fat hoax, and they were bribing her for thousands to keep the footage out of the public eye. She would have paid, and slept better with that – there would be no reprisals or revenge in mind. Instead she descended the steps, knowing she had agreed to an arrangement Patrick wouldn't have.

Patrick stepped back as the door swung open. He stared at Valda as if she were an ancient relic, millions of years old. She walked out into the drizzle, hailstones cracking beneath their feet. They walked back to the car.

"What happened? You Okay?"

"I'm fine."

"I tried to get up there, but I couldn't. I was just about to call the law."

They got in the car. Valda removed her hood and baseball cap.

"I told you not to."

Patrick turned round in the front seat. "You've been in there for two hours."

"Two hours!"

"Yeah! I tried to call Alex but his phone kept going to voicemail. I was starting to get worried."

"It felt like five minutes, though."

Patrick shook his head and pulled up his sleeve, revealing his watch.

"Five on the dot," he assured.

"Shit."

"Hmmm."

Patrick turned round, started the engine and turned the heating dial up.

"You ready?" he asked.

"Yeah."

As they pulled away she looked up at number 18. As it grew smaller, she closed her eyes and wished she could start the day again.

Gaudium

The evening rolled its canvas across the sky; there was nothing spectacular to display, the day hadn't many colours left in its palette. The rain eased, leaving large puddles, for people to consider.

They pulled into her driveway. Light shone out from her home's rectangular window, signifying someone's presence. Patrick killed the engine and turned in his seat to face Valda. The pair had travelled in relative silence, both deep in thought.

"Will that be all for tonight?"

Valda placed her hand on the door handle.

"I would say so."

"You sure?"

"Yes."

Valda opened the door and got out.

"Valda!"

Valda stopped and looked back.

"Goodnight ..."

The pair stared at each other. Valda sensed he had more to say, but held back. She lowered her head, turned and walked towards her house, the bean and bracelet accessories to a temporary happiness and, unbeknown to her, an inevitable hell.

Patrick watched her stride away like a man on death row. He put the car in reverse and proceeded out of the driveway, feeling more than uneasy about things.

Alex opened the door, took one look at Valda then behind her at the Ford driving away, then back to her, wearing his clothes, damp and baggy, looking like a badly-dressed rapper.

"What the hell is going on?"

Valda stepped forward. She walked past him and stood in the space between the two staircases and the living room, her feet creating a small damp patch. Alex shut the door and faced her.

"We need to talk," Valda said

"We certainly do."

"I'm gonna change."

"Yeah … maybe you should."

Valda slinked past him, up the staircase, looking like shit. Alex watched her every step until she disappeared from sight, shaking his head in disbelief. She re-emerged minutes later in a figure-hugging silk nightgown, a BBL best-seller. She had tied her hair back and done her make-up. She wore a pair of high heels. She had gone from rapper chic to seductress in an instant.

Alex stood in the same position she had left him. He watched her descend the stairs, his confusion deepened.

"What the hell is going on with you?"

Valda walked past him and stood besides the sofa, leaning against its back, one fishnet stocking-clad leg on display.

"I'm fine. Why wouldn't I be?"

Alex shifted his weight from one hip to the other, and licked his lips.

"Well, there's a hole in the TV screen, your lip looks like you're on crack, ten minutes ago you got out of Patrick's car wearing my clothes and now this – something's definitely up."

Valda smiled with nerves.

"I can explain. I went to see someone, a specialist—"

"A specialist?"

"A fertility specialist. She has agreed to help us."

Alex blew his cheeks out. "Okay, and that explains why you were driving around in Patrick's car wearing my stuff?"

They both froze. She pictured how it would have looked to him, and realised he must have thought her a liar. She began to feel a sense of panic, panic that she wouldn't be able to fulfil Lilif's requirement to use the bean tonight.

Alex wasn't like other men. He was sensitive, thoughtful, more human than most. The brain in his head ran the show, as opposed to the one below. If he felt any sort of confusion about their relationship he'd call time on the sexual aspect of it until all had been resolved. She feared they weren't in a good place already; the direction of this conversation had to appear to be one of resolution and honesty.

"I can't just walk around the streets of London and pop into somewhere like that. You know there'd be some asshole with a camera trying to make a pound."

Alex nodded. "Who's the consultant?"

"I got the number from a friend—"

"Friend!" Alex scoffed.

"Look, why does it matter? The fact is, she can help us."

"How much?"

"Twenty thousand."

The lie rolled off her tongue with such ease it scared her – and her track record for honesty was appalling.

Alex frowned. "Wow! Twenty? Is there a guarantee?"

"More or less. She came highly recommended."

Alex stroked his stubble. Valda forced out a laugh.

"My God, you're worrying about twenty thousand pounds."

"I'm not worried about that. I just hope it works; we've been here before."

Valda leaned away from the sofa, walked towards him and wrapped her arms around his waist. He wrapped his arms around her.

"It'll work, and we'll finally have a beautiful family."

"What does the procedure involve?"

"It's homeopathic, natural … I can't explain exactly, but loads of stars have used her services and been successful."

Alex smiled, rubbed her back and closed his eyes, resting his head on her shoulder. The pair swayed gently; Valda sensed the time was right. She began to rub his crotch softly then harder, her other hand pulling down his zip. Once down with no objection or resistance, she began to stroke his penis back and forth. His breath became softly laboured with passion and her hand became sticky. He pulled her in closer and began to grab her ass cheeks, squeezing them, pushing aside her thong. She spread her legs for easier access. He travelled her curves and located her entrance deep between her legs. He began to stroke her clit, his hands moistened, they both began to pant and kiss, both their hands moving all over each other's bodies like ants over sugar; panting, kissing, stroking, fingering. Alex ripped off her gown and pressed one of her breasts into his mouth, his tongue flicking her nipple until it stood erect. She moved her hand back and forth as if her life depended on it. Her mind split between mission and passion, she stroked him with such vigour he left their embrace, swung his head back and moaned, on the verge of climax. She felt his shaft throbbing and she knew she had to stop or he'd ejaculate. She pulled him in closer.

"Not now. I want you to fuck me," she whispered.

His breathing calming, he grabbed her face with both hands, kissed her passionately, then turned towards the staircase, one hand in his, the black bean cradled in her other clenched fist.

As they ascended the stairs she attempted to place the bean, but it wouldn't stay put; each time her forward motion forced it back out. She retrieved it and held it once more. They entered the bedroom, the lights fading in on entry. Alex clapped and they went out. He grabbed her and kissed her again, then began taking off his clothes, the pair no more than silhouettes in the darkness. She lay on the bed, already dressed for the occasion.

Valda began to masturbate, pushing the bean further in with each stroke. Alex stood over her and did the same, then climbed on top of her, pulled her hand away and entered her. His entry forced moisture out of her and wet the sheets. The first, second and third thrusts were normal; she recognised them, but the fourth was laboured. By the fifth, he had slowed to a virtual stop, his arms on either side of her, holding him up, the inflation and deflation of his naked chest visible in the darkness. He shook his head slowly and erratically, as if to disperse a horrible thought.

"Alex …" she whispered

Alex whipped his head up and bent his neck and upper body back like a wolf howling at a pregnant moon. He groaned quietly and looked down at her. From what she could see in the darkness, his face looked hardened as if he were another man. He held so tightly it unnerved her. A hellish heat began to radiate off his naked body; ungodly amounts of sweat dripped from him.

"Alex!" she called out.

Then he started to thrust again, the first one slow and firm.

"Ale—"

The second stroke was faster, the third and fourth so fast and hard she didn't recognise them, the sixth, seventh faster and harder still. There was no sound besides hers. At first she moaned with pleasure, then with pain, pain shooting up from her pelvis, across her stomach, up her back, into her neck. She screamed in agony and he moved in and out of her like a robot, programmed to fuck with no sympathy.

She looked up again at his face, tears streaming down her cheeks, and she recognised it – she recognised her father in the darkness; the creature her mother had slain. His eyes looked directly into hers and he smiled.

He moved faster and faster. She attempted to rise but her arms were held in place, so tightly he pushed her flesh up against her bones. The pain was so unbearable that it siphoned sound from her screams, and tears rolled into her open mouth. She looked up again and Alex had returned. Staring, wide-eyed and expressionless, he hung his head again and slowed to a humane rhythm, whispering a concoction of inaudible sounds, mad ramblings that covered her in goosebumps.

He let out a bass moan and ejaculated. Within seconds a million faces had formed and flooded her brain, distorted and twisted, their eyes nothing but black orifices, dripping with black goo; she felt a colossal amount of pain and suffering, and imagined flames and frost, unthinkable levels of panic, terror, dread and loss.

Alex toppled over to her side, his back to her. Beads of sweat rolled off him; his ribcage inflated and deflated, his body steamed and radiated unearthly amounts of heat. Her vision became blurred and darkness crept in from the corners, covering her pupils until it was absolute.

~

Sunday morning began with a smell of pancakes that curled and swirled around the house, raising the dead from their slumber. Valda's eyes cracked open to a concerto of birdsong from the garden below. Sunlight flooded the room and smudged it, giving it the appearance of a dream or that place good souls are rumoured to go.

She swam around her sheets looking for Alex, his side vacant. She groped the mattress, expecting dampness, but it was dry. She sat up and examined her wrists, expecting bruising where he had held her so tightly, but there were none. She stood; her fish-netted feet hit the floor.

She spread her legs and inserted her fingers inside her to feel for signs of the bean. Pulling her finger out, she expected to see at least the smearing of a black substance, but there was none. She sat for a second and looked into space, considering how plausible that it was: could it have all been a nightmare? The visit to Lilif, the agreement, the terrifying sex, all one long, vivid, drawn-out nightmarish dream? The thought filled her with joy.

She stood, went to her wardrobe and pulled out a white cotton gown and slid it over her slut-wear, tying both sides together at the waist. She hummed a little, enjoying the smell that emitted from below. She walked around her bed out into the hallway and looked over the banister.

The TV showed a Sunday morning breakfast show with the sound muted. Sunlight kissed every piece of furniture, and the marble floor below glowed. She walked down the staircase to her left and towards the kitchen, past the chipped Olympian frozen in stone.

Before she could open the door she could hear the radio playing smooth music. She stood outside and listened for a few seconds, two of her main senses appeased, smell and sound.

Slowly, she pushed open the kitchen door. At the far end a tap ran in the sink, unattended. To her left, on the island's built-in cooker, a pan sat at rest with pancakes in it, frying lightly. Valda stopped and observed the set-up. Something wasn't right. Alex would never have been so irresponsible: he virtually had OCD; he was the type to check the front door was shut a few more times than was necessary, and always made sure that all electrical appliances were switched off at night.

Valda walked forward. The door leading from the kitchen to the conservatory was open. She walked further, the sunlight so bright the white window frames hummed with its rays. She walked in and stood in the centre of the conservatory looking around. Nothing seemed out of place; the table, the bookcase, the sofa chairs neatly positioned on the outskirts of the glass room.

She walked over to the door on the other side, the one that led out to the garden, and tried the handle. She pulled down and it opened out, so she could hear the sound of nature un-muted. She stood on the step and looked out into the garden. Alex was nowhere to be seen, but among the sound of nature was a sound that she had never heard out there before; the sound of slow creaking, like an old door, its hinges encased in rust, being moved back and forth, back and forth … creak, creak, creak.

She stepped out onto the grass, which softly stroked her feet. She could smell the sun as well as basil, parsley and mint. She walked beyond her vine arch, little trees and massive evergreens that blocked people from looking in. The deeper she advanced, the louder the creaks grew: creak, creak, creak, creak.

She passed under another vine arch and continued towards the end of the garden, where suddenly her vision was hampered by extreme sunlight. She shaded her eyes with her hand. When she looked more closely at the largest tree in the garden, an object swung back and forth, breaking the sunlight's concentration.

As she neared, clouds began to ease in, making her vision 20/20. In an instant her legs became sponge tubes and her heart almost tore through her ribcage. She brought her hands up over her mouth; her eyes widened and watered.

Alex swung back and forth, a large fisherman's rope tied around his thin neck, the skin and flesh around his throat gathered into one heap, making his face look fat and bloated. His eyes were wide and staring, fear trapped in them. His upper body was naked, his lower half covered only by shorts, his skin pale grey. Valda stumbled back and let out a scream that came from the pit of her stomach, born from loss and love.

Six black birds, their wing span easily two metres, whooshed overhead, commanding her attention. So big they blocked out her vision of the sky, she watched them fly and traced their movement towards her bedroom behind and above her.

When she looked up, her gaze was caught by a figure standing in her room looking out on to the garden. The figure was too far away to make out gender, ethnicity or anything else. They stared at each other, while the creaking continued. The figure raised an arm and began to write on the glass, producing a red dribbled scribble, spelling out 'Welcome'.

Valda stood rooted to the spot. She hadn't noticed the creaking had ceased; they continued to stare at each other. Suddenly Valda felt an ice-cold breath on her neck and the smell of rotting flesh made her heave. She spun around and Alex had untied himself, his neck still in the noose, gathering flesh from his face into a heap. The diagonal knot made his head crooked, the whites of his eyes completely bloodshot, both bulging. His teeth grated against each other, some broken from where he had bit down.

He stood before her, maggots falling from cavities in his decaying flesh. She let out a scream, scrambling backwards, falling as he advanced, the floor giving way into darkness.

Alex became a dot above her and she fell for what seemed like an eternity.

Valda shot up in her bed, her breathing hard and determined. Her arms ached and her pelvis pained her. She looked around. The early-morning sky coloured her room a beautiful calming caramel. She looked over and Alex wasn't there.

She got on her knees, propped herself up and looked out of the window onto the garden. The tree at the far end stood, Alex-less, just a few birds perched on it, waiting for whatever the day would bring. Insects flew about from flower to flower. She scanned across the whole garden for any signs of foul play, until a sudden jolt of pelvic pain shrank her into a ball on the bed. She let out a small whimper and rocked until it passed.

She knelt on all fours and twisted around until she sat on the edge of the bed, where she took a deep breath and stood up. Pain radiated all over her body, almost making her collapse, but she held on and shuffled over to her wardrobe to dress.

Every step towards the hallway brought surges of discomfort, pains shooting up her legs, back and pelvis. She got to the banister in between her dual staircases and looked over. Alex was sitting watching television, the volume low; she watched him for a while until he turned and looked up.

"Hey."

"Hey."

The pair paused again, snapshots of last night's events replaying in both their heads.

"You coming down?" he asked.

Valda nodded and began to shuffle down, trying her best to keep her discomfort contained. Alex watched her move like an old woman and stood.

"What's wrong?" he asked.

Valda stopped half way down and held the banister.

"It's nothing, just … ah, a little cramp."

Alex began to shuffle towards the staircase, pain slowing his movement. The pair stopped, looked at each other and began to giggle, both held their stomachs and sides moaning.

"Jesus, you too?" he questioned.

Valda nodded and Alex put his arm around her. The pair limped to the sofa, and plopped themselves down. The table had an array of food on it: croissants, ham, cheese, bananas, oranges, chocolate spread and bars, a multi-pack of crisps, two jugs of water and orange ice afloat in both. A stack of takeaway leaflets and a credit card sat on top of them.

Valda reached out, grabbed an orange and began to peel it.

"What's all this in aid of?" she asked.

Alex looked at her and raised an eyebrow.

"Can you see either of us moving from this sofa today?"

She continued to peel and smiled.

Alex cracked his neck. Valda looked at him, envisioning the version of Alex from her nightmare: his neck twisted, his lips pale grey, and the noise his body swinging made – creak, creak, creak. The vision bred unwanted nostalgia: her dear brother hanging in the flat from the light fixture, his face so peaceful and calm. She felt tears gathering but fought them.

She thought it odd she had never had such a horrendously vivid dream in all her life, even when her father was molesting her and life was a little slice of hell. It had been a dream so vivid she could touch, feel and smell it, a dream that utilised elements from the one memory she wished she could forget.

"Welcome."

They both looked at each other as if the other had said it.

"Pardon?" Alex asked.

Valda looked at him, baffled as to how a word could slip from her mouth and not register with her brain first.

She shook her head.

"Sorry, I-I mean the food is welcome."

She bit into the orange.

"No problem. You sure besides the pain, you're fine? You seem a bit out there."

"I'm fine, just puzzled as to why we're in so much agony."

Alex smiled and reached for a croissant.

"You don't remember?"

"Kind of."

"What! Kind of? Last night was something else. I think we pulled off every position in the Kama Sutra. I'm not in the slightest bit surprised we're in agony."

Valda spat out pips and placed them into the orange peel on the table, beginning to question her sanity; her version of events was completely different to his. Valda forced a smile and brought a slice of cheese to her mouth. Alex fell silent and looked pensive.

"Tell me something. Did your specialist say when?"

Valda dropped the last shred of cheese in her mouth.

"I'm not sure, but she assured me it would be soon."

Alex rubbed his face.

"Okay … you still haven't told me what we have to do for it to work."

"I take a few homeopathic remedies and God does the rest."

Alex nodded slowly.

"You don't do 'vague' well and you certainly don't do God. I want to meet this specialist who has calmed the beast and given her religion."

Valda felt anger rolling around in her stomach. Alex was severely pissing her off; she wanted to leave the subject and wasn't used to having to lie so much. She was the owner of a multi-million pound business and when she called Tuesday Monday, calendars got corrected at BBL – not her word.

She took a deep breath, universally recognised by sensible adults as an annoyed one, and smiled as her father had taught her to do when he had finished and actually gave a fuck about her mother knowing 'their little secret'.

"Don't you believe me? Do you think I'm lying to you?"

"Look, I'm just concerned; you know how much we want this. She might be some quack giving you something harmful. Let me check her out online, and make sure she's cool before we go eating twigs."

Valda sighed. “Alex, on my worst day, I’m sharper than you on your best.”

Alex squinted in thought and smiled.

“Judge Judy?” he responded, clicking his fingers.

“No, Valda fucking Payne.”

They both paused then fell about laughing.

“My God, you just quoted Judge Judy. I like this version of you. Can we sign you up for more visits to this specialist?”

Valda punched his arm, they both let out moans of discomfort and went back to laughing. They spent the rest of the day, afternoon and evening, watching television, eating, drinking and chatting like teens on a first date.

Valda forgot about Lilif and the bean, she even forgot about the bracelet tucked in the pocket of Alex’s hoodie slung in the laundry basket. This was to be her undoing: this convenient slip of the mind would eventually bring another world into hers, a world that questioned everything maturity had taught and dismissed as fiction and fable, a world that would push her sanity to the brink, eventually forcing it over, kicking and screaming.

For today she laughed and drank; for today she was happy.

Miraculum

Drew walked over to Valda's table. Her black heels click-clacked. Many called it the P45 walk. Urban legend had it that between the door and Valda's table she would have decided if your face still fit around BBL.

Drew pulled a seat out and sat. She was a buxom blonde from Poland, her eyes were wolf grey, her native accent eroded away from being in the UK. She was head of PR for BBL and her résumé was fantastic.

Valda had poached her from the Dunwick's supermarket chain, impressed with the way she single-handedly steered the company through its bad meat scandal. It had emerged that meat sold from their stores had made a thousand people sick in the UK and abroad.

When the media wouldn't let the story die, the Dunwick family appointed Drew and she went to work. She was able to divert and attribute all blame to a small family-run factory that supplied the supermarket chain with all its poultry. She sought out and paid disloyal workers small fortunes to go to the press with stories of bad working conditions and practice at the factory, raising false flags and creating a fictional feel of chaos there.

The press began to run these stories instead, turning away from facts and opting for sensationalism. The real truth was that Dunwick's had opted for cheap meat storage, leaving meat at room temperature for 24 hours and more, as well as using warehouses that were also used to store manure and waste to store supplies, and changing use-by dates to shift old stock.

Drew's work began to take its toll on the factory, which began to lose contracts hand over fist, its good name dragged through the dirt. Bills piled up, as well as law suits. One day the owner, Cyril White, went home and shot his whole family, then went on a rampage around his factory, killing ten workers before killing himself. The factory went into liquidation and all its assets were seized, leaving workers without jobs and final payouts. Dunwick's was off the hook and Drew was paid handsomely for it.

Drew's reputation preceded her, and the only question she was asked by Valda at her interview was if she felt guilty about the events surrounding the Dunwick's scandal, to which she simply replied, "No."

She placed her folders on the desk. Valda coupled her fingers together and leaned forward. "Talk to me."

Drew sighed. "This underage advertisement thing is resurfacing again. My contacts have told me a story will hit the front pages tomorrow, about a young teenage girl who's had underage sex with an older guy. The boy told authorities he thought she was older after she posed on social networking sites wearing our range."

Valda rolled her eyes.

"I know … the problem is, it's national child protection week and all eyes are on the brats. We can't afford to be having scandal of this magnitude spinning around the globe, when we're so close to sealing the Braga move – they may get cold feet," Drew continued.

"Well, what are you suggesting?" Valda replied.

"Pull advertisements from all teen sites, so that we're seen to be doing something about it. Let a month pass, let the press get back on Gaga and Bieber, then we can slowly creep back in."

"You make it seem so simple. Are you aware that teenage girls make up at least twenty per cent of our income per year? Besides, if we pull advertisements it could be seen as an act of guilt and acknowledgement that we are in the wrong, not to mention Braga thinking we're flaky."

"I know, but my only fear is that we'll get protesters outside shops throwing paint and all that shit they did last summer, Braga may also think the business is more trouble than he needs."

Valda suddenly saw Drew separate and merge. She shook her head and her sight was normal again.

Drew looked at her. "Valda…"

Drew's voice echoed, distant. Valda drew her palm down the front of her face. Her brown eyes shot with blood.

"Valda, you Okay?"

Valda shook her head once more. "I'm fine, just tired. Anyway, I want the adverts kept: find another way to sort this out, you've got until tomorrow."

Drew cut a concerned look.

"You sure you're fine? You don't look too well…"

Valda rolled her head to relieve tension. "Stop with the bullshit, Drew, you couldn't give a fuck about me. Just get on with your job and get us out of this."

Drew looked down at the table, gathered her folders and stood. "Sorry."

She turned on her heel and marched out of the office. Valda watched two Drews walk out and four doors open and close. She went to her phone and buzzed through to her PA. "Claire, unless it's Braga or Alex I will be unavailable for the next two hours."

"Got it," Claire replied.

Valda leaned over in her chair, grabbed a waste-paper bin, placed it on her lap and vomited into it, her throat burning like fire. Her stomach muscles clenched so tightly she thought they were going to tear. She came up for air and the room was spinning out of control, the London skyline outside jumping up and down as if the city was built on a bouncy castle.

She vomited again until everything she had ingested had exited. She hung her head for a few seconds then looked up. Her vision was clear once more; in fact, it was better. *What the fuck?* She thought. She reached over and pressed the phone for Claire again.

"Claire, call Dr Ryan and tell him I'm on my way. Get Patrick and tell him to come immediately. Give me confirmation of both."

"Okay, call Dr Ryan and Patrick. Got it."

Valda ended the call, stood up from the table and leaned over the back of her chair, twisting and turning to get comfortable. Then the phone's display lit up. Before it had a chance to sound, Valda snatched the phone out of its cradle.

"Ms Payne, I have called Dr Ryan. He's waiting for you to arrive and Patrick's on his way. Will you come down to wait, or shall I call you when he gets here?"

"I'll make my way down."

"Okay, will that be all?"

"Yes."

"Thank you."

Valda took a deep breath, gathered things off the table and swept them into her bag. She walked towards her door, mild stomach pain radiating around her waist, and stood by it, fighting for composure. She stood straight, fixed her clothes and walked down the corridor to the lift; once down, she walked towards the exit where Patrick waited by the main entrance.

The sun was out, illuminating a sparse blue sky, with wisps of cloud. The air was cool with a lovely breeze.

Patrick opened the Bentley door and she practically threw herself in, letting out a mild groan. Patrick rushed round to the driver's side and got in. He turned in his seat and watched her clutching her stomach.

"You sure we shouldn't go to a hospital?"

Valda held her palm up. "No! Just get me to Dr Ryan."

Patrick sped through afternoon traffic with ease, the London roads clear for a Wednesday. They pulled up at the surgery in Harley Street. Patrick pulled over, parked then jogged around to let Valda out. She moved across the seat, jaded. Patrick took her hand and put his arm around her back; she bent over, hunched, and he covered her face with his body.

They rushed inside, and the receptionist put them straight through to Ryan's room. Dr Ryan met them at the door, helping her to the examination bed. Patrick made his way back out to the car.

Dr Ryan stood by the table. Valda groaned, he placed his hand on her stomach and palpated her belly, each prod causing further discomfort.

"Have you eaten anything out of the ordinary today?" Dr Ryan asked.

Valda held the corner of the bed; her nails dug into the foam mattress; pain brought her knees to her chest. The feeling of sickness spread from her stomach to every node of her body, her vision split Dr Ryan in two and brought him back together. Ryan's mouth opened and closed, but the words that emerged seemed foreign and jumbled. She closed her eyes and her memory began to paint pictures, first her mother's face, distraught, her eyes big and brown, her hazel hair a wild mess the day the police came, the day both her brother and father's decay had become too obvious for neighbours to ignore.

Four days after the day of treats, neither Valda nor Leon had gone to school, one for obvious reasons, the other for safety. Clover had caught her daughter crying in the bathroom while getting ready one morning.

Her mother knelt down before her and held her hands together.

"You promised you'd be able to handle this, didn't you?"

Valda looked her mother in the eyes, huge and needy, waiting to hear a response – she needed to know her daughter wouldn't break and fold under pressure, assuring her she would have enough time to figure things out.

"I-I-I-I, I'll try, I promise."

Clover shook her head, unconvinced. "You won't."

Clover leaned forward and kissed her daughter's forehead. When she pulled back Valda saw it for the first time: a flicker in her eyes, a spark destined to become a raging inferno of madness.

The first few days flew past. A mild smell seeped from the cracks of the door. Clover bought masking tape to seal up the gaps, as well as incense, scented candles and sprays to conceal death's aroma.

Once the smell had been dealt with, the days felt as if they had been sent from heaven, as if they had been stolen from an American TV programme, where the family dynamic is perfect. Clover rummaged around Eric's side of the wardrobe and found his stash of cash, bound together in hundreds, stacked in a giant sweet tin. Valda stood by her mother's side, while she balanced on a chair retrieving the money; cash that almost killed her mother one afternoon.

~

Valda and Leon had come home, their toes virtually frozen from walking in snow up to their ankles in nothing but plimsolls. Leon had told Valda not to make anything of it, as it would surely lead to trouble. He wiped warm tears off his sister's frozen cheeks as they stood on the doorstep, and told her that tomorrow he'd give her his socks to double over her feet. He was loving like that. He always looked out for Valda where he could. He wasn't a small boy; at thirteen he was the biggest in his class. People never gave him trouble; they just didn't interact with him, and he liked that; his father's behaviour had made him numb and uncaring for strangers. He trusted no one with a smile and people with frowns even less.

When Clover met them at the door she pulled them in close and gripped them in love, knowing their little feet had felt the cold. She moved her gaze from Leon to Valda, making sure she had their attention.

"I promise you I'll get money for winter shoes, I promise," Clover said.

Leon looked away, fighting tears, aware his father was almost home, and aware his father could read situations like Batman or Colombo. He would take puffy eyes as a display of emotion; emotions that could lead to acts of spontaneity, spontaneity that could lead to his exposure.

"Leon, look at me…" Clover commanded.

Valda looked up at her brother and he looked at his mother reluctantly. He felt sorrow for her; sorrow, pity and anger.

"You won't ... You won't do anything, you never do," he protested.

Clover looked down at the floor, the weight of truth and shame dragging her head there. She knew he was right, yet she looked up, determined to prove a point.

"I will ... Take off your coats and go and sit down."

Clover stood up and ascended the stairs. He knew where she was going: his father had taken him up there many times before to show him where he kept his stash and to warn him that if a penny of it was touched he would "kick the shit" out of his son.

Leon told Valda to take a seat in front of the heater in the living room while he kept a look-out of the kitchen window. In a way, he wanted his mother to be caught. He had watched a TV programme once about a woman who had been beaten one too many times and had finally snapped. She had grabbed a knife and stuck it in her husband's heart – and was found not guilty of murder. He wished his mother could have found that woman's ferocity, guts and courage, but he doubted it; she was delicate and too beautiful to be capable of such gruesome acts.

The snow started to come down quickly and thickly. Eric emerged around the corner carrying shopping bags, smiling, laughing and walking with a neighbour, who probably thought, like the rest of the estate, that he was husband, father, brother and human being of the year. He walked with great strides, his eyes always on the window Leon stared from. Firm, piercing and cold: if only the neighbour paid attention to those baleful eyes, she would have seen they didn't match his smile; she would have seen the wickedness that lay beneath his skin.

Leon closed the small gap in the curtain and came away from the window before he could reach the stairs to warn his mother. He heard a loud crash from above, followed by a scream of agony. Valda came to the living room door, her little face concerned. Leon stared at her, hiding his worry.

"Eric's here. Go and sit down and keep quiet."

"But …"

"No buts!" he barked.

Leon stared at her, she obeyed and slinked off. He turned and jogged up the stairs, where he found his mother lying on the floor holding her back and groaning, bundles of money everywhere. Leon knelt down to pick his mum up. She waved him off, speaking through gaps of pain.

"Leave me – pick up the money and get it back in the tin."

Leon froze, torn between love for his mum and the love for his mum. His heart said to pick her up, but his head knew that the money being everywhere posed more of a threat to her than the fall. He went about the room scooping up the cash bundles and placing them in the tin. A sudden sound of a muffled male voice froze him, Eric was home. Leon sped up, making sure he had all the money.

On the last bundle, Clover grabbed his wrist before he could place it in the tin; she plucked a twenty-pound note out of it and stuffed it down her bosom. From below, a deep growl travelled up the stairs.

"Clover! What the fuck is going on up there?"

Clover looked at Leon. Leon quickly spun around, grabbed the tin's lid, placed it on the tin, tiptoed over and shoved it to the back of the wardrobe. By this time the sound of angry footsteps had begun to grow closer. Clover reached out her arms, and Leon hoisted her up onto the bed. Too late for Leon to escape, he sat beside her and waited for Eric's arrival.

Eric turned into the bedroom and looked at the pair sitting on the bed. He scanned their faces slowly then spoke.

"Didn't you hear me fucking calling? And what the fuck are you doing in here?" pointing at Leon.

Clover swallowed a little, the pain from her back radiating up her neck.

"I-I-I was just talking to him about school."

"Why the fuck up 'ere? I told ya I don't want these shits in 'ere."

Clover paused and looked at her husband. His crew cut looked freshly done and as menacing as ever. He broke eye contact and looked at Leon.

"Get out."

Leon hesitated and didn't move; instead, he placed his hand in his mother's as a show of support, hoping to anger his father so much he would give him the lashes instead. Eric's face went red. He stormed from the doorway and grabbed the boy's collar; Leon grabbed his hand and pulled back against him. Eric froze at the act of defiance, and his eyes widened.

"Ohhhh, you wanna be the big man now, huh?"

He pulled back, taking Leon out of his sitting position, off his feet.

"For God's sake just leave him," Clover pleaded.

Eric looked down at her as if she were a tramp.

"Oh, I'll leave him, but you'll take every lick he had coming, how about that?"

"No! Just leave her alone!" Leon screamed.

Eric's eyes moved from one to the other, and he started to laugh.

"What the flying fuck is going on 'ere? You both been on the gear, or what?"

He dragged Leon out of the room and slammed the door, locking it behind him. Leon landed on his front at Valda's feet, resting in a shallow pool of her urine. He looked up at her, her eyes puffy and sombre. When the hitting started, he rose to one knee, picked her up in his arms and went to their room.

Eric didn't disturb them that night; he had overexerted himself beating their mother. He had broken a belt in the process, and had been forced to use a bit of plastic cord, its whistling sound a prelude to a low, bloodcurdling scream, which forced tears from Leon while he held his hands over his sister's ears.

The morning after was extra quiet. Both Leon and Valda sat eating their cereal, aware their mother hadn't joined them, terrified she might never again. Their father sat watching them, his greedy, baleful eyes always looking for a reaction, looking for signs of anything he didn't like: signs that they might talk at school, or elsewhere.

When they heard the sound of shuffling, they looked at each other, Leon rubbed his knee against Valda's and she rubbed his back. Their mother walked around the kitchen door, bent over by the beating, her face totally unmarked, as always. She walked over to Eric and kissed him on the cheek. Eric looked straight ahead, at his kids.

He got up, and Clover flinched in preparation for a blow, Eric didn't: instead, he walked to the sink and placed his bowl in it, then left the kitchen. He grabbed his coat, pulled it on and left the house, slamming the door behind him.

Leon rose from his seat; his mother and sister held their breath. Leon waited before going to the window to watch Eric disappear round the corner. Leon turned back to the other two and nodded; everybody exhaled, Valda got up and walked to her mother, helping her to sit. Clover hissed in pain as she lowered herself to a chair.

Leon stood in the middle of the kitchen, his hands balled into angry fists, his face set like a warrior.

Clover looked over at him.

"You mustn't do that, Leon … you mustn't allow him to make you angry like him."

They stared at each other, Valda looking from one to the other. Clover broke off the stare, and slid her hand into her bosom, producing the twenty-pound note secured the night before.

"Come here …" Clover requested.

Leon stood still.

Clover waved him over.

"Come."

Leon sighed and walked over to the table. She raised her arm in agony and pulled both her babies in.

"I want you both to remember that, in life, sometimes you must face pain to gain more …"

Leon looked down, and a single tear rolled down his cheek; neither Clover nor Valda noticed. Clover slipped her hand into his, her grip so faint it barely registered.

"Take your sister, go to Harlesden and buy you both some boots ..."

She placed the note in his hand, gripped it and forced a smile that embarrassed both of them. He wanted to call her weak; he wanted to call her many things but for Valda's sake he held back. Three months later, he would take his own life, unleashing a version of his mother he would have been proud of.

~

Valda took the tin from her mother and placed it on the bed. Clover got down off the stool and stood beside her. She opened it and turned it upside down. The money formed a neat pile. The day was grey and cold, but to Valda it was as bright as the surface of the moon. Her mother looked happy and in control.

Clover ordered a cab. Valda buzzed about in excitement, as she had never been in a car before, let alone a cab. She imagined a grand car with huge wheels and tinted windows, the kind she saw movie stars get in and out of on TV. While they waited, she sat, legs crossed, watching cartoons, the volume so low it was almost inaudible, the visuals mirrored in her eyes. Clover came downstairs and stood at the living room door.

"Turn it up."

Valda looked over her shoulder at her mother, her eyes big and watery with worry.

"Go on, turn it up … He can't hurt you any more."

Valda turned back to the television and reached out. Her hand shook, hovering just above the volume button. She turned once more to look at her mother, her eyes asking for reassurance.

Clover gave it. "Go on."

She pressed the button so hard the tip of her finger went pale white. The volume began to ascend, and the sound of Daffy Duck and Bugs Bunny filled the room.

Clover began to giggle. Valda looked at her mother's beautiful mouth, wide as a country mile, her bunched rosy cheeks making her eyes slits in her face. Her giggle became a full-blown laugh, infectiously spreading to Valda. Oh, how she loved that sound her mother made: she pressed the volume button again, hoping to make it last.

"That's right, turn that fucker up!"

The neighbours must have thought them mad, but neither of them cared. They had passed that point the day their beautiful brother and son had had enough and had taken his own life. The same day the devil had swum around on the kitchen floor, bleeding from his ass and other orifices.

Valda stood up and ran towards her mother, wrapping her arms around her waist and laughing. Her mother held her so tightly she couldn't breathe, but their embrace was cut short by the doorbell. Clover looked down at Valda.

"It's the cab. Come on, let's go."

They opened the door. The cabbie was a fat Indian gentleman with a large moustache, a cigarette hanging from his dry chapped lips. Valda flinched at the sight of him; her father had told her stories where men of colour were no more than cannibals, who would eat her brains if she touched one. She had suspected the tales to be untrue, she had seen many collect their children at school; but she clung to her mother's leg and stared with caution, a slight look of fear etched into her face. He looked concerned. Clover cleared her throat.

"Sorry; she's never been in a cab before, that's all."

He looked at Clover. He took a long drag on his cigarette, bringing its head back to life.

"Well, there's a first time for everything, hey?" he questioned.

He flicked his fag over the balcony, went to his pocket, withdrew a Murray mint and knelt down, the mint flat in his palm. Valda moved back further, and her mother gently pushed her in front of her and whispered, "It's Okay, I promise, take it. Go on, it's not true."

Valda looked at the man, who extended his hand further, and Valda shot her hand out and grabbed the mint.

"What do you say?" her mum asked.

Valda looked at him. "Thank you."

He smiled and rubbed her hair. His smile was organic and she began to warm to him.

They walked down the estate staircase past a group of teenage boys who were listening to music from a boom box and smoking weed.

The cabbie led them to his car, a clapped-out Ford Sierra, its hubcaps missing, dents and rust spots plaguing its paintwork. He opened the front passenger-side door for Valda. She froze and looked at Clover; her mother smiled and waved her to get in. She climbed in, remembering how elegant Julia Roberts had made it look on the TV. She sat down; the seat was riddled with tears and burn holes. When she sat back, dust rose from her seat's fabric, making her cough. Her mother got in behind her and closed the door, then came the driver, his stomach just shy of the steering wheel.

His dashboard had strange ornaments: a blue lady, an elephant with several arms and a beautifully sculpted mini-building that looked like a palace fit for a king. The driver turned to Clover behind.

"Where to, love?"

"Staples Corner, please."

"Let me guess. Ghostbusters?"

Clover smiled.

"Okay, that'll be £2.50."

Clover handed him a note. Valda sat still, looking all about the car as the transaction went through. She looked at the air vents, sun visor and the cab radio, which crackled with funny voices, wondering what their uses could be; her attention was suddenly drawn by the cabbie, who took his seatbelt, pulled it across his belly and clipped it in.

"Belts please," he shouted.

Valda looked up behind her. Her mother's hand dangled the belt from above her head rest. She reached up and pulled like he had, but struggled to get it into the clip, so he reached across, clipped it for her, then winked.

"Right, let's go."

They pulled out of the car park and took off. Grey clouds began to produce little droplets that gathered on the windscreen, obscuring Valda's vision, until the wipers washed the screen new. He reached down and twisted a knob. The air vents came to life, blowing out warm air – and one of her questions had been answered.

The radio played music she had never heard before, everything from George Michael to Stevie Wonder. The cabbie drove so fast that the houses and shops she normally walked past blurred one into the other.

Clover sat staring out of the window, thinking about her next move. They pulled into another car park filled to the brim with other cars and people heading towards the building her mother had called a cinema.

The cabbie unclipped his seatbelt, pulled the sun visor down and stuffed some notes from his pocket into the elastic pocket beside the mirror. Valda looked over at him, her second question answered.

Clover reached over and rubbed her head from behind, opened her door and got out. The cabbie walked around to Valda's door and opened it for her. Valda undid her seatbelt and slid out, and the cabbie knelt down before her.

"Hope you enjoyed your first cab ride?" he asked.

Valda smiled. He stood and closed the passenger door. Clover grabbed his arm gently before he walked round to the driver's side.

"Thank you."

"No problem. Enjoy the film."

He got in, picked up the cab radio, spoke into it and drove away, her third question answered.

Valda sat gobsmacked at how real the film's special effects were. Ghostbusters had brought the stuff of nightmares and dreams into the real world, and she sat in awe glued to the silver screen. Her mother watched her watching the film, so happy she was able to enjoy, if only for a moment, a chance to be a normal child, carefree, careless and loved.

After the film they took the number 258 bus to Kilburn, discussing the film at great length along the way. Valda asked how they made it look so real, if it wasn't. Clover's only reply, unable to elaborate further, was, "It's just special effects." They got off the bus and walked to McDonald's, another first for her. Valda had a small cheeseburger and chips with ketchup. To wash it down she drank root beer. She told her mother it smelled like Savlon; they both laughed until drink spilled out of the corners of Valda's mouth and nose.

A family approached from the counter and sat at the neighbouring table. A father with his wife, daughter and son, they exuded happiness.

He kissed his daughter's crown the way Valda imagined the cab man would kiss his own child that night, probably giving her a mint, then rubbing her head the way he had hers. Nothing like the way *her* father had kissed her on the mouth, forcing his tongue down her little throat every other night, his saliva sour, rancid and warm.

Clover put her arm around her and whispered, "You Okay?"

Valda remained silent and watched how the girl and her brother laughed and messed about, their parents' only concern their children's happiness. Clover reached out and touched Valda's shoulder, making her jump.

"Let's go."

Clover placed their rubbish in the tray and slid out. Valda took one last look at the family, and began to follow. Then her mother did something she didn't understand. As she left, she stuck her head back through the door and screamed at the top of her lungs, "You selfish, selfish fuckers!"

Valda looked up at Clover. Her nostrils flared, her eyes widened and homed in on the family. Everyone in the restaurant froze and stared at the door. She pointed at the family, her finger shaking.

"Keep your shit to yourself, there are other children here!"

The man rose out of his seat, analysing the situation. His wife grabbed his arm and stared at Clover. Clover took a breath and let the door close, tears spilling from her eyes. She drew her arm across her face, exhaled and looked down at her daughter.

"Sorry."

As they walked away, the entire restaurant watched them until they were out of sight. Valda felt a strong feeling of shame; her head buzzed with confusion, unable to comprehend how her mother could change tone and attitude in ten steps, unable to see the cracks that were beginning to show, cracks that nothing or no one could stop growing.

The night had grown chilly but they didn't take a cab. Instead Clover opted for the 98 bus from Kilburn to Willesden, then the 266 to Church Road estate. They travelled in absolute silence.

They walked around the corner to their home. The teenage boys had moved from the staircase to the pavement in the distance, music still playing but lower. A few girls had joined them, spliffs in between their fingers, the glowing tips floating from their mouth to waist like erratic stars in the night. They didn't even look at her and her mother, too busy with their own existence.

Valda looked up at their kitchen window and for a split second thought she had seen someone looking out of the darkness inside, but as they approached she realised it was just the way the curtain had been left.

They took their coats off in silence. Clover turned the light on in the kitchen, ran the tap and emerged with a glass of water.

"Here," she said.

Valda took the glass and drank, Clover stood watching her.

"Good girl … get some rest, it's been a long day."

They both ascended the stairs but stopped at the top, the smell of rot so strong it beat them back down. Clover lit incense and sprayed air freshener up there but the smell was still present. By tomorrow, these measures wouldn't be adequate, and Clover knew it.

They both took blankets to sleep downstairs. Valda lay down on one sofa, her eyes threatening to close. Her mother sat on the other sofa, cigarette in hand, picking at her lip, wondering what to do with the dead.

Valda woke briefly from a dream in which she was the fifth Ghostbuster, sitting on the shoulder of the marshmallow man, who had the face of the cab driver. Instead of destroying the city, he roamed around it handing out gigantic Murray mints to children. She looked around the room. Her mother's place was empty, just ruffled blankets laid across the sofa. Valda stood and walked out of the living room. Along the passage walls were huge bluebottles at rest. Her presence awakened them, and they flew up around the light, clumsy, as if their bellies had been filled with beer, baguettes and wine.

Valda waved them away from her face and stood at the foot of the stairs that travelled up into darkness. From above came the sound of her mother's voice, filled with tears. The only word Valda could make out was 'Leon'. Valda contemplated walking up but decided against it, as she too spoke to Leon through the door and wouldn't have wanted anyone to interrupt.

The next time she woke up, her mother lay across the sofa. Daylight shone through the windows, polishing all the furniture with its reach. Her mother's eyelids twitched constantly.

She had a strange taste in her mouth: root beer mixed with decay, stronger than it had ever been. Flies flew around in the living room now, their numbers increasing with the decaying process. The doorbell rang and Clover stirred a little. Valda stood and walked towards the living room door. The hallway was full of flies, crawling on the floor and ceiling, with more in flight; their unified hum made her feel sick.

The bell rang again, and the person's silhouette moved restlessly. Valda stood at the living room door, looking. The doorbell rang again, this time more prolonged and angry. Valda walked forward, crushing flies on the floor into the carpet, while swatting the rest from her face.

At the door she reached up but, just before she could turn the handle, Clover's hand shot out from behind, grabbing hers. Valda jumped and turned around to look up at her mother, whose face was tired and angry.

"Whatdya think you're doing?" Clover whispered

Clover held her hand tightly.

"I was answering the door," Valda whispered back.

"Really? After I told you not to?"

Flies flew around her head like a black halo. Clover's grip tightened in anger.

"Y-y-you're hurting me."

"Shut up and get in the living room."

The bell went again. Clover pushed Valda towards the living room and fixed her with a menacing stare, then held the door handle, opened the door and slipped out quickly, closing the door behind her.

She remained out there for ten minutes, lying through her teeth to neighbours on either side about the origins of the smell they were getting through their walls, as well as the flies. Clover claimed that misplaced meat was the issue and she was working on it.

Of course, they didn't believe her, as neither they nor the rest of the estate had seen Eric or Leon in two weeks. What her mother had failed to understand was a council estate is like a body: some people who lived there were nothing more than replaceable blood cells, small and insignificant, easily replaceable, people who moved about by themselves, cats and birds their only companions, able to die and be undiscovered for weeks without so much as a raised eyebrow. Some people were major organs, and unfortunately for Clover, Eric was one of those, always going about the estate helping where he could. No women carried their shopping upstairs when he was about; he would give a pound to a kid in the shop for sweets – he was a regular gentleman. When the body missed organs like that, everything within it noticed. Clover didn't know that, but within two days she would.

She came back through the door and pressed her back against it. She let out a sigh then walked towards the living room, swatting flies from her path. She entered like a rocket and fixed Valda with a look of disgust. She pointed her finger at both sides of the living room walls. And spoke through tightened lips.

"These bitches were asking about the smell and flies … they wanted to know where your fucking dad is."

Valda sat looking up at her; a feeling began to float in her stomach that she had never felt for her mother – a feeling of fear. Her behaviour was becoming more and more erratic.

"I told them it was lost meat, fallen down the side of the unit."

She began to pace the living room like a caged bear.

"We have to get rid of the bodies – chop them up … put them out."

She clicked her fingers and pointed at Valda.

"That's it. We'll chop them up and put them in the waste bins downstairs. Collection's on Monday."

Valda sat transfixed by her agitated movement and the conversation she was having with herself. Things seemed a million miles away from the great time they had shared last night and the week before.

This situation appeared to have aged Clover. Over two weeks her once beautiful face had been marred by murder and the suicide of her first-born. Worry lines and crow's feet were permanently on show.

The rest of the day she spent upstairs in her room, mumbling to herself, spraying both fly sprays and air fresheners while relighting incense. Valda wished this could end and for a second or two she wished her father was alive, abusing both her and her mother. She knew where she stood with that; she had trained herself to accept it as a way of life, but this situation was too much for her eleven-year-old mind to handle.

That night Clover insisted they turn off all the lights, convinced that neighbours were peeking through windows, trying to catch her out. Valda didn't want to sleep that night; her mother was starting to scare her, walking around in the darkness, a big blade in her hand, talking to herself in incoherent ramblings, sounding as if she were possessed.

Valda cried in silence until sleep kissed her and she went down.

She was awoken in the middle of the night by frantic rocking. When her eyes opened, her mother stood there, her finger pressed against her own lips, a meat cleaver in the other.

"Shhh … It's time," Clover whispered.

She pulled Valda's arm and dragged her upstairs into the darkness, then turned on the light in the hallway, revealing thousands of dead flies and incense sticks stuck to the wall, all at various stages of burning. The tape around the door cracks had been broken; maggots twisted and curled in a liquid at the door's base. Clover looked back at Valda through a smile that said, "Ready?"

Without any further warning, she opened the door and more liquid seeped out, carrying a smell that made them both hold their stomachs. A mist of flies flew out like bats from a cave. The hum they made was so loud Valda thought they would shake the house apart. Valda bent over further and vomited. Clover walked in and slid on badly decomposed flesh and began to vomit violently. She turned on her belly and crawled out of the room, maggots and rotting flesh in her hair and face.

Valda turned away and attempted to walk back downstairs but was brought to her knees on account of the smell and vomiting. Clover pulled herself to a crawl, got back out of the room, then rose to a knee, shutting the door before collapsing to the ground. Liquefied flesh was jammed underneath her fingernails and ran up her arms, her hair and face. She lay on the floor and cried in between vomiting, vomiting until she had nothing left.

Valda lay in a foetal position and closed her eyes. The hum above and around her changed from that of horrible bluebottles to some beautiful device that helps insomniacs sleep.

Both awoke to an earth-shattering crash from downstairs that was so loud they both jumped up and looked around for the source. It came again and Clover rushed past Valda, cleaver still in hand, her appearance that of the walking dead. Her top was stuck to her with waste, and her hair was stuck to her face with the rotten and rancid substance from the room upstairs.

"Shit, it's your dad; the fucker's come back for us, call the Ghostbusters!" Clover screamed.

Clover descended the stairs in three jumps, each making a large thud. Valda stood frozen to the spot. The last crash from below brought with it a confused concoction of screaming and shouting male voices. At first she thought it was her dad, then she heard them say, "Police! Police! Police!" Valda walked to the stairs and sat on the top step, looking down.

Two police men squared up to Clover and the cleaver, Clover screaming random obscenities. The officers held their truncheons out and pulled back as she advanced, cleaver held above her head like the last Red Indian fighting four crazy cowboys. From behind the first officer, one jumped up and used his walkie-talkie like a sling, throwing it at Clover with full force. Her forward motion doubled its impact; it hit and stunned her in one go. She bent and held her face, the meat cleaver falling to the ground.

Clover stumbled all over the passageway, holding both her jaw and the wall for support. The police rushed in, kicked the cleaver away and brought her down to her stomach, pulling her hands behind her back and cuffing her.

Where fear and sorrow for her mother should have been grew a strange sense of relief that curled over Valda like a fluffy blanket. She had seen on a TV programme that children with no parents got given to good ones, ones who took their children to McDonald's and the cinema every other weekend, ones who tucked them into bed at night and read them a story, their stomachs filled, their thirst quenched, love all around them. She wanted that … she wanted that more than to be a Ghostbuster, more than anything.

One police officer looked up and saw Valda sitting on the step looking down. He rose up from restraining her mother, turned and shouted something to an officer out of sight, then stood aside, allowing a female officer to come through. She walked past Clover and came half way up the stairs, a few steps down from Valda. The pair paused, sizing each other up. The police officer's stare said 'I'm here to help', while Valda's screamed 'help me'. The officer read that pretty well and extended her open hand for Valda to take.

They walked hand in hand out of the house. Outside was grey with drizzle that pelted her face softly. When she reached the bottom of the block and walked out to the car park below, it was as if the world had come to see a hanging. A sea of nosey neighbours, mostly women, were outside, clucking like chickens over feed, crossing their arms over their housecoats, long T-shirts and jumpers.

Valda never saw her mother alive again after that day. While in custody she had used a jumper as a noose and hung herself in her cell, leaving Valda an orphan. Valda went to live in a care home and mostly kept herself to herself. The staff were good despite all the horror stories she had heard. Although they weren't all loving, they did their jobs correctly, and Valda was able to find a peace she had never before enjoyed in her life.

The gruesome tale didn't make the newspapers or TV, local or national, as all British media outlets were occupied with news on the Provisional Irish Republican Army, who had attempted to assassinate the British government by bombing the Brighton hotel where they were staying for their annual conference. Prime Minister Margaret Thatcher escaped without injury, while five people, including one MP, Anthony Berry, were killed.

~

Dr Ryan hovered over Valda, holding a needle. "Okay, you're going to feel a small prick."

She looked up and nodded, pressing her lips together. Dr Ryan injected her, placed the needle in the bio waste box then walked over to a cabinet in the corner for another syringe.

"I'm just going to take some blood for the lab."

Valda sat up, her arm in Ryan's gloved hand. Dr Ryan massaged it for a vein, and once satisfied he looked over his glasses at her, his grey eyes as calm as the sea at night. She looked down at the blood filling the tube like thick red wine. She looked back at his eyes, so calm and soothing. From above her a quiet hum and the soft white glow of the light aided her eyelids to shut. She slurred a word she had no warning was coming. "Welcome."

Dr Ryan pulled the syringe out and watched her slip into sleep's hands. A patient at a NHS surgery would have been woken and tossed out immediately, but Valda and the calibre of the patients who attended surgeries like Ryan's were stinking rich and highly influential – everyone from film stars to oil-rich Arab sheiks. The amount she paid for his services meant Dr Ryan smiled, stood, dimmed the lights and left.

Valda had begun life as Valda Wright, until she was adopted at the age of thirteen in 1985. Valda was adopted by the Payne family, a middle-class, middle-aged couple who had spent their youth pursuing careers instead of raising a family. Ronald Payne worked in finance and Donatella Payne in fashion.

Ronald was a slender man, always in a suit, his brown hair pinned to one side of his head by a pen, his oversized mobile phone glued to the other. He would pace the house up and down, down and up, speaking quietly but firmly to someone on the other end, telling them to sell, buy or stall.

Valda loved that he never raised his voice and always kept his cool. When she first arrived on their doorstep, one of the first things he gave her was a long stare and gradual smile, extending his huge hand for a shake. He was the reason she was there.

Ronald had had testicular cancer which doctors had found very late, which almost took his life. While in hospital, he and Donatella had had serious time to re-evaluate their lives. They wondered where the time had gone. They had gone from weekly movie nights to coming home late with extra work, from joint holidays to places of wonder, to individual business trips with pricks in suits and fashionistas, from dinner with friends to takeaways for one: in fact, they barely spoke to each other or their friends any more. Their joint obsession with money and work progress defined them. They hadn't even realised that they had been together for over twenty years, and they hadn't even thought of children.

Scared they would die and leave no legacy, they enquired about the likelihood of having their own children. Doctors told Ronald he would never be able to produce sperm again after his operations and chemotherapy. They spoke to a counsellor, who suggested they adopt, so they did.

His hospital stay had saved their lives and had given Valda a new one. He was a loving man who always had time for Valda and understood when she never had time for him: when she went to her room to cry sometimes after good things were given or done for her, sorry her brother couldn't have tasted what a good life should have been like.

Donatella was as mad as a March hare, more of a friend to Valda than a mother. She wore wacky clothes, like Vivienne Westwood. Her hair was dyed unnatural colours humans couldn't make, like neon pinks and acid greens. Teachers and children at Valda's school made fun of her, but Valda loved her very much, especially all her quirky idiosyncratic ways.

Donatella had come to England from Italy as a fashion student and had planned to go back, but met Ronald at university. She would call Valda 'Little V' and introduced herself to everyone as Donatella Payne of the house of Vaughan. Her flamboyant introduction always made people laugh. One day Valda was standing on a stool, her arms outstretched like a scarecrow, masking and measuring tape hung from her as it did when Donatella had a flash of inspiration and borrowed her to use as a model to try it out. Valda looked down at Donatella and asked, “Don’t you care when people laugh at you for your style?”

Donatella looked up and smiled. Crow’s feet radiated out from her ageing brown eyes behind pink-framed spectacles.

“I’m not bothered; my style is just my way of trying to be an individual within a world where I have become a sheep. Ronald and I are slaves to the system. We let our wage packets determine the trajectory of our lives, enjoying things that only the foolish lust for.”

Valda dropped her arms, her brain fully engaged. Donatella rose from her knees and sat back on a chair, a pair of scissors in one and material in the other. Donatella pointed the scissors towards Valda.

“You’ve had a terrible life so far, but you must not let it dictate where you are going in life. Take being here as a second chance, aim to own your own business – not for money, but for the freedom and options it brings. Live life to the fullest and, most importantly, get married – be happy, have children and leave your legacy.”

Valda swallowed hard and locked eyes with Donatella, seeing regret and pain, acknowledging that she would have much preferred to have a biological daughter standing before her. Valda didn’t like her look; it reminded her of how her own mother slid around the house trying to be small so her father wouldn’t beat her, ignoring what he did to her children.

Donatella’s words that day created a personal mantra for Valda: “Be the wolf over the sheep.” Valda aggressively applied it to everything she did in her adult life until it would eventually harden her, having the complete opposite effect to what Donatella had intended.

One afternoon, in 1998, Valda received a phone call at Ellen's from Donatella, asking her to come home urgently. She wouldn't say what was wrong, but she sounded upset. Valda rushed back and met Donatella at the front door. Her make-up ran down her face, giving her the appearance of a sad clown. She swung her arms around her and held her so tightly that she almost crushed her ribcage. She began to cry. Valda didn't need to be told what had happened; she knew that only loss could invoke such profound sorrow.

Valda whispered in her ear. "How?"

Donatella loosened her grip and took a deep breath. "You'd better come in"

She led Valda into the living room, which was just as she had left it five years before, with wooden flooring and a clear glass table in the middle with fresh flowers at its centre. All their family photos still stood on the units surrounding white leather sofas. They took a seat. Donatella placed her hand on Valda's knee.

"He'd been ill for a while now."

"Ill! Why didn't you tell me? I was here last month!"

"I know, I know. He didn't want to bother you, you'd just started your new job and he was so happy for you."

Tears gathered in the corners of Valda's eyes, on the verge of flowing over.

"His cancer came back three months ago—"

"Cancer! Again!"

"I know. The thing is, it came out of the blue. Even the doctor said he was shocked that it took him so quickly …"

"Well, where is he?"

"Given's hospice."

"Have you seen him?"

"I was getting ready to visit him before they called to tell me, then I called you."

Valda held her head in the palm of both hands, tears dripping between her fingers. Donatella rubbed her back. Valda looked up and put her arm around her neck and they pulled each other close.

Death has a funny way of revealing elements of lives that were hidden when the person still breathed. As they planned for his burial with the rest of the Payne family, out of nowhere came Tyler and his horrible mother Pam, from the USA. Tyler claimed to be Ronald's long-lost son who had heard about his death and wanted to begin a relationship with the Payne family or as Donatella put it, "like vultures looking for all the flesh they could scavenge from Ronald's bones."

Both Donatella and Valda were shocked by the revelation and ordered his will to be read. The only problem with the request was he had written one stating half his estate should go to his first born, which left her praying that DNA tests proved the man, who looked a lot like him, wasn't his, or she could be fighting for everything they had worked hard for their entire life.

When the results came back, Donatella almost fainted: they showed he was indeed his child and legally entitled to half of Ronald's estate and, boy, did they take that entitlement to its limit. They grabbed half his share of their savings, totalling £500,000, and Donatella's home be sold so they could get their half of that as well. Donatella had ploughed half her savings into fighting them, and lost the majority of it to legal bills.

Donatella never recovered. The problem wasn't the money: it was the humiliation and feeling of betrayal, and the fact that at some point in their happy relationship Ronald had been unfaithful, leaving a legacy, as horrible as the man was. She left England for Italy, with mere shrapnel of her former life, vowing never to return.

At first she and Valda spoke on the phone weekly, then monthly, then on birthdays and holidays, then not at all. Valda was once again alone in the world at the age of 28 all alone in a world that never respected the rules of karma, where good people always seemed to get fucked over and bad guys laugh loudest.

She had learned a valuable lesson from Donatella's situation; a lesson that would stay with her, and change her forever. Trust no one: get what you can at all costs and by any means necessary. Fuck everyone, man, woman or child; be the wolf, never the sheep – never the weak, never the weak.

~

Half an hour had passed and Valda began to stir, a gentle sway pulling her from her slumber. Dr Ryan stood over her, his smile huge. Valda rubbed her eyes and sat up, her legs hanging off the bed's edge. Dr Ryan held a piece of paper in his hand. Valda stopped blinking and rubbed both hands across her stomach, the pain gone as if it had never been. Dr Ryan pushed his glasses back up the bridge of his nose.

"I have some good news for you."

Valda perked up. "What is it?"

"You're pregnant."

Valda gasped and brought her hands to her mouth. "Oh my God!"

Dr Ryan nodded. "I don't know how, but it says so right here."

He turned the paper around for her to see. She snatched it and read it, then read it again and again, then looked him dead in the eye.

"Are you sure this is accurate?"

"We ran the test at least five times. There is no doubt you are one hundred per cent pregnant."

Valda jumped off the bed as if it were on fire, right at Ryan, who held her weight. He smiled and she smiled, then began to cry; tears of joy, tears of triumph.

Renasci

A pale sickle moon hung in a fading blue sky, waiting with stars behind stage curtains to perform in the longest-running show on Earth.

They say the night in all its beauty has the ability to draw from us the worst versions of ourselves; as if the dark has the ability to cloak both our intentions and actions from God. It is beyond these twilight hours where some sign treaties with demons, fiends and devils. It is in the dark where you must dwell for eternity when the ink dries and the deeds bartered for have been done. A baby born from a barren womb was not God's intention, yet it has come to pass.

Alex stuck his head out of the shower door, his hair bound together, dripping, drawn away from the shower for the second time in ten minutes. He scanned from left to right. The living room had begun to take on the caramel tone of fading daylight, a perfect manifestation of dusk.

Boom! The noise came from above. Alex looked up, unable to see anything but the door frame and ceiling. He paused in that position, contemplating his next move. Boom! The noise came again, and one by one the hairs on the back of his neck stood upright.

He grabbed a towel, wrapped it round his waist and walked slowly towards the twin staircases. He stood between them, looking up. While the light was bronze below, it appeared that the floor above was operating in its own time zone, swallowed by pitch-black nothingness.

Alex's mind began to craft and create, drawing from the depths of him a man standing at the top with an axe, blood dripping from its blade. He wore a clown's mask, with tufts of green hair springing from its sides. He wore blue raggedy overalls, too small for his frame, exposing his ankles and hairy wrists.

Of course, the clown was eight feet tall, and of course when Alex tried to run, the doors in the house would be locked and the keys hidden from reach. Alex laughed, sighed, shook his head and reached for the light switch, a part of him expecting them – in true horror-film fashion – not to work. The lights came on and dispersed the dark, bringing rational thought back to him.

Alex retied the towel round his waist and walked slowly towards the staircase, looking ahead and behind, his feet sinking into the thick carpet. At the top he stood facing all the rooms. All the doors were slightly ajar, shrouded in darkness, except the nursery, whose door was closed as if it held secrets.

He stared at the door and its gold plaque; his eyes looked back in its watery reflection, his gaze broken by a smaller noise that sounded like movement in their bedroom next door. Alex looked towards the room, then down at his damp bare body, his nakedness bothering him. He sucked on his bottom lip, his eyes dancing rapidly around as his brain went through several rational explanations for random unidentified noises in the house.

He took a deep breath of courage, put his best foot forward and walked sideways, his right hand on his towel knot, the left trailing against the wall as if he were blind. His heart began to flutter as if it housed a harem of butterflies. His breathing accelerated very slightly. He stood by the entrance of the bedroom, sideways, swallowed a hard, deep breath then pivoted round, pushing open the door hard and fast. The door swung open and the room's lights clicked on within a second.

Alex panned the room from left to right, his heart crashing. He looked to his left and noticed the wardrobe door was open, the dirty clothes basket on its side, having fallen out from where it belonged, its flap opened by the mound of clothes falling out across the floor.

Alex walked slowly towards the mess and pulled the wardrobe door open further to look inside.

Inside the wardrobe, two of the shelves had collapsed, the top one breaking the one below. Alex attributed the booming noise to the shelves and their collapse the reason the basket had been pushed out.

He placed his hands on his waist and smiled to himself, thanking God it was what it was. He bent down, picked up the basket and moved it to one side. He reached into the wardrobe, pulled out the fallen shelves and dragged them over to the bed's edge for examination. He looked at the side that had given way and realised the screws that had held them in place had broken. He looked over into the wardrobe to see if anything heavy had been placed on them, but all he could see were clothes. He thought it odd that not one, but two, shelves could collapse with nothing heavy on them.

He sat with the shelves between his legs, his eyes moving gingerly across the wardrobe's open mouth. *Ghosts, maybe?* The thought made him spin his head round to look at the room. It felt as if someone were watching him. He took a small breath of maturity and quickly opted for *wear and tear* as the reason for the breakage. He tried to think back to when they had bought the wardrobe, but had no recollection of them doing so, which led him to conclude that it had been in Valda's life, long before his arrival. This gave it age and his theory possible credence.

Alex stood and dragged the shelves to the corner of the room, leaning them against the wall. He walked back to the wardrobe, knelt before the open doors and looked in at the fallen mound of clothes. He picked up one jumper, folded it and placed it on the floor. By the fourth jumper, after he had detangled some material that had attached several jumpers together, he thought, *Fuck it, let her deal with this, she'll only complain about how it's been done anyway.*

He stood looked over at the shelves in the corner and an idea washed over him. *Put all this shit back in there and let her discover it when she gets in; that way she can't say I left the mess for her*. The idea was sneaky but harmless. He walked over to the shelves, dragged them back over to the wardrobe and placed them back in. He picked up the rubble of clothes and slung them all back into the wardrobe, including the folded ones.

He stepped back, grabbed the dirty clothes basket and lay it on its side, half hanging out of the wardrobe, as he had found it. He stepped back to admire his work. On the second step, a sudden sharp burst of pain shot up his leg from the ball of his right foot, sending him falling back onto the bed.

"Fuck!" he screamed.

He held his foot and writhed around on his back.

"Shit!"

He pulled his foot up as high as possible and noticed severe bruising, then looked down for the culprit. Valda's wooden bracelet lay on the floor: beads and triangle-shaped pieces of wood threaded together with black string. Alex leaned forward from the bed's edge and picked it up in his palm.

The pain faded, becoming secondary as he focused on the object, which was of a peculiar design. The wood pieces were dark matt mahogany. He looked more closely at each one and realised that each piece had a period of the human life cycle etched into it, from a baby crawling to upright walking.

He counted the number of pieces, which totalled thirteen. The thirteenth one appeared to differ from the rest. Engraved into it was what looked like a goat's head, circled. He didn't like that piece; it looked satanic. It made him wonder about Valda; wonder about the facets of her life she could be hiding from him, made him think about all the unscrupulous things she had done in the name of business. He thought about the way he'd turn a blind eye to so many of things she'd done, occasionally throwing up hollow protests, to make himself feel better; to make himself feel comfortable with how far he had fallen from the ethical roots his parents had laid down for him.

The doorbell dragged him out of his reflective state, making him jump. He rolled the bracelet into his palm and closed his fist around it and looked around the room, making sure the set-up was flawless. He jogged down the stairs and looked at the picture on the CCTV screen, Patrick's face appeared on it.

Alex opened the door and poked his head out, looking for Valda then at Patrick.

"Patrick! How's it going? Where's Valda?"

"She sent me to come get you."

They both paused, Patrick waiting for him to receive the message and Alex receiving it.

"But she knows how I feel about the whole driving thing."

"I know, but I think she expects you to have a drink today."

Alex paused.

"Why, what's the occasion?"

Patrick smiled. "Well, that would be telling."

They both paused.

"Not gonna give it to me, are you?" Alex stated.

Patrick shook his head sideways.

"All right, give me ten. You want to wait inside?"

"I'm all right. I'll wait in the car."

~

Riku's was a beautiful Anglo-Japanese restaurant in the heart of the City, frequented by the rich and famous or those with connections. They made sure they kept their clientele to a certain calibre by charging almost £20 for plain rice alone. The place had a beautiful white dragon sculpted into the wall, the designer ensuring it stretched and covered all corners of the restaurant. The floors were white marble and shiny. The tables were black frosted glass and the chairs white wood. The front facing window of the restaurant was tinted so diners could see out but fans, paparazzi or – God forbid, the common man – couldn't see in.

Riku's buzzed with laughter and drunk talk. It was full of rich men with their wives, mistresses or both; pop stars with friends, associates and leeches, unable to see they were mere moths spending old money heading for flames, flames that would see their wings burned, engulfing them whole, until their fifteen minutes of fame were up and the machine found others to replace them. Valda sat with her elbows on the table, her fingers interlocked under her chin. She couldn't understand how some of these pop stars and celebrities ended their careers broke, when they had the world at their feet, opportunities ten a penny. *Surely they would think about investing for the future?* At that point, a mature couple walked in through the door, the flash of paparazzi cameras lighting up the tinted restaurant windows from outside as if a shooting star had fallen to earth. The couple walked over to Micky D's table. He was the latest big thing whom young girls and corporate radio stations had placed on a pedestal. The mature couple both looked like him; Valda concluded they had to be his parents. Instead of rising to greet them, he looked up over his shoulder with such disregard that any onlooker would have thought they were begging vagabonds. It then clicked: the reason these people ended up with nothing was because they simply didn't know what it is to want. They didn't know what it was to burn from the inside out praying for death when the very person who should lay their life on the line for yours is slowly sucking it from you. When you've never lived in hell, you'll never know how badly you'd want to escape from there.

"He who feels it knows it," she whispered.

She became aware that someone was standing on her right. She looked sideways, expecting to see a waitress, but standing beside her was a young pretty girl with auburn hair cut short with a funky diagonal fringe. She looked nervous. Valda widened her eyes, tilting her head slightly as if to say, "Can I help you?"

"Hi, my name is Jenna Todd, you're Valda Payne, aren't you?"

Valda looked beyond and behind Jenna and observed a table of people looking over at them, one space empty, obviously her uninvited guest's. Valda sighed.

"That's right."

Jenna stuck out her hand. "I'm Jenna Todd."

Valda looked at her. "Yeah, you said that already."

Jenna laughed nervously and brought her hand to her forehead. "I'm so sorry. You're my idol and I'm a little nervous."

Valda laughed. "Idol?"

"Yeah, I really respect your business acumen … I mean, I've just made my first million selling custom-made hampers for kids' parties and you gave me the drive to run with my idea. I want you to know that."

What a ridiculous idea, Valda thought. *Who on earth gave that notion legs?* Then it clicked. Valda saw how her cheeks were rosy and her hair was full of bounce, her figure faultless – all signs of being brought up with optimum nutrition. Jenna was full-fat perfect, her diction middle-class. She was one of those who had wanted for nothing; she had been born with pounds in her palm, Daddy's favourite. She reminded Valda of the girl in McDonald's that night her mother began to fade; the happy little shit whose father would ensure that every business idea she had would materialise, to stop her having a bitch fit. Valda hated girls like her. She hated those who pretended they had come from nothing when in actual fact they had more at birth than some people died with.

"Well, now I know. Isn't that a pip?" Valda said.

Valda looked her in the eye, deadpan, and Jenna stared back, her smile fading. Suddenly their attention was drawn to bursts of camera flash exploding across the tinted window. The door opened and in stepped Alex. Valda raised her hand for him.

"Thanks for the chat," Jenna said

"If you wanna call it that," Valda smirked.

Alex arrived as Jenna slinked back to her table. Valda watched until she sat, then looked back at Alex, smiling.

"Who's that?" Alex asked.

Valda turned her fingers into inverted commas. "I'm her biggest idol."

Alex frowned, looked over at Jenna's table, then back at Valda.

"O-Kay. Anyway, to what do I owe this invitation?" Alex leaned forward and laced his fingers. Valda drew a breath maintaining eye contact with a smile.

"Well, how can I put this? ... How about … you're gonna be a dad."

Alex's jaw dropped, and his eyes opened so wide that it looked as though he was about to have a heart attack. He grabbed for her hands, but Valda drew them back.

"Stop it, you'll make a scene," she said through tight lips.

Alex's bemused look gave way to a smile. He leaned back in his chair, interlocked his hands behind his head, and exhaled. His cheeks puffed out and his lips created an O. "I wasn't expecting that at all."

Valda stared into his eyes, which were a little too still for her liking, the kind of stillness people with questions have, questions that upset the apple cart. Valda broke his contemplation.

"I, ah, went to Dr Ryan's with a stomach ache. He did a blood test, and it turns out we're having a baby."

The pair paused. Alex's smile weakened, not much but visibly to anyone who was searching for it. Alex laughed nervously and adjusted himself in his chair.

"Just like that, huh? Crazy!"

Valda sent her brain to amber alert. "Is there a problem?"

Alex leaned forward, arms half stretched out across the table towards her. His thumbs tapping, she could feel his knee going against the table leg. Something was wrong.

"Don't you think it's a little weird that, after all these years of us going to top fertility specialists, we're able to conceive all of sudden?" Alex questioned.

The murmur from other diners faded away. All Valda's senses fully focused on everything he said and did. She shook her head slowly from side to side involuntarily.

"Where's this coming from? I thought you'd be happy." Valda questioned.

"I am happy, trust me, but I have concerns …"

"Concerns … what is there to be concerned about?" she said, bringing her voice down to a whisper.

Valda's brow furrowed and she tilted her head, waiting for elaboration. He took a deep breath.

"Well. First, I find it little odd that the information surrounding this specialist is all cloak-and-daggerish. All you've told me is it cost £20,000 and she's some sort of holistic health doctor."

"Well, that's how much it cost, and that's what she is. What more do you want me to say?"

"Talk me through the process, then, tell me what holistic herbs or medicines were used to make this happen."

A waitress walked up. They stared at her, their faces projecting their tense exchange. She kept moving. Once out of earshot, Valda continued, "You're starting to piss me off, with all these silly questions."

Alex smirked. "Look how defensive you're getting about this. What's really going on here?"

Valda looked around at the other diners, making sure no one was tuned into their exchange. Satisfied, she continued, "I'll tell you what's going on here. You're a complete asshole who should be happy about this, not questioning this gift. You know how much it means to me."

Alex leaned in closer over the table and whispered, 'Gift?'

The restaurant doors opened, letting in the sound of the city and cameras. Micky D's table erupted into applause and cheers upon seeing the newcomer. The noise drew both Valda and Alex's attention. Riku's manager Ryu emerged from and stood in the door way that led to the back of the restaurant. He called over one of the floor staff, spoke with them and sent them over to Micky D's table.

They brought their focus back to each other.

"What are you getting at?" Valda said in a low growl.

Micky D's table began to remonstrate with the staff member, their protest getting louder than normal social murmur.

Alex shoved his hand into his pocket, produced the bracelet and placed it in the centre of the table. It sat curved like a wicked smile, commanding Valda to explain its presence. Valda looked up at Alex. He stared back, his lips pressed against each other. He looked genuinely concerned. Valda laughed with such a lack of conviction she worried he knew she was about to lie.

"What's this?" Valda asked.

"I don't know – you tell me."

At that point Micky D and his camp all got up and marched out of the restaurant, making as much noise as possible, throwing the money for their bill up into the air like confetti. Valda looked over at the commotion, hoping Alex would follow, breaking the tension.

The manager and waitress walked over to the door and knelt down to collect the funds, mumbling to each other and tutting. Valda shook her head and looked back at Alex, who continued to stare deep into her.

"These kids …" Valda said.

"Valda, what's with the bracelet?"

"I told you – I don't know anything about it," she snapped.

Alex reached across and slipped it onto his hand.

"Well, I'll tell you this. This bracelet was in our dirty clothes basket and, seeing as we barely have people over, let alone upstairs, with neither of us knowing where it's come from, I'm more than concerned. I'm about to go into an all-out fucking panic."

"Calm down."

"I won't calm down! Look at the pictures on it … especially this one."

He pointed to the goat's head.

"Are you hearing yourself?" Valda questioned.

They both looked to Alex's left and a waitress stared at them then diverted her gaze. Alex lowered his voice to a whisper and placed the bracelet back on the table.

"I know how it sounds, and I feel stupid even asking about it, but you have to look at it from my point of view," Alex replied.

"You watch too many films. What do you think I've done? Sold my soul to the de"

Alex's hand shot out and closed over hers, so quickly it stopped her in mid-flow. He looked at her and shook his head.

"Don't."

His reaction sent cold throughout her and brought clarity to the seriousness of the situation.

"Forgive me for what I'm about to say, but if you have, you have to get rid of that baby, Valda …" Alex whispered.

Tears began to form in the corners of her eyes, like small crystal pearls. Alex looked around, then back at her.

"We can adopt," he pleaded.

Valda pulled her hand out from under his, and pushed her fingers into the corners of her eyes to get rid of the tears.

"I told you already, I don't know where that thing came from."

She stood, took a breath and walked towards the toilets, holding back tears, aware she was on show. People looked up from their meals as she passed, and whispered, looking everywhere but at her.

Valda pushed the toilet door open and walked into one of the cubicles. She went to take a seat but realised the toilet lid was slimy to touch. Upon closer inspection it became clear the slimy substance was vaseline. Ryu had been forced to take this drastic measure due to the excessive use of cocaine on his premises. Valda leaned against the door instead.

Maybe I should have the damn abortion and be done with this. Alex sounds scared and he doesn't even know the half of it! Okay, Okay, think, think, think ... Come on, this is ridiculous, the whole fucking thing. I should never have gone. Patrick was right, he always is. That's it – I'll ask him what to do, but he'll say some wishy-washy nonsense like "she has no power over anything and only God can decide," which would be right, wouldn't it? I can't believe I'm even thinking about abor—

The toilet door opened and someone walked in. Valda paused in her thoughts, all her attention drawn to the visitor.

She looked through the gap in the door but couldn't see anyone. She heard the rustling of clothes, then a tap being turned on for a few seconds, then off, then no sound. Valda twisted her head to see if she could see who it was from another angle, but the person was out of her visual range. She listened harder, but it was so quiet it was as if no one was there. Valda pressed her ear up against the door, but still heard nothing. She suddenly became aware of the length of time she had spent in the toilet. Knowing that among the diners would be journalists who would have read her and Alex's body language or may have heard bits of their conversation and were now measuring the length of time she had been in the toilet, using the latter to further validate the story they were going to print in the tabloids, next to the one about BBL's smutty approach to business. Valda knew these guys better than they knew themselves.

Valda rubbed her stomach, then stopped. She looked down and lifted her top to stroke her bare belly, and tears began to breed. Unable to stop them, they rolled down her face. She closed her eyes tightly and shook her head. Visions of her and her daughter came into her mind, Valda pushing her on a swing, her laughter so bright and naive.

The sound of someone exiting brought her back to reality. She looked out of the gap in the door, then opened it. She poked her head out and looked from left to right, concluding she was alone. A thought popped in to her head, so clear it was as if it were illuminated by a floodlight.

I'm not getting rid of you. He must be crazy. I've been waiting half my life for you. I deserve this.

She inhaled, fixed her face and walked towards the exit. Valda took a seat at their table. Alex watched her. Valda leaned forward and whispered, "With or without you, Alex, I'm having this child. End of."

Alex paused, his finger pressed up against his lip. He, of all people, knew that when she had made her mind up, she wouldn't be moved. He shook his head and sighed.

"I'm telling you, if—"

"Like I said, with or without you," she said, cutting in.

Alex shook his head.

They travelled home in silence, sitting at opposite ends of the back seat, looking out of their windows, watching London's nightlife crawl by. They pulled up outside the house. Patrick drove in and came to a stop, unclipped his seatbelt and went to get out, but was halted by Alex placing a hand on his shoulder, Patrick turned to look at him.

"I wish you wouldn't do that. I really don't like it – I can open my own door."

Alex turned and looked at Valda.

"We both can."

Valda fixed him with a wicked stare. Alex slid his hand off Patrick's shoulder, opened his door, walked across the gravel towards the house and went in.

Patrick got out and opened her door. Valda slid out and leaned against the car, looking beyond him towards the house. She exhaled, exhausted by thinking, shattered by the situation. She stood straight and began to walk towards her home, her head slumped in sadness. Patrick shut the car door and stood watching her.

"Valda!" he hollered.

She stopped and turned to face him. Patrick paused as if he had to construct every word from scratch.

"Sometimes, dog ah sweat and long hair hide it."

Valda looked at him then into herself, her slight eye movement showing that she was thinking about his words.

"I don't … don't get it."

Patrick took a step closer and for a second Valda felt scared of him, scared he would hurt her with his translation, powerful truths that would reinforce what Alex suspected and she already knew. The problem with truths is that they are both intrinsic to real love and a major cause of its destruction.

His chiselled cheekbones shaded his cheeks. His pupils were small, sucking in the driveway floodlight. He moved closer and stopped just in front of her.

"Things are not always as they seem; be mindful of this."

Valda looked up at him, towering and thin. She swallowed and spoke.

"Well, I appreciate your concern, but I don't know what you're referring to, so we'll leave it there."

They paused, Patrick aware he might have said too much. He adjusted his stance and jacket then cleared his throat.

"Will that be all for tonight?"

"Yes."

Patrick smiled, turned and began to walk around the car to get in. Valda turned and walked towards her front door. She touched her cheeks and felt the wet of tears and was thrown by it; she hadn't realised she was crying. Her head had become a swirling mess of confusion and chaos, Alex and Patrick's words colliding. Alex didn't understand love's song lived where his doubt had been cast, its sound and feeling, bigger than he could have envisaged.

The car pulled out of the driveway and drove off. Valda watched the gates shut. The floodlights cut out in the absence of movement, plunging the driveway into darkness. She suddenly appreciated how patient, quiet and non-judgemental the night was. She hadn't realised how peaceful her driveway could be, surrounded by its high walls and evergreens that swayed like large tufts of candyfloss in the breeze.

She stepped back from the front door, sat on the step and blocked out the world, enjoying the night's calm in the company of her growing child.

Lovis

Their lack of eye contact was normal but their body language said something else completely. They kept their heads low, entrenched in their work, as if their lives depended on it. Normally, a Thursday was a winding-down day, a day where loud conversation and laughter could be heard from down the hallway until Valda arrived. Today there was no laughter or conversation, just work – hard work, Valda felt she should have been pleased by this, but a break from the norm meant change, which is something Valda rarely embraced unless she had endorsed it. A designer got up and carried a piece of cloth across to a neighbouring designer, his shoulders slumped and his pace sluggish as if someone had died.

Valda hadn't, in a while, stood and watched the intricate workings of BBL: the clusters of little people who made her huge business tick, day in, day out, the cells, tissues and organs that made BBL the leading brand of lingerie in the UK.

She looked at the design table on her right, where a man and woman sat with scrolls of paper adorned with beautiful etchings and sketches. To her left was a designer table with more sketches, but these had colour, beautiful deep reds and purples that gave life to outlines. Of course, she knew what the two tables did: the one on the right sketched ideas and the one on the left gave them colour before they … Her mind went blank, as the next stage of development eluded her. She looked over towards the back of the room and saw two handfuls of people buzzing about, scraps of cloth between their teeth, scissors and bobs in hand. Still her mind ran bare, unable to name the next stage of development. This sat uncomfortably with her; it meant there were facets of her business that were alien. She had become too complacent, simply smiling and nodding when things were brought to her, not questioning the process, preferring to give the impression she had a clue about how things were begun, maintained and finished, hiding ignorance behind an incredibly ruthless approach to man and business management, similar to those who ran Ellen's – and she knew how that ended.

Charlie Gibbs (design manager for BBL) emerged from nowhere, glimpsed Valda and began visibly giving instructions, his arms and attention going this way and that. The floor sprang to life with movement; people looked at Valda out of the corners of their eyes as she stood, surveying them.

She only met Gibbs once a month. He was thin and olive-skinned with a strong, camp Yorkshire accent that really jarred her. He would bring up pieces his team had designed for the coming month for her to judge whether they were good, bad, current, in season or unsellable – sort of like a pre … Her mind ran vacant once more, unable to name that part of the process either.

Valda nibbled her lip. She began to realise she had become more concerned with the company's appearance in the media than the stuff that went into the process, more concerned with the money she would receive than where the rest went. She recognised in her approach the ingredients for downfall, the same ingredients that were thrown into the mixing bowl and baked when Ellen's Brassieres went under, when the owners had been too busy enjoying the produce of others' labours, unaware their captain had gone rogue and was steering their ship into a jagged cliff face.

Gibbs began to look nervous, and made a beeline for the designer floor doors. Valda held her palm up and waved him away. He paused and moved his weight from one foot to the other, then turned back. Valda watched a little while longer then walked towards the lifts, her mind racing.

Hang on a minute, it was never my idea to advertise on teen websites that was Rachel and Dean from marketing ... That's it, they told me how much it could generate from an untapped market, but where was Drew then? She wasn't there to say this is bad PR, but now we're in the shit, she's in my office every minute, appearing to do her job.

The lift doors opened and Valda stepped in.

You're losing it here; you're losing control of the ship.

The lift doors opened, Valda stepped out and walked towards her office. Waiting outside her door stood Selen and Drew. Selen was black with bushy hair and caramel skin. Selen held paperwork and Drew held a bundle of newspapers.

They stopped talking as Valda approached.

"Morning," they said in unison.

Valda forged a smile, took out her key card and opened her office door.

"Come in."

Valda walked towards her desk and took a seat, the pair sat in the two chairs opposite.

Valda crossed her arms and leaned back. "How can I help you?"

Drew looked at Selen and Selen nodded for her to go first. Drew placed a newspaper on the table. The front page had a picture of Valda and Alex looking as though they were about to rip each other's heads off. Valda's eyes moved across the headline; she unfolded her arms and picked the paper up.

"Is tycoon Valda's relationship with her toy boy feeling the strain after a rough few months for her ailing company BBL? Get the full breakdown inside."

Valda huffed and threw it down on the table. Drew looked at Valda.

"What does it say?" Valda asked.

"It says you and Alex were arguing and you walked off to the toilets, then it goes into some stuff about BBL and your past …" Drew replied.

Valda leaned forward, her eyes wide. "Past! What about my past?"

"Oh, nothing personal, just your business past from, Ellen's to BBL et cetera."

Valda leaned back.

"Okay, do you know who wrote this?" she asked.

"I don't know her. She's new. Her name's Jenna Todd, she's a Globe in-house reporter."

"Little bitch," Valda responded.

Drew and Selen looked at each other.

"You know her?" Drew asked.

Valda laughed sarcastically. "Yeah, she approached me on the night and told me she was an entrepreneur who really looked up to me, blah, blah, blah. These fucking roaches never stop."

"It doesn't matter anyway. This might go in our favour – at least it shows a more human side to you. I'll make some calls and see if we can get it phased from radio and TV until it's forgotten about."

Valda nodded and looked at Selen.

"What's the latest?" Valda asked.

"Well, sales are down another ten per cent this month. The team has put it down to the media campaign against us. The news is affecting morale throughout the company; people think they're going to lose their jobs," Selen replied.

"Explains a lot. What are you putting in place to stop this going any further?"

"Well, I know it's not within my jurisdiction, but I would suggest we bow to the pressure and remove the ads before it's too late."

Drew cut in. "She has a point; a lot of female celebs are joining in with the condemnation of us. Mary Donto weighed in last night on Twitter saying we were a disgrace of a company. With her having a current chart number one, she has a lot of influence. Young people do listen to these people, like it or not."

Valda cupped her chin in thought. "We have a Twitter account? Since when?" she asked.

"Since last November. I run it personally. We have over 10,000 followers. I'm sure we went over this at the time…" Drew replied.

"Okay, here's what I want you guys to do. Drew – sort out the phasing, Selen – get me an accurate breakdown of our accounts for the last five months. I want both things done by the end of the day."

Both looked at Valda and nodded, accepting her orders, then stood and walked out. Valda watched them leave then went to her phone and called her PA, Claire. The phone rang and was answered immediately.

"Good morning, Valda, what can I do for you?"

"Get me a croissant and fresh orange juice from Miguel's. After that, get me an independent auditor, and make sure the meeting room is vacant for 6 pm. Inform all heads of departments they are to attend a meeting at six sharp. Make sure only they are told, and Claire, absolutely no one is to know about the auditor."

"Okay. Should I provide refreshments for the meeting?"

"No."

"Okay. I'll bring the croissant and orange juice up immediately and get straight onto the auditor, then meeting invites. Sorry, Valda, should I attend as well?"

"Yes."

"Okay, I'll be up soon."

Valda stood up from her chair and looked out of the window, across London's skyline, where she could see cars and people moving like ants, making the capital tick. She sighed; second guessing is a tiring business and will drain your spirit if you let it. At times it can break your heart when someone who you think is close turns around and sidesteps you. Her father and Ronald had been the best teachers in life when it came to understanding how sick, sneaky and dishonest humans could be. She had never missed one of their classes, and had graduated with full honours. She trusted nobody.

BBL was falling and she could only attribute blame to decisions she had hired experts to make. Heads were surely going to roll tonight.

~

Valda buzzed Claire in. Claire placed the goods down on her desk.

"Claire, before the auditor gets here, I want you to go down to Selen's office and gather the files I've asked her for. I want you to give them directly to the auditor and provide them with the meeting room to work from. I want them to tell me in layman's terms where all expenditure is going from the company and whether there are any areas for concern. Give them my email address and tell them to email me with their findings."

Claire nodded.

"Be sure to stand outside the meeting room until they have finished their work and let them know that if they need anything they can ask you. Oh, and make sure they're out of there by 5 pm. If you can't find an auditor, call me. If you don't, I will assume they have come and gone, got it?"

"Yep."

"Good, I'll see you at the meeting."

Claire turned around and walked out.

Valda opened the paper bag and slid out the croissant; its sweet buttery smell filled the office and relaxed her. Her thoughts drifted to the unborn child growing inside her. She thought about how the feeling trumped making her first million or buying her first piece of expensive jewellery, even meeting Alex.

The rest of the day flew past. Valda filled it by surfing baby forums and visiting websites for baby clothes, accessories and shoes. She went to Twitter and looked over BBL's account and all its 10,001 followers that she hadn't been aware existed. She would do well to rein Drew in tonight, she thought; humiliate her just short of firing. Selen would remain, depending on the auditor's report, but Dean and Rachel were going and would be replaced by their assistants there and then. The whole online advertising thing had done more harm than good and was now forcing BBL and Valda to be reliant upon Braga – this was not a position she desired to be in.

Five o'clock rolled around and Valda was sitting looking out across London's fading day. She sipped on Fugi volcanic water, recommended by several online forums for older pregnant women, as the sulphur aided in the development of unborn babies. Claire had rung round for an hour trying to find stockist and had only found one health store in Richmond which sold the bottles, at £25 per unit. Claire bought a caseload and had it delivered by cab.

Valda had an hour to kill. She spun round in her chair and placed the water down on the table, picked up an apple from her fruit bowl and bit into it. She looked at the front page of the paper and read it again.

"Is tycoon Valda's relationship with her toy boy feeling the strain after a rough few months for her ailing company BBL? Get the full breakdown inside."

She shook her head in annoyance. She took another bite of her apple, opened the paper, turned three pages and stopped at her story. She rarely read articles about herself as it put her in a bad mood for days. The thought that somebody would have the effrontery to bare elements of your personal life to the world without permission angered her immensely.

She skimmed through the Jenna Todd exclusive, looking for anything she could sue the paper for, but – to her extreme displeasure – everything had been written in prudence where needed and fact where required. She took another bite of her apple and looked at the photos, wondering how on earth either of them had been unable to see the photographer.

The first two were taken at close range from the shoulder up. The third and final photo was wider and included other diners in the background. Valda scrutinised the last one. In it, Alex held the bracelet and she seemed to be pointing at it. She thought how the world would think the lame-looking accessory held no significance, when in actual fact, it was the reason they had had the dispute; the argument the media had seen fit to project to the world.

Valda took one last bite of the apple and threw the core in the bin. She turned and looked out across London's skyline slowly fading to black. Conscious of the time, she turned back to the paper and went to close it, but something caught her attention.

In the wide picture, three of the furthest-away diners appeared blurred and all appeared to be looking in the direction of the camera, as if they knew the photo was about to be taken.

She hadn't noticed them before. She rubbed her eyes and looked at it again. With every second passed the figures appeared to be coming into focus, until their identities were certain, making hairs stand up all over her body: looking back at her were what seemed to be her mother, brother and father. She shot back in her chair, away from the desk, her heart beating so hard she thought she was about to have a full-blown heart attack.

She stood up and walked around the table, twice.

You're imagining it, you're imagining it. Breathe, breathe.

She stood by the edge of the table and looked at the open paper from a distance. She walked around once more and stood above it. She took a deep breath and looked down. They still remained, but now their faces were high-definition clear, her brother's skin a pale grey, his lips blue and his neck bent awkwardly. Her mother's once beautiful hair looked wild and untamed, as it had looked in her final stages. Her father looked awful; he sat and stared directly at her, his eyes as black as her table, his smile as wicked as sin; he looked both angry and happy. She stared at him and him at her, then he took a breath and Valda held hers, bringing her hands, cupped, to her mouth. He stood slowly up from his seat, as did the rest. They began shuffling towards the camera, slowly, like zombies, past other diners towards her. Her brother dragged his bare feet; her mother's hands were twisted in frightful un-human ways.

Valda stood frozen stiff, physically unable to move, her body felt as though it weighed a hundred stones. They edged closer, right to the foreground of the picture, her father's mouth salivating black liquid, the same colour as the stuff that had spewed from him on the day of treats. Just as they looked as if they were about to climb out of the newspaper, there was a knock on the door and Valda jolted backwards, clattering against the window behind her.

She leaned against it, her breathing laboured, tears rolling down her cheeks. There was another knock. She looked up at the clock, which read 6:15. She leaned off the window and gathered herself, then went back to the paper, and the picture was normal: the table where her family had been was occupied by some other diners frozen in time.

Thank God, Thank God.

She closed the paper and ran her hand down her face. There was another, louder, knock. Valda stood up straight and went to it, then remembered the door entry camera. She looked down at the screen and, looking back, was Claire.

Valda gathered herself, took a sip of Fugi water and buzzed her in. The door opened and Claire entered. Valda stood on her side of the table.

"Is everything Okay?" Claire asked.

"Of course, why wouldn't it be?"

"It's just that everyone's waiting downstairs for the meeting to start and we've heard nothing."

Valda looked down at the paper again, then back at Claire.

"Come," Valda commanded, waving her over.

Claire looked apprehensive, but walked over. She stood by the table and looked at Valda. Valda pointed down at the paper.

"Open this paper and go three pages in to the story about me."

Claire looked at her, bemused by her request.

"Go on."

Claire pulled the paper round to face her and opened the paper to the page about Valda, then looked up for further instruction. Their eyes met, Valda's stare intense.

"In the third picture, look at the people in the corner and tell me what you see."

Claire looked at the people, then looked up at Valda.

"Two people eating and drinking."

Valda looked at the picture, closed the paper and brought it back to her side of the table. "Good. Tell them the meeting's cancelled until further notice and get me Patrick," Valda requested.

Claire looked confused.

"Cancel the meeting and get Patrick," Claire repeated.

"Yes, right now."

Claire jumped and realised she had lingered too long. She began to walk towards the door. Valda stopped her. The thought of being alone induced dread.

"Claire, wait. On second thoughts, I'll come down with you."

Claire looked at her with genuine concern. "Are you sure everything's Okay?"

Valda wagged her finger at Claire. "Don't ask me that again, you're walking a very thin line."

Claire paused; Valda walked around the table and approached her with the paper in her outstretched hand.

"Here, I want you to take this and dispose of it on your way home."

Claire slowly raised her hand and took the paper, trying her best not to show that she felt Valda was losing it. Valda opened the door and stood by it, waving Claire out.

"Come on, out!"

Claire walked out hurriedly and Valda followed behind her.

"On second thoughts, don't worry about Patrick. Just cancel the meeting and, above all, get rid of that paper on your way home."

Claire nodded. "Okay, will do," she responded.

"Claire, I mean it. Make sure that paper is out of this building."

They shared a look.

Valda shot out of the lift at the bottom and walked as if she were an Olympic power walker straight past Mercy's replacement on reception, past security, who obviously didn't realise Valda was still in the building, since he sat slumped in his chair, playing on his phone, while eating a pack of crisps, securing fuck all. He jumped up, crumbs on his dark-blue uniform, and watched her power-walking so fast towards the door she would have collided with it had he not pressed the release button in time.

Veronica, Claire and the security man all stood inside, watching in sheer amazement as she rushed towards Patrick's parked car. Claire looked down at the paper and stared outside, intrigued.

Valda slid in and lay on the back seat, both hands covering her face. She spoke in a muffled voice through laced fingers. "Take me home."

Patrick looked over his shoulder, surveying her for ailment or injury, and was shocked to find her lying along the seat. He had had enough experience with Valda to know he wasn't to ask her a thing at a time like this. He started the engine and drove away.

Throughout the journey he looked back to find her still lying down, face cupped in her hands. At certain points he definitely heard sobbing; seeing her like that reminded him of his first serious job, driving for a limo company called Ting's. Patrick had laughed to himself when he had come across the company name, innocently derived from the owner's name, Mr Ting Ju-ch'ang. In Jamaica, ting, or tings, had a whole array of universal meanings, ranging from describing a loose women and the apprehension from her of sexual favours, to other more serious contexts, such as narcotics, firearms and more.

In his interview for the driver's job, Mr Ting had remarked that he was extremely tall and happy, as Patrick couldn't stop smiling every time Mr Ting said, “So, you want to work for Ting’s, huh?”

Patrick considered Mr Ting at least a partially good man for giving him the opportunity to work and earn a fairly decent wage, but the other half of him was tight, greedy and cared very little about the roadworthiness of most of his limos. As a result, the vehicles were beautiful outside, but a mess under the bonnet. Duck-tape bound, rusty old parts kept the limos just about moving and money in his pockets.

One of Patrick’s very last jobs for Ting’s was a prom night pick-up for a little girl called Shelia Bradford. Patrick hated prom season; the girls or boys were usually loud and rude, drinking and smoking underage, and if he had mixed groups he expected sexual vulgarity. He was sure these were good kids normally but something about prom night made them rat-shit crazy.

Patrick pulled up outside 13 St Mary’s Road and prepared to do the whole ‘knocking at the door then waiting by the car’ VIP thing that he thought was unnecessary for people who weren’t actual VIPs, but Mr Ting insisted all his drivers did it so he did. He could see curtains twitching, people shocked by the sight of a limousine on their working-class road.

Shelia’s mother answered the door and sent him a warm and welcoming smile. She stepped out of the doorway and walked halfway down the path towards him.

“Thanks for coming. It’s Shelia’s big night. I’m so happy for her, I never even knew she had friends. You do know you’re doing another pick-up, don’t you?”

Patrick nodded.

“Great! She should be down in a minute – you wanna come in?”

“I would, but I have to wait by the car.”

“Limo, you mean, It’s a bloody limo, my baby’s going in a limo,” she said, punching her fists in the air.

Patrick smiled.

“Indeed,” he said to himself.

Normally, such jubilation and salivation over luxury would annoy him, but he sensed more happiness for her daughter than anything else.

She looked over her shoulder and signalled she was going to see what was delaying Shelia. A group of boys stood across the road looking on, while several residents, mainly women, suddenly felt the urge to sweep their doorsteps and oil the hinges of gates. Patrick was used to this; it happened everywhere he brought the limo. People were inquisitive by nature.

The sun was high and the sky clear; his black suit absorbed the sun's heat and held it in its fibres; if he wasn't as thin as he was, he would have cooked. The door opened and Shelia stood on the step. The first thing Patrick thought was …

Lord have mercy, she fat ee?

Her rosy cheeks were swollen with fat, stealing territory from her mouth and eyes, making her lips small and her eyes mere pimples in her face. Her dress was pink satin with a large cream sash tied around her hefty stomach; her hair fell into beautiful golden ringlets that glistened in the sun.

Patrick looked around at neighbours who were doing their best to hide their amusement at her appearance. She walked towards him, nervously watching her step in her pristine white shoes. Patrick walked towards her, opened her front gate, took her hand and escorted her to the limo, while her mother stood at the door with a smile so large, you would've thought she had won the lottery. Tears of joy rolled down her cheeks.

"Make sure you have a good time and be safe," her mother hollered.

Shelia sat half way in the limo.

"I will – love you!" she replied.

Patrick closed her door and walked around to the driver's side.

At first she sat quietly in the back, her hands under her huge thighs as if her mother was there, then it clicked that she was alone and more or less in charge. Her eyes began to look every which way, capturing every contour of the limo, and she moved seat several times, bouncing up and down on them like a seat inspector. At one point she lay across the back seat, her fingers laced together.

Patrick looked up into the rear-view mirror and met her eyes there.

"My name's Shelia, what's yours?"

Patrick hated conversation, especially with minors. It took an incredible amount of effort to remember the things you could and couldn't say.

"Patrick."

A wrinkle formed over her nose as if his name were so foreign, it deserved immense wonder.

"You sound like Mister Johnson from 53. Are you from St Lucia?"

Patrick smiled and glanced up from the road into the slice of mirror.

"No, I'm from Jamaica."

"Oh, Jamaica, like Mrs Daley at number 11. I like her, she always gives me funny pastries called dumplums or dumplims or something like that."

Patrick grinned.

"Dumplings, fried dumplings," he corrected her.

"That's it – dumplings."

She paused for a second, the way old people do.

"Patrick, would it be okay if my friends had a drink and smoked in here?"

Patrick didn't look up.

"They can smoke if they're sixteen, but unless they're eighteen, drinking is against the law, so no, your friends cannot drink in here – but what they do before they get in is up to them and Jehovah."

There was a pause; Patrick looked up to see why. She looked worried, her bottom lip tucked into her mouth, as if it was being eaten by the top. Her eyes wide and darting all over, she looked on the verge of panic.

"Shelia! You Okay?"

She looked up, her eyes worried.

"She won't like this. She told me to get a limousine she could drink and smoke in. She's gonna be angry with me," Shelia replied.

Patrick didn't like the 'she' already.

"Who's she?"

"Katherine Braithwaite. All the girls are meeting up there, where we're going now."

"Well, I'm sure if they're your real friends, they'll understand."

Shelia looked down, her fat jaw squashed into her neck, forcing out four chins. Patrick glanced at her, then back to the road, feeling a little sorry for her. The turning for Katherine's road came, and they took it. He stopped just shy of the house, unclipped his seatbelt and turned to face Shelia.

"We're here."

She looked up, her eyes watery and uncomfortable for him to look into. Patrick had people cry all the time in the back of his limo, in both joy and sadness, but they were adults and usually had people with them for consolation or celebration.

He knew what her situation was; she was buying friendship on Katherine's terms, which couldn't be met. He felt he knew her whole story: lonely, fat, no friends at school, no interest from boys; she just existed, wishing one day her time would come and this was it – and he was fucking it up with good old legislation.

Patrick considered letting them drink, for Shelia's sake, but opted against it. His ass would be on the line and he would be out of the country if found out, given the fact he hadn't any papers to stay. In the UK in the 1980s it was hard for Jamaicans to gain citizenship, thanks to a small number of bad Jamaicans the media had titled 'Yardies' who had come to England with ideas and intentions other than work, corroding away at the positive legacy their countrymen and women from the Windrush era had created.

He sighed, turned around, grabbed a handful of tissue and gave it to her to mop herself up.

"Thanks."

She blew her nose, her pudgy fingers making the tissue look like two sheets of tiny rizla paper.

"They aren't really my friends; they just said I could go to the prom with them if I paid for the limousine and they could drink and smoke in it."

Patrick shook his head, wanting to advise her, but decided it was best to stay out of teen politics, keep his mind on the job and his thoughts to himself.

"Well, they must be waiting," Patrick said, starting the engine.

Shelia looked up and sighed. Patrick drove a few paces outside Katherine's house. He jumped out, walked around the car and opened her door. The curtains on the road began to twitch; a small crowd of kids stopped what they were doing and stood watching the limo.

Patrick held the door open for Shelia to step out, then stood awaiting her return. Katherine's house was beautiful; painted entirely white, it glowed in the sun. Her front garden was well maintained, easily outshining all the other houses it nestled among. Her front door was red with gold trimmings. Healthy tulips and variations of coloured roses lined the walkway to the front door.

Only wicked people could live in a house like this, he thought, looking around at the other homes that lined the street. Some had windows put out, with black bin liners taped to the frames. Some other houses were in such bad disrepair he wondered if anyone lived in them at all. The dilapidated houses he observed more or less personified the struggle the early 1980s had brought for those ill-equipped to deal with the 'shut up – pay me' capitalistic society that had emerged under the Tories. A Tory mantra that saw greed and self-indulgence praised. The rich got richer and the poor got poorer. Things were tough all round – south, east, west and especially up north. The Braithwaites were obviously playing the game well; better than most.

Like the cosmetics of a house or style of an item can personify the owner's taste, the same can be said for the attitude of their child. In the case of Katherine it was disturbing to Patrick that such a young child was aware that their company/time was a sellable and exchangeable commodity, and was brazen enough to request another child take their own money and pay for a limo with specific specifications for carriage. With all the information laid bare, one could safely guess that Katherine's outlook and approach to life had been influenced by undesirable parents, who almost certainly had projected and taught their child, either overtly or covertly, an attitude of fierce materialism. The Braithwaites' daughter was a child of capitalism, selling herself – no better than a prostitute.

Shelia stood waiting, and eventually a tall thin women answered. She looked Shelia up and down, her nostrils flared, her eyes judgemental. They spoke for a few seconds, then she stepped to one side to let Shelia in. The woman stood on the doorstep looking at Patrick as if he were a weeping sore. She shook her head and closed the door.

Patrick grinned.

Five minutes passed, and the road was awash with gate checkers and driveway sweepers. Katharine's front door opened and out came Shelia, her cheeks so red she looked as if she was about to burst with rage, sadness or both. Her head hung as she dragged her feet down the pathway.

As she neared him, he noticed her dress was no longer clean: there appeared to be food smeared all over it, and her ringlets looked like they had been dragged out. From the house came loud oinking and pig noises, mixed with laughter. Patrick stepped forward and looked past her. Out of the door came four girls in prom dresses, wearing pig masks, throwing what looked like cake at Shelia's back and hair. One broke away from the rest and smeared a piece into the side of her cheek, and Shelia simply allowed it.

Patrick's blood boiled so hot he almost jumped over the gate to assault the aggressor. The girls stopped just shy of the gate, all laughing and dancing at Shelia's expense. Katherine pulled up her mask and spoke.

"You fat pig – did you think I would be seen dead with a fat pig like you?"

They all started laughing again. Shelia looked back and began to cry, and Patrick put his arm around her like a referee does a finished fighter.

He looked Katherine in the eye and she looked back.

"Watchya looking at?" Katherine asked.

The girls went silent, then fell about laughing. Patrick looked up and saw Katherine's mother standing at the door, her arms crossed, a look of sheer wicked amusement etched across her face. They held each other's gaze, then Patrick broke away and turned, with his arm around Shelia. He opened the door and she virtually threw herself across the back seat, sobbing. Patrick peered in at her, words escaping him in the face of such senseless cruelty. He closed the door and turned back towards little Katherine and her merry men, who were skipping back towards the house, each squeezing by Katherine's mother until the last. Katherine's mother stood motionless, her arms folded. She mouthed 'Black bastard' then slammed the door.

Anger rose in him, curling his fists into a ball and making his heart pound to rage's beat. Surprisingly, it wasn't so much the word she mouthed that stoked his flame – it was her sheer lack of humanity and empathy for another child. Patrick bit down on his bottom lip, shook his head and walked around the limo to get in.

He sat down and exhaled, his hands shaking. He looked up into the mirror; Shelia lay on her front, her arms crossed under her face, her back shaking.

Patrick commenced driving, parting the children in the road like the Red Sea. He drove down another road, thinking of things he could say to make things better, but nothing came to mind; he just wasn't equipped for situations like this. Eventually he decided it best to pull up and ask her what she wanted to do, as she had paid for nine hours and was highly unlikely to get a refund from Mr Ting.

Patrick let out a loud elaborate sigh to summon her. She raised her head above her crossed arms. The pair shared a stare, her eyes and cheeks red. He adjusted his tie then spoke.

"You have eight hours to run. What would you like me to do?"

She looked out of the car window, getting her bearings, then sat up and hung her head as if she were ashamed. Patrick looked at her and began to feel such pity it almost brought tears to his eyes.

"Take me home," she whispered through wet lips.

Patrick dismissed her suggestion immediately, as if it were his choice to make. He felt it was too closely related to giving up and letting those little wicked bitches have their way.

"You sure?" he asked.

"I can't go to the prom. They'll be there."

At first, he thought, *I'll go with you,* then realised how ridiculous a suggestion it was, then he had an idea.

"Well before I take you home, would you do me the honour of having dinner with me?" he said in his best posh accent.

She looked up and a wrinkle formed across her forehead.

"Ah yes! One will be eating at M. C. Donald's, it's all the rage in Paris, I hear."

Shelia's brow lifted and a smile crept across her face.

"Wha you ah say?" he said, smiling, knowing she'd ask him to repeat himself.

"What did you say?"

"You coming or not?"

"Yeah, I want to come."

"Good."

Patrick turned around and turned on the radio. The Jets shot out of the speakers singing about their crush; Patrick turned it up and began nodding to the beat. Shelia's smile widened and her feet began to tap to the rhythm, then her shoulders started to jiggle. They drove off. Patrick looked in the rear-view mirror to find Shelia standing up, literally shaking a leg. He smiled and turned it up.

They pulled into McDonald's car park and Patrick turned the radio down. Shelia stopped dancing and looked over at him. He pulled on his chauffeur's hat, which he reserved for real VIPs, got out, walked round to her door, opened it, and reached inside with his open palm. She slipped her hand into his and he eased her out as elegantly as he could, cake and icing stuck to her hair, face and clothes.

She hooked her arm into his; he looked down at her and she looked up at him. They walked towards the entrance and he held the door open for her to enter. Several individuals and families dining looked up from their burgers and fries and whispered among themselves at the bizarre pair they made.

He was a tall black man dressed like a chauffeur and she was an overweight sixteen-year-old white princess. The UK in the 1980s was still very much an intolerant place when it came to race relations; a lot of blood had been shed on both sides since the surge in migration from the West Indies. Hatred, fear and widespread general ignorance had led to riots and countless occasions of civil unrest over the years. By the 1980s, things had calmed down and improved some what.

Patrick ordered two Big Mac meals with two root beers, and looked down at Shelia, who was bopping away to music being played overhead: the Miami Sound Machine's 'Conga'. Her shoulders were going, her feet tapping, as she held on to the counter, twisting her waist to the beat.

Patrick looked around at the rest of the diners, who were looking at her as if she were crazy, unaware that Shelia Bradford would shed her puppy fat and go on to be one of the greatest dance choreographers the UK would ever produce, teaching the best dancers worldwide.

Patrick grabbed a handful of straws and napkins, placed them on their tray and walked towards a free table, slowly balancing their beverages. Shelia followed behind.

The pair sat in a booth, across from an older couple. The man had a skinhead and wore a white T-shirt, his arms littered with tattoos, the most pronounced a British bulldog and Union Jack. The woman's hair was blonde, greasy and slicked back into a ponytail. As soon as Patrick and Shelia sat, the skinhead packed his half-eaten food, all condiments and drinks back onto his tray, sighing loudly. Patrick and Shelia looked up at the man, his cheeks red and flustered as if he were about to faint.

Shelia began to laugh at how animated he was. The man stopped and looked at her directly.

"What you laughing at? You think it's funny this country's going down the shitter 'cause blacks are coming 'ere? Should be ashamed of yourself."

Patrick shot up and walked out from behind the table, his height astounding in comparison to the man's. The restaurant fell silent and everyone looked over. The man swallowed and looked around at the rest of the restaurant, blinking, beads of sweat dribbled from his balding head.

"Don't act like you're not all thinking the same fucking thing," the man shouted.

Patrick walked towards him and smiled, the man's head just about reaching his chest. The skinhead began to shake, the contents of his tray vibrating, giving away his feelings. Patrick looked down at him and crossed his arms; the man broke eye contact and looked away. His partner grabbed his arm.

"Frank, you're making a scene, come on," she screamed. She tugged him and they left the restaurant, with the tray and everything. Other people started sniggering as Frank was led away, no resistance in his body; he was glad to be out of there.

Patrick looked around and everyone went back to their meals and each other. Patrick smiled and went back to his seat.

Shelia looked at him, her mouth agape. Patrick picked up some fries, dipped them in sauce and held them between his fingers. Before eating them, he leaned forward over the table and whispered, "Always stand your ground; you have as much right as anyone on earth to be here."

Patrick leaned back and pushed the fries into his mouth and chomped away. Shelia smiled, opened her Mac and removed the gherkins, placing them on a napkin.

They spoke for hours, until the sun began to sink in the sky and the moon rose.

"You ready?" Patrick asked.

"Yeah."

The evening was still warm with the heat of the day; they pulled up outside Shelia's house and Patrick turned to her.

"Remember what I said. Don't allow anyone to take you for a fool; you have as much right to be great as anyone else … Stand your ground or people will stand on you."

Shelia nodded and smiled. Her front door opened and Shelia's mother stood there, waiting, her smile wider than before. Patrick got out, opened Shelia's door, took her hand and helped ease her out. She stood in front of him; he clenched his fist and she hers, they bumped knuckles and she walked off towards her mother, who wrapped her arms around her, happy that Shelia looked happy. Shelia turned from the embrace, waved then slid into the house. Her mother gave Patrick a thumbs-up, and Patrick nodded and winked.

Patrick returned to base, the sweet and sour elements of the day still playing out in his head. As soon as he stepped in, Mr Ting called him into the office. Patrick entered and Mr Ting handed him the phone and a number scrawled on a piece of torn-off newspaper.

"Da Bladfods call to say call dem."

Patrick took the newspaper and wondered how on earth Mr Ting could conduct business with such terrible English at times.

"They want me to call them?"

"Ya, maybe wapeat business, ha?"

Mr Ting jigged at the prospect of repeat custom.

"Yeah, maybe."

Mr Ting slapped Patrick on the arm with sheer delight as he walked out.

"I go do somfing. Don't stay on phone so lon – cost money."

Mr Ting walked out and left Patrick. Patrick wondered what it could be; a feeling of dread took hold of him and he assumed the worst – maybe Shelia had accused him of touching her. He stood looking at the number, his hands sweaty, his stomach rolling.

He took a deep breath and picked up the phone to get it over with. The phone seemed to ring for ever, then it was answered.

"Hello, Bradford residence."

Patrick's mouth felt as dry as sandpaper, he realised he had paused for too long.

"Heeee-llo," Mr Bradford repeated.

"Oh, sorry, hello. I'm Patrick from Mr Ting's limo service. You wanted me to call?"

"Yes … yes I did."

Patrick tried to decipher how he was feeling by his tone, but couldn't. Mr Bradford took a breath.

"My name is Earl, I'm Shelia's father, and I wanted you to know we really appreciate what you did for her today. You didn't have to bother, but you did. She's had a horrible time at school over the years, which has affected the whole family. Anyway, I won't bore you with the sob story, let's cut to the chase; she told me you're trying to get your papers."

Earl went silent, awaiting a response. Patrick wasn't sure if by saying yes he was showing his hand, but something felt right about this, as if it was meant to be.

"Ahhhh, yes, yes I am."

"Well, a man of your calibre deserves a chance here. I'm going to sort your stay out – take it as a thank you for your actions today. Come by tomorrow and we'll go over it in full … Oh yeah, and make sure you keep this to yourself. If not, we'll both be in the shit."

If it wasn't for him looking at his reflection in the window, Patrick wouldn't have noticed the smile that had developed across his face, or Mr Ting heading back towards the office.

"Okay, thanks sir, thank you so much."

"No, thank *you* Patrick, you're a good man. I'll see you tomorrow – let's say 7 pm."

"Seven. Yes, I'll be there, thanks again."

"Okay, tomorrow."

Earl put the phone down and Patrick held his to his head in absolute shock. Mr Ting walked in with a look of worry etched across it.

"Hey! Patwick! You cwayze? You been on phone too long!"

Patrick turned and flung his arms around Mr Ting's thin waist, hauled him up a foot and swung him round in joy.

"Patwick, you so happy, you must have got wapeat business, ha?"

Patrick smiled.

"You could say that, Mr Ting, you just could say that."

Octo et unum

"Blessed be Providence, which has given to each his toy: the doll to the child, the child to the woman, the woman to the man, the man to the devil!"
(Victor Hugo)

Valda's world developed a funny unfamiliar hue after the picture had brought back the dead. She began to wonder about the concept of good versus evil and which side she stood on after her arrangement. She dared not tell anyone about the incident for fear of her sanity being brought into question. She was good at lying, good at keeping secrets from the world with which she felt no connection. She was an orphan, walking around with her ghost story stuck to her back like a huge parasite, which sucked a little whenever she got too close to happiness, reminding her she deserved none. For a few nights after the newspaper incident she would wake with nightmares so horrible she dreaded sleep.

Before she knew it, her time was being filled with scans, antenatal classes and expectant mother matters, her memory of the incident fading with every day passed.

She began looking into religion; she loved the concepts Christianity housed, she began reading about it on the internet and was brought to tears after reading certain passages, thinking back to rough times in her life where some of these scriptures could have helped her get through the darkness. The internet readings led to her ordering a Bible, the first she had ever owned, touched or seen. The front cover was dark brown, made from leather; the pages were tipped with gold and felt like baking paper.

She found a church to attend, where she sat at the back. St Mary's C of E church, which sat behind Church Road estate. She could neither understand nor explain the overwhelming urge to go there, of all churches, but it felt right and that's all that mattered.

Inside was brown and brass. There were two sets of wooden pews, with a single aisle to divide them. Upon the altar stood a large golden crucifix. Behind it lay a platform with two large tables littered with candles and holy ornaments on top. Beyond the tables was a grand organ, aged and sturdy. The church smelled old and musty, but sweet from large incense sticks that stuck out of shiny golden orbs, all at various stages of life. Whenever she left she could taste them in the back of her throat and smell them on her clothes. On her third day there, she waited until everyone had dispersed and walked around the building, looking up at the windows: pictures colourful and vibrant, telling tales of sorrow, grief and betrayal.

She loved the church, its services and people; kind-hearted calm, of all nationalities, who kept conversation to hellos and goodbyes, but gave you a look that said when you're ready to further our communication I'm here and you're welcome. To Valda, that felt beyond good: it felt great, a complete contrast to the ruthless world she was used to.

Father David was St Mary's priest. He was round, with a balding head, pale skin and intense grey eyes that sat behind spectacles which rested half way down his nose. When he spoke, his voice would echo and clatter around the church with such immense authority and amplification, she thought at first he was aided by speakers or a sound system.

Patrick routinely dropped her off by Neasden Tube station, half a mile from the church. From there she would walk, a ladylike hat slanted to disguise her face, fearful she would draw paparazzi attention and bring the circus that was celebrity to the church. She believed no one knew who she was there and, if they did, no one appeared to care.

After the service, on occasion she would stroll down Church Road's high street, one half littered with dilapidated shops run by London's latest influx of immigrants. Their shops appeared to have no rhythm, reason or genre, just loads of old and young men loitering, looking worse for wear. The other half were proper family-run stores, a few from her past, the rest newly owned. Sometimes she'd sit at the bus stop opposite her childhood flat, looking up at its windows, contemplating how far she'd come. In one moment of reflection, she played with the notion of visiting it, or possibly buying it – for what reason, she couldn't decipher. She dismissed the awful ideas as soon as they had come, and stopped walking down there altogether. Her memories were too vivid at times; the feelings she had felt back then manifesting in her current reality.

Alex wasn't a religious man and barely believed in the concept of God, but he observed how religion had begun to change Valda and liked it. He put her new approach to life down to the pregnancy. She had calmed. The fire that consumed her daily, making her an almost unbearable force, had dwindled down to a rudimental flicker that smoothed her rough surfaces and rounded her edges. There was diplomacy where it didn't exist before, and she allowed him space to be a man and expectant dad.

At four months pregnant, Valda's stomach had begun to globe and the baby began to kick, turn and make itself known. When she first felt it, she jumped up from her chair, spilling her bowl of salad everywhere, and brought her hands to her mouth in a gasp. Alex ran in from the kitchen, frying pan in hand, apron on, with a look of terror on his face. She explained, and they both laughed with elation.

With every passing day Lilif, the bracelet and bean receded further and further in her memory until it faded and failed to exist at all. After their lunch at Riku's, Alex had placed the bracelet high in a wardrobe, to be researched at a later date. That date never arrived, on account of day to day life eroding away his questions and fears, replacing them with optimism and anticipation. The baby had become their world, their universe and star, inducing a selective amnesia in both.

Valda's clothes got tighter and the days she actually spent on BBL's premises dwindled down to near zero. Things had begun to go so well for the business. The auditor's report came back and showed no signs of foul play, so Selen stayed in employment. They had decided to fold and remove all advertising from all teenage websites. Drew and the rest of the world believed it was about the preservation of money, but in actual fact it was about Valda's newly-found desire to do the right thing, which she kept to herself. Instead of losing money through pulling the advertisements, BBL gained. Selen came in with a report showing sales were up twenty per cent on last year. Rachel and Dean were still replaced, for making the initial suggestion. In their place, she hired marketing managers who prided themselves on having higher senses of integrity and ethics. She put Drew on a final warning for not foreseeing the problem Dean and Rachel's decision would create, setting a new precedent for her to follow.

Valda arranged to spend a week with all factions of the design department. Gibbs thought it was her way of saying she was worried about his management abilities, but she reassured him that she just wanted to get back into touch with the process of how everything worked. After spending a total of three weeks with him, she had a better grasp of what they did and how hard they worked to keep BBL ahead of the pack. She was so impressed with their work ethic, attitudes and abilities that she gave them a pay rise and gave hefty bonuses to each member of staff.

Out of the blue, Valda made a move that shocked the business world: on the verge of a signing a deal worth millions, she backed away from the prospect of dealing with Braga, for no apparent reason. Reports said that Braga was absolutely furious and vowed to "never give insignificant no-bodies a chance again". Valda backing away from the deal only made business pundits and analysts wonder what she had seen behind the scenes that made a shark like her keep swimming and not attack a deal that would expose her brand to the Americas and, more importantly, millions upon millions of pounds. They couldn't fathom that she could or would have done it because it was the right thing to do: ethics and morals didn't really exist in business, they were just something you stuck on a label, website or packaging, but they did in Valda's new world and she was proud to stand by them.

The Cog, a business magazine, ran a story titled "Has Valda driven a final nail into her own coffin?" The article, written by Ravi Singh, began to question Valda's business acumen and her ability to steer BBL in the right direction. He was adamant that not getting into bed with Braga was probably the biggest mistake she could have made. He wrote that the British brand would have gone down a right royal storm in the Americas, making them virtually invincible to threats from others trying to survive.

Alex didn't know why she was making so many drastic changes: even when he questioned her, her only reply was that she felt a deep spiritual need to purge her world of all the evil she had let into it, either willingly or unknowingly, and felt she needed to clean the roads and woods around her before she brought this baby into their lives.

By now people, could see her face had begun to fill out and her movement appeared somewhat laboured. People began to whisper and speculate about everything from cancer to arthritis, then pregnancy, which stuck.

Five months in, Valda had stopped going into BBL altogether. She released a statement via Claire informing colleagues that she was expecting a child and she would be absent from the office until further notice. Valda expected a big deal to be made of this, once the press caught wind of it, but the news barely made a small column on the fourth page of any paper.

Alex and Valda sat at a table in their garden. He drank a chilled beer and she Fugi water. A bowl of fruit sat in the centre of the table, flanked by a basket of bread lightly marinated in olive oil. Several newspapers were spread across the table top as if they were war schematics. A warm breeze circled, the sun's dying glow casting a rose-gold light.

"You see, they only want to know you when you're in the shit or doing the dirty; I hate the press." Valda protested.

Alex digested her words.

"Well, isn't this what we want? We would hate some big circus."

"I agree. But it shows that when it's something positive, these vultures don't want to know."

Alex took a sip of his beer and placed it back down.

"Just be glad we aren't Kate and Will. Can you imagine that level of harassment?" he replied.

Alex licked his finger and turned to the sports pages. Valda picked up a slice of bread and chomped down on it, the olive oil squeezing out around her mouth and fingers. The rose-gold cast had darkened, bringing forth the beginning of night. Valda rubbed her belly and felt a kick. Although the novelty had worn off for Alex, for her every time was like the first, bringing a smile to her face.

"We'll need to hire some help around here," Alex stated.

Valda looked across at him.

"You know how I feel about people in the house," she replied.

The pair paused, Alex's finger between pages, Valda's hands on her bump.

"Well, let's look at this seriously. Neither of us have ever raised a child, my parents aren't here and yours are …"

In an instant, a flashback to the moving picture played out in her head, making her subtly recoil. Goosebumps sprang up on her skin, and she began to feel a sense of impending doom. She picked up her water, her hand shaking, and drank; Alex reached across and placed his hand over her arm, his face worried, sure he had upset her.

"I'm sorry; I didn't mean to bring it up."

"Don't worry about it; I just wish they were here to support me."

The lie rolled off her tongue as smoothly as the warm olive oil down her throat. She had painted a picture to Alex and the rest of the world of her life before the death of her parents and brother. A glowing place, filled with love, only to be cut short by a house fire that ripped through their home, killing everyone but her.

She had never – and would never – disclose to Alex how her father had stuck himself in her mouth and vagina; or that it was due to his depraved acts (which had physically damaged her internally) that, with all the money and the best will in the world, the finest doctors and surgeons on the planet were unable to make her fertile.

Alex stared at her.

"I'm just saying we've a few months to go and neither of us have a clue. We need support on this, and I know you want my parents' involvement but, trust me, they cannot be relied upon. We need to start vetting a nanny from now," Alex insisted.

She knew he was right about his parents, but wished he wasn't, and hoped the baby would bring them all together. The only problem was that his parents had loathed her from the get-go: they were what Valda considered new-age hippies. They were anti- corporations, capitalism and anyone who stood for them; however, his parents hadn't started life that way. His father, Adrian Cambridge, of average height and slender build, with brown eyes and a mop of clean-cut hair, was a former Liberal Democrat MP for Camden; and his mother Janelle, short, round, with creamy Mediterranean skin and full lips, was a former prison manager.

The beginning of Alex's life went the way a child with a father in politics and a highly-paid mother would: private schooling, lavish holidays, opulence – and scandal, dirty filthy scandal.

Adrian got caught up in the 'money for lobbying' witch hunt, which saw five Lib Dem MPs laid bare trying to influence parliament for personal interests. Adrian was exposed, for trying to push for investment to knock down shabby estates in his constituency and have new ones built in their place. The estates were only ten years old and although they looked a little grubby all they needed was a good cosmetic overhaul. A building company called McBride & Co paid Adrian £1 million to try to have the refurbishment proposal pushed through parliament. If successful, a total of £50 million regeneration money would be awarded to Adrian, who would give the job to McBride, skimming a little off the top in the process.

Things looked as though they were going Adrian's way – until he was forced to fire his PA Brian Keane, after it had been reported in the press that Keane had been caught dogging on Clapham Common. Adrian stood by him at first, but went on to dismiss him after pictures emerged confirming the claims. Disgruntled, Keane almost immediately went to the media to air Adrian's dealings with McBride, then the shit really hit the fan. This had a cascading effect for other MPs who were involved in similar dealings. But to the British people, suffering the effects of the economic depression in the 1990s, it looked like the rich looking after the rich once again (which, frankly, it was, which didn't sit well with the public or his already struggling Liberal political party).

Keane sold meeting minutes and recorded telephone conversations to the press; bank receipts were photocopied and printed in the papers. The leader of the Lib Dems at the time distanced himself from Adrian, as did the rest of the party. Technically and legally, he had done nothing wrong as there was no specific law against lobbying, so the party couldn't fire him. However, they could ease him out, which they did; they didn't take his phone calls and letters he sent were returned to sender. They ignored him in public; he was virtually exiled by people he had known for twenty years, all to keep the heat off them. Adrian was hung out to dry in both private and public.

His wife wasn't exempt from the heat either. Her ability to manage the prison she ran was brought into question. The press discovered that there had been an abnormally high level of inmate deaths and illness over the years. They wouldn't normally have given a hoot about this, but it was necessary to keep the fire roaring under a phenomenal bit of news. Janelle was brought before her superiors to explain the papers' findings. She was made to answer questions surrounding the lack of nutritious food on the menu, why the prison was in such a bad state of repair, with conditions akin to prisons in

Eastern Europe, the inadequate, ill-trained medical staff, and terrible lapses in security.

The final straw came when an undercover reporter took a picture of himself inside a cell wearing a prison guard's uniform, showing just how easy it was to get in. She was fired immediately. Things got still worse. The papers reported that Alex was going to a top private school; the headline read:

"We suffer while Adrian's kid gets the best education a nation can buy."

Fed up, Adrian left his constituency and politics altogether. It was a confusing time for Alex: one minute he had all the toys money could buy; the next, his high-calibre hobbies were scrapped and he stopped going to lavish kids' parties. Whenever he called at friends' homes, their parents would make up weak excuses for why little Timmy couldn't come over to play with him. One afternoon he had overheard his father curse at one parent, screaming and using foul language.

"What the fuck do you mean 'people like us' can't come to your fucking party? We were bloody invited when I was an MP though, weren't we?"

Alex sat at the top of the stairs each night, listening to his father try and keep his world together, trying to soften the blow for his son and wife, who had become a recluse who rarely left her room. Alex scarcely went into see her; he hated this version of his mum, and he hated this version of his life.

A month into Adrian's living nightmare, three butch Irish men in hi-vis vests with 'McBride' written on them came to the house. His father let them in reluctantly. They barged past him and he followed them into his own living room. Before he walked in, he slowed to a stop and looked up at Alex. He smiled, though his eyes didn't. In fact, they looked worried, bordering on frightened. He closed the door behind him and Alex heard a growl of voices, none of them belonging to his father.

Alex covered his ears and kept his eyes on the door. It opened suddenly with vigour; the three guys walked out of the front door, leaving it ajar, drizzle raining onto their beautiful Persian carpet.

The van they had pulled up in roared away angrily, as if possessed by a wicked sprite.

Alex stood up, aware his father hadn't yet emerged. He looked upstairs towards his parents' room where his mother had sat for the last couple of weeks. He looked down again at the living room doorway, hoping his father would surface; still nothing. He gulped and walked downstairs. Fearing the worst, he stood beside the doorframe for a second gathering his courage, then walked in gingerly. What he saw was far worse than he had expected.

His father was sitting, his head in his hands, his elbows digging into his knees, with no tears or expression on his face. Alex placed his hand on his back and rubbed it. His father looked up, his eyes red and wet; he looked beaten spiritually. The pair held their stare until his father broke, as did Alex, both crying without restraint. He drew his son close and whispered, "I'm so sorry, son. I'll fix this … I promise."

Things moved quickly after that day. Adrian sent Janelle to their small family home in Goa so at least she was out of his hair. For a peaceful life, he paid back McBride partially by the sale of their home and the savings he and Janelle had amassed over the years.

Both he and Alex stayed in a hotel until all their affairs in the UK were resolved, then his father took what remained of the money, totalling £60,000, and flew out to Goa to start afresh. Their home in Goa was in a compound, with other Westerners, mostly Americans with a small handful of Brits.

The country was beautiful. Driving to their home, they passed tall palm trees that sprang out of patches of sandy earth on surprisingly well constructed roads. His father sat in the front seat, smiling and laughing with the driver, wearing a beige sunhat which looked like one of the hats explorers wore in the 1920s. The radio played music in another language; Adrian occasionally looked back at his son. Alex smiled, happy he was himself again. Regardless of the mistakes he had made, he was a kind, gentle father, husband and man, who would do anything for his family.

They passed women walking in saris that swayed behind them, their beautiful vibrant colours bringing them to life. They all had things to sell in hand, from wooden trinkets to incense and food. Alex stuck his head out of the window; the warm air smelled of heat and mixed spices. It filled his nostrils and lungs, making his belly growl.

When they approached the gate, Adrian got out, walked towards the gateman and spoke for a second, then the gate opened and they drove in. The houses inside the compound were detached and large with decked porches in front. The greenery and trees were well kept. Beautiful red, yellow and blue flowers sprouted everywhere, with massive prehistoric-looking green leaves popping out of their stems.

They pulled up outside their house, which was painted baby blue with a white front door and window frames. Janelle was standing on the porch with another woman and hadn't noticed their taxi arrive. The woman alerted her to their arrival and his mother turned and ran towards the car, her hands outstretched, pulled open the taxi door and literally grabbed Alex out of his seat.

She had lost a lot of weight in the two months she had been there; she had also acquired her smile again. Her olive skin was now a healthy bronze colour. She pulled Alex so close to her that his face was submerged in her mane of hair, which smelled of spearmint and lavender.

She held him away from her to look at him, her hands clasped around his forearms. Alex noticed she wore a necklace with a pendant attached. It was a silver hand with palm welts etched in it. She smiled and stared at him. His father walked up behind her, flung an arm around her shoulders and kissed her head.

"Look at you … I missed you so much," she said to her son.

"I missed you too," Alex replied.

That night both his parents sat up late discussing UK politics and their total hatred for the 'idiots' who were running Britain.

They spoke about how everyone had turned against them in their hour of need. Alex sat by the window absorbing the fact this beautiful place was home and, judging from the way his parents were speaking, he'd never see England's green and pleasant land again.

His father walked around the room, a glass of brandy in hand, and looked at the bizarre Buddhist pictures and symbols on the walls. He asked why they were there. His mother went on to reveal that when she had arrived in Goa she was functioning but was in a worse state mentally than she had let on. She explained that a fellow resident called round to find out who owned the vacant house that had stood there for years. They got talking about everyday things, until Sandra was set to leave. Out of the blue, it had become frighteningly apparent to Janelle that if she didn't get how she was feeling off her chest there and then, nobody else would ever have seen her alive again. So she asked her to stay, and ended up baring her soul. In the end, the women embraced each other, and Sandra asked Janelle to stay with her and her husband Jeremy. It turned out that Jeremy had become a Buddhist after leaving his high-powered job in the States. He had had a nervous breakdown due to work and the religion had helped him get back on track.

A tear rolled down his mother's cheek and his father put his arms around her, pulled her close and shot Alex a wink from over her head as if to say 'I've got this'.

She wiped her face and mouth to continue. She went on to explain that the month she had spent with Sandra and Jeremy had been the best month of her life. They had helped her purge herself of Western wants and needs. They helped her to understand how insignificant opulence really was in the grand scheme of things. Her diet improved, helping to cleanse her body and mind. At first Adrian laughed, but stopped when Janelle didn't. She went on to explain about the benefits of meditation and how it had taken her out of the dark place their situation had placed her in.

Adrian asked if she was now a Buddhist and she said yes. He took another sip of his brandy, the last sip of alcohol he would have.

Alex attended an international school in Goa, where he took his GCSEs and went on to take A-levels. At the same time his parents delved deeper and deeper into Buddhism. Two years passed. One day, Alex came home to find his parents, Sandra and Jeremy sitting around the table discussing setting up a Buddhist commune. Their plans would come to pass and his parents, Sandra, Jeremy and several other people simply packed up and left for a plot of land they had purchased for twenty people, with scope for growth. Not only were they a commune, but they also formed an anti-capitalism movement that campaigned to prevent Goa becoming any more Westernised in terms of its approach to life, politics and people.

Although Alex believed in their cause he just couldn't get used to commune living. He felt he could make more of a change back home and at the age of nineteen, five years after arriving, Alex Cambridge decided it was time to return to England.

He applied to universities in London and got a place. He flew over to England to study politics at the School of African and Oriental Studies at the University of London, with the aim of starting a political movement that could effect change in British politics.

His mother and father laughed at him, reminding him how easily they had ended up in that terrible mess in the first place. They warned him about the allure of luxury in the Western world. His father explained that before he had joined politics, he had had the same dream: that he could change things – until he had got in and it had changed him.

When Valda located Alex months after the TV show they met on had been cancelled, he was virtually squatting in a shitty flat, up to his eyeballs in debt, on the cusp of rummaging through rubbish bins for food from sheer hunger. The appeal of her warm freshly baked opulence was too much for his famished stomach to dismiss and he gave in to her advances. She paid off his debts, fed, sheltered him and polished him up like the little trophy she saw him as – and he was hers.

When they finally flew over to Goa so she could meet his parents, all white linen, Gucci glasses and Versace handbag, they were furious. She was everything they stood against; his father shook his head in disbelief and reminded his son how short his memory was and how close they had come to total ruin chasing the almighty dollar.

Janelle looked her up and down and stormed off. Adrian put his hand on his son's shoulder and whispered in his ear, "As long as she's in your life, count us out."

His father walked away, a spade in one hand, off to do his duties in the commune, no doubt. The commune had grown to accommodate three hundred people and was now considered a village, which his father, mother, Sandra and Jeremy governed, with zesty quotes on love, spirituality and social and economic freedom.

~

Valda lay in bed that night, the light dim. Her tablet lit the crevices of her face as if she held a torch beneath it. She read through baby forums, looking for recommendable nanny agencies to begin her search. The TV's glow from the living room below clicked off, plunging the house into darkness. She looked up over the tablet and waited to hear Alex ascending the stairs. After no more than a few seconds of continued silence, she began to feel an unwarranted sense of unease. She put the tablet down and leaned forward awkwardly over her bump to get up. Just as her feet hit the floor, Alex began to climb the steps, his feet heavy and lumbering. She sighed with annoyance. *Great; he's drunk.*

From out of the darkness Alex walked in. She looked up at his silhouette, one arm braced against the door frame for balance. He walked in like Saturday night in Leicester square, reeking of alcohol.

He stripped off his shirt and collapsed into bed, his back to her.

She looked down at him, shook her head and went back to her tablet. She searched for more agencies, then spent some time looking at her company's website and Twitter. Exhausted, she turned off the tablet and placed it down on her night table beside her. She lay on her side and stroked her belly; the baby gave a small kick that brought a smile to her face.

The small sound of her ticking clock began to ease her to sleep, then she heard another sound that made her hairs stand on end: a sound that could only be described as warped child's speech, coming from the pitch-black hallway outside; a childlike whisper that made Valda sit upright and made her stare into the dark. It came again.

'Welcome.' It hissed.

Valda held her breath.

A small darkened figure slid in to the room and stood in the doorway, its eyes bled red light. It seemed to carry a smell she was all too familiar with – the smell of rotting flesh and decay. It raised an arm and pointed at Valda. Her stomach churned; her heart dared not beat.

From besides her Alex began to stir with a childish giggle, which quickly developed into a laugh, a terrifying impious laugh, Valda looked down at him, then he rolled over suddenly and his face looked as if he had been embalmed, frozen in a grimace of terror, his eyeballs missing, black gaping holes where they had once been, his neck deformed as if it had been broken. He spoke through lumpy, rotting black lips.

"Pay what you owe, pay what you owe," they said in unison.

"Pay what you owe, pay what you owe," their voices warping.

Worms fell from his mouth onto her lap. He wrapped his arms around her waist as she tried to get up from the bed, but he held on tight, placed his head against her stomach and bit into her belly. Valda screamed and the creature in the doorway laughed louder and louder and louder and louder.

Valda shot up, screaming, from the nightmare. Her face and neck were as wet as grass in March, her breathing deep and laborious. She flung off the covers, pulled her top up and looked at her belly, still intact. From outside, she could hear the sound of running on the staircase. Valda jumped out of bed, tablet in hand, backed up against the wall and held it high above her head to strike.

Alex ran through the door. The light faded on to reveal Valda breathing hard, sweating as if she had run ten miles. They both stood in silence, their eyes searching each other, his face riddled with questions, hers with pure fear.

Alex woke early the next morning, to find her space empty. He got up and walked out of the room, turned towards the bathroom but slowed past the nursery and stopped. Its door was ajar. He looked through the crack made by the hinges and the door, but saw nothing, then Valda walked past suddenly, eclipsing his vision, making him jump. She walked around the cot, slowly drawing her fingers across the top of the frame, looking down into it. She stopped and looked directly at Alex's peeping eye; both held the stare, neither blinking. Alex walked to her and the pair stood in the centre of the room. Alex slipped his hands into hers.

"You okay?" he asked.

She nodded and he tightened his grip.

In the morning, he washed, dressed and gathered his things for the day, his head full of questions and concerns. He stood by the front door putting on his shoes.

Valda descended the left staircase and stood before him.

"Is everything all right?" she asked.

"Everything's fine, I'm just running a little late."

They both fell quiet, neither wanting to talk about last night.

"Okay, got to go, call you later."

He pecked her cheek, turned, opened the door and left.

The door closed, leaving Valda alone. She turned and walked back to her bedroom. She popped open the wardrobe door, stood on tiptoes and felt around for the box with the bracelet. She slid it across towards her, took it down and sat on the bed, looking at the pictures etched into the individual pieces. *Phases of human growth*, she thought. It wasn't the twelve pieces that played on her mind, but the thirteenth – the goat's head outlined by a circle. The implication of the symbol troubled her somewhat: her nightmares were back and becoming so real they had begun to bleed over into her days, and not being at work didn't help, as it gave her too much time to think and dwell, her thoughts coming so fast she couldn't ignore them – or the insistent notion that she had commitments to fulfil, like it or not.

Wear it the day the child is born for twelve months. The first year, I'll give you the first year, yes I will. If I don't? She smiled, a wicked smile, her horrible wicked eyes, my eyes, her candle, her candle, her candle ...

Valda had never dreamed – let alone had nightmares – on this scale. Even when she was being abused, her brain would create a defence against her reality that gave her peace in her slumber.

A warning, her end of the deal was met, now I must meet mine, but she knows I ... But how?

Valda turned and looked across her bedroom, scrutinising everything.

She knew I wouldn't.

Valda focused on the bracelet, as if in a trance, feeding it through her palm, round and round, faster and faster, until it was spinning at an unnatural speed, her thoughts becoming words.

"Lilif, Lilith, Lilif, Lilith," she began to chant.

She began to hyperventilate, the sound of the nursery door creaking could be heard and then it started opening and slamming, slowly then faster and faster and faster, until it was banging, shaking the house. Valda fell back on the bed, her arms outstretched across it like Christ on the cross, her eyeballs rolled back. Her mind became a jumble of thoughts and voices. She began sweating profusely, the bracelet gripped tightly in her palm.

A voice spoke from within her that she didn't recognise. It was soft but firm.

"Amanda Brace … Mariah Wray … Jane Heckle have all been treated, all treated, all treated," she chanted to herself.

Valda's conscious mind came back, the nursery door stopped banging and she pulled her arms back into her sides as if she was emerging from sleep paralysis. She shot up from her bed, looked to her left, out of her bedroom door and saw Lilif standing there – in her true form. Her face was wrinkly, grey and old, her eyes black shiny ovals, her teeth jagged. She appeared to be screaming, with no sound, at someone or something beyond Valda's right-hand side. Valda turned to look and was met with a light from above that shone so brightly it forced her to shade her eyes. Her bedroom appeared to stretch for an eternity. The light flickered, and everything went black, then white. Immense heat overcame her, and she closed her eyes; the heat was on the verge of burning, melting her joints, then she heard a voice. Lilif. Her voice raspy and rusty, its reverberation overwhelming all of Valda's senses.

"Free will, she came of her free will … Welcome, Valda, you are mine."

A spiteful laughter sounded out, so loud that Valda was forced to put her hands over her ears. She fell backwards onto her bed. Blackness and absolute silence prevailed.

~

Her eyelids snapped open and her pupils were immediately focused. She rolled over onto her side, sat up and took several deep breaths. She rubbed her stomach and her baby adjusted its position. She raised her right hand, the bracelet still held tightly within it; the wardrobe door still open. She tried to stand but pain radiated throughout her body, forcing her back down.

Her head buzzed as if she had drunk a litre of over-proof white rum. She stumbled forward, like Bambi just born, and leaned against the wardrobe's open door, and then the seriousness of her situation hit her. Warm tears rolled down her cheeks and, for the first time in years, she felt like little Valda Wright; eleven, vulnerable, and in the hands of evil. Valda slid down into a helpless bundle at the foot of the wardrobe.

She said she didn't want money, but a year. I chose the first year, you accepted with free will ... Gladly, with free will, yes you did...

Valda looked at the bracelet; a whisper spoke in and around her head – a voice; soft, gentle, persuasive and credible. It sounded like an echo from a distant star travelling through space on the back of light created trillions of years ago.

Just wear it, wear it when the baby comes, wear it and repent after... Yes! Wear it and the nightmares stop, the pain stops. We are an old creed, as powerful as the stars, powerful like the stars, powerful like the stars, pow-er-ful li-ke th-e staaaaaaaaaaaaaars

Valda shook her head as if she had taken a punch. She reached up, placed her hand on the wardrobe knob and pulled until she was standing. She walked across to her side of the bed as if remote-controlled, lifted the mattress and placed the bracelet under it for safe keeping and sanity.

Aevus

Patrick partially woke to the sound of pre-daylight birds talking. He rolled to his left side and reached down to pull the covers up against the impending morning that would spell the end of slumber. He felt around, but couldn't feel them there; then he saw them crumpled on the floor. A glow of the light twisted and straightened folds in the sheets; casting shadows, shaping it into a person lying in a foetal position.

Patrick stared at it, reassuring himself that all was above board and the presence on the floor was truly his sheets and not anything untoward.

He sat up, dusk rapidly fading, giving way to beautiful baby-blue light that shone through his thin curtains. He took a deep breath, resigned to the fact he was up and the moment for extra sleep had passed.

He rubbed his fingers into his eyes to clear his vision; by now the light had begun to whiten.

He walked over, picked up the sheets and tossed them into a corner. He knelt down, pulled a lever and folded his bed up into a sofa, his bedroom becoming a lounge in an instant. A television sat on a wooden stand opposite the sofa-bed. Beside the TV was the door to the flat, to the right a small kitchenette and to the left a small shower room. In its entirety it measured the same length and width of Valda's upstairs bathroom, but who was measuring? Certainly not Patrick – he had lived in worse, sometimes just existing, in the darkest moments of his life.

After he had got his papers to stay in the UK, he took the little red book he had earned and began to explore his options; going back to Jamaica a comfortable man, his ideal scenario. By getting the book, he had joined an elite group of Jamaicans who could now raise their heads above the parapet; they knew their own, just by the way they walked and talked, big, bold and brazen. They kept the burgundy gold in their pockets, their accents suppressed and their nostrils flared at any notions of similarity between them and their less advantaged fellow countrymen. The rest were forced to live below the radar, living and working in poor conditions; the embarrassing possibility of having to return home from the UK broke and penniless ever looming.

Rough living, scarce job opportunities and at times horrendous levels of mistreatment by a small percentage of the indigenous population equated to failure, gradually turning work-minded men into petty criminals. Petty crime aggravated and further alienated them, making things worse. The country pushed back harder; the pursuit of rights became a pursuit for respect. Out of desperation came greed and resentment, out of those two mindsets came the Yardies, ruthless street gangs that sold drugs and murdered for territory and power, a far cry from the well-dressed, well-spoken and well-educated Windrush generation that preceded them.

In 1987, work at Mr Ting's had begun to dry up for Patrick. The summer months faded and the recession bit harder, resulting in the majority of the illegal immigrants Mr Ting employed or exploited (depending on which side of the table you sat) being let go. These drivers were the ones he allowed to drive for people like Shelia Bradford going to the prom, or the average Joe, trying to make his wife feel special on her birthday. These drivers spoke little English and would smile and nod when asked questions by their passengers, barely able to read a map. They never complained about working conditions or pay, and drove the 'shit bricks', a term coined by Patrick and the other two fluent English-speaking illegals, Luigi from Italy and Podolski from Poland. These three were Mr Ting's most valued migrants, who had the privilege of driving for businessmen occasionally, if his *crème de la crème* drivers were unavailable.

His best drivers drove the pristine limos for diplomats, government officials, actors, singers and the rich. When you drove for that calibre of client, you'd better speak English with no accent, you better know Baker Street from Battersea, you'd better be groomed – and, preferably, white; in Mr Ting's eyes anyway. The majority of his elite drivers were black-cab rejects, who had done the Knowledge but failed the exam.

Mr Ting paid them handsomely for three reasons; they were white, English, knew the city like the back of their hands and also knew, despite Mr Ting's best efforts, about his dodgy cheap, illegal workforce, giving them leverage to request what they wanted when they wanted it. Coupled with the slow pace of business, their demands were killing the company. They shouted for big bonuses and pay rises when they felt like it, at a time when outgoings needed to be frozen. The subtle threat of exposure amounted to no more than blackmail.

Under pressure, Mr Ting decided to do away with the economy service by scrapping the cheap limos and getting rid of all illegal drivers, hoping the act would remove himself from under their thumbs. He sat Patrick, Podolski and Lugi down individually to give them the bad news. Podolski didn't care much, as he had amassed a bit of money over ten years and was returning to Poland anyway; Luigi had just got his papers to stay in the UK and was going to begin work in a restaurant in the city. This left Patrick.

"Patwick, I so sorry I have to let you go; de wankers bleed me dry, for having you guys."

Patrick's heart instantly sank. He liked his job, he got to meet great people and one job was never the same as the next. More importantly, it kept a roof over his head, food in his belly and dignity in his heart. For a second he felt like telling him he had gained his stay, but refrained, feeling wary about telling anyone, scared he would draw unwanted questions and attention to how he had got it, so he exhaled and accepted his fate, unable to do or say much else.

Mr Ting held his hand out over the table and the pair shook on it, his handshake soft and reluctant. The saddened and desperate look in his eyes made it hard for Patrick to feel anything but sorry for the position Mr Ting had found himself in: at the mercy of vultures, picking the flesh from a man who probably deserved it.

As Patrick walked home that evening, the realisation that he was jobless began to sink in. The rent for his room was due in two weeks and his aunt Edith, who had looked after him since his parents passed away, awaited her monthly instalment for her upkeep back home.

Patrick lived in Willesden, a forty-five-minute walk from Mr Ting's limo rentals, which was located just off the North Circular where years later you would find a national car rental company dwarfed by a beautiful white and gold Hindu temple.

A bronze sun faded above him as he walked, his blazer folded over his arm, his sleeves rolled up, his top button gaping, his mind trying to find a solution to this unexpected termination of employment. He lived in a room within a shared building above a shop that sold bits and bobs on Willesden High Road. Directly opposite his building was a club called the Conference Club where older Jamaicans in the community had been going since the 1960s to socialise and connect. It was a home away from home, where you could play dominos, eat jerk chicken and fried fish, listen to reggae music and enjoy uncensored loud chatter.

The Conference used to be a respectable haunt for gentrified men and women, but during the late 1980s undesirable elements of the community had started to filter in, seeing it as a convenient place to go and scheme or sell drugs, safe in the knowledge that even law-abiding Jamaicans had very little dealings with the police and were too scared to challenge these young men about anything. On approach, Patrick slowed to hear muffled music and the smell of chicken escaping through the cracks of the Conference's door. He stopped, considering a glass of Wray and Nephew, a piece of fish, hard-dough bread and maybe, just maybe, the possibility of finding a young lady to keep him company for the night.

This would be his first time back in the Conference in over a year. He had stopped going once it had lost its innocence, after poor old Percy Twig had had his wages stolen from him at gunpoint on his way home, by a man he had broken bread with earlier. Twig's wasn't an isolated case either; there had been a spate of similar robberies, stabbings and even one rape. Poverty has a beautiful and horrible way of dragging the best and worst out of people: the pauper's own community always the first to bear the brunt of degradation.

Patrick sighed to himself and pushed open the door. The smell of food and cigarette smoke hit him in an instant; the music went from muffled vibrations to Burning Spare; he had already begun to relax and could taste the rum. Inside, the windows were painted black and the lights were dimmed to a point just above absolute darkness. People ferried cigarettes and cigars to and fro, from their lips to ashtrays in the darkness, floating like fireflies over still water.

Twelve tables with floral cloths laid across them were ahead of him. To his direct right sat a small bar, made from a long stall table with two chairs behind it, occupied by two elderly gentlemen. On top of the table were stacks of plastic cups, several bottles of Wray, E&J and coke lined up beside each other. The place was shabby at best, but clean. Right next to the bar was a walkway which provided the only source of light. The walkway led to the toilets and kitchen. A sound system occupied two corners of the room.

Patrick made his way to the bar, and heard his name being called out from the darkness. He slowed and looked in the direction the voice had come.

"Yo, Patrick!"

A hand waved him over to a table occupied by two. As he got closer he realised it was Leroy Prince and Sheldon Johnson. Sheldon pulled out a seat for him to sit.

They had a bottle of Wray's on their table and two cups. As Patrick lowered himself into the seat, he noticed how Sheldon's eyes followed his descent.

Leroy shot out a clenched fist and bumped fists with Patrick. Sheldon just nodded, his fingers laced around his cup, as if protecting its contents. Leroy smiled but his eyes didn't. Sheldon's gaze drifted from Leroy to Patrick and back again.

"Wha gwan?" Leroy asked.

Patrick exhaled.

"Bwoy, nothing really."

Everybody fell silent.

"Ya still ah drive for the chiney man?" Leroy asked.

Patrick looked at Sheldon, who stared at Leroy, his eyes moving from side to side like a slow tide.

"Na," Patrick replied.

"How come?"

"Bwoy, him jus let me go ta-day."

Leroy sucked his teeth.

"Fuckery."

Silence again. Sheldon sipped his drink, his eyes still drifting between the pair in conversation. The DJ switched track and a few people at a distant table applauded. Patrick and Leroy looked over in the direction of the applause, but Sheldon didn't, keeping his eyes on the pair of them.

Leroy leaned forward, picked up the bottle of Wray, poured a shot into a plastic cup and slid it over to Patrick. Patrick didn't really know much about Leroy, except that he had once held down a job as a janitor in a school and, when he was fired, he went rogue, wheeling and dealing, ducking and diving. He was short and thick; he had a faded haircut, shaped-up beard and moustache, and was always in the nicest clothes.

Sheldon he knew even less about, except, it had been rumoured, he was a shooter and was responsible for slaying many men. He was tall, thin and light skinned his hair a small shaped-up afro, his face hairless.

Before leaving for England, Patrick's aunt Edith had made three statements that had stuck with him. The first was, "When ya reach England, be careful of women," the next, "Don't bother move with no criminals, abide by the law," and the last, "Nobody can call your name, if ya not there." Yet here he was at a table with a thief and murderer. Something didn't feel right; it was if they were buttering him up. He knew these types of Jamaicans, he knew how they moved when hungry; slow and steady, pulling you in gently, so you couldn't see it.

Letting you know so much, so that you knew *too* much and must go along for the ride.

Patrick wanted to leave, but could find no reasonable excuse to do so. Sheldon looked across Patrick to the door as if waiting for hell to come through.

"So Patrick, tell me something. Ya want to make a lickle money?" Leroy asked.

Patrick felt like saying no, but refrained from doing so. Sheldon continued to sip and stare.

Maybe he means legally. He was once a worker. Maybe he's seen the error of his ways, maybe it's work, work I may need. I'll hear him out ...

"Doing what?" Patrick replied.

Leroy smiled a little.

"Doing what you do, my fren."

Sheldon became alert and sat forward, his hand at his waist, and watched as evening light poured in as the entrance door opened. He watched two women walk to the opposite side of the room. Satisfied, his menacing gaze fell upon Patrick once more.

"What do I do?" Patrick asked.

"Drive."

"Drive who where?" Patrick asked.

Leroy leaned forward over the table, his gold chain dangling out from his shirt.

"Us."

Patrick and Leroy held each other's gaze. Sheldon looked at Patrick's profile.

"Before ya answer, mek me tell you what ya stand to gain," Leroy elaborated.

Leroy slid closer until his lips almost touched Patrick's cheek.

"Five thousand pound."

Instantaneously the devilish part of Patrick's brain killed the voice of reason. He thought of the financial respite he could receive with that type of money, especially now he was jobless. One thousand pounds could pay for five months of rent; another could see Aunt Edith set for a year; and the remaining three could give him enough time to get himself back on his feet and back into work again.

"Where to?" Patrick asked.

Sheldon kissed his teeth and appeared inappropriately annoyed.

"Him ah ask too many questions," Sheldon said to the table.

Leroy looked from Sheldon to Patrick.

"Look, ya want to do it or not? If you agree, we'll tell ya where and when."

"I'm interested, but I have to know, what it's all about?"

Leroy paused. His eyes began to move, scanning, roaming over Patrick's face, searching for trust, searching for weakness.

Leroy began. "Look, if I—"

Sheldon leaned forward and cut in.

"Ya sure you want to do this? Ya sure you want to let him in?" Sheldon questioned.

"Yeah man, Patrick's cool," Leroy replied.

Patrick watched Sheldon lean back, take his glass and neck the contents.

Leroy began again.

"Ya know Red Wayne, from over Stonebridge?"

Patrick nodded.

"Well, it turn out that him work in ah hotel over Paddington, an' him say one actress has been staying there; and him say, one night she make for him and him fuck her. They got chatting and it turns out she has a necklace worth a whole heap of money tie round her neck. He say she ah go to some award show tomorrow - wearing it. Him say she nah walk with security."

Leroy looked up and around at his surroundings as if to make sure he wasn't being listened to, then continued. "Anyway, to cut it short, we wan take that! Sheldon know a man over Hatton Garden that will take it off us and give us money for it … All you have to do is drive, and we'll do the rest."

Patrick sighed, resurrecting reason, thinking, *Just ten minutes ago I came in here looking for a drink, food and a place to unwind, and now I'm having a conversation about robbing a movie star, an act that could see my passport revoked and me sent to prison, then back to Jamaica in shame ... The last thing Mr Bradford said to me was keep your nose clean or we could both be in it. There's no way I can do this; God will provide ... He has so far.* Sheldon huffed, commanding attention. He looked at Leroy and Patrick shook his head softly. "I can't."

"Wha ya mean can't?" Leroy asked.

"It's not for me." Patrick elaborated.

Sheldon leaned forward.

"So why are you wasting we time fa?" Sheldon hissed.

Patrick stared into Sheldon's eyes, the whites yellow and aged, the pupils big in the absence of light; cold, callous, ruthless and turbulent. Patrick exhaled and looked back at Leroy, his elbows on the table, nodding gently, his face disappointed. Patrick stood and looked at the pair.

"Sorry about dat."

Patrick turned and attempted to walk off, but Leroy shot out a hand and grabbed Patrick's tightly and spoke. "Mek sure this stays with you."

Patrick looked down at Leroy, who looked at Sheldon; Sheldon had his shirt pulled up, revealing a brown and silver gun handle peeking out of his trouser waist. Patrick swallowed and began to feel panic setting in. His palms became sweaty and his heart raced.

"C-c-c-come on Leroy, you know I don't play."

"Hmmm, cause you know…we kill man for less, right?"

Leroy paused, making sure his message hit home, then let go of his hand. Sheldon lowered his shirt and went back to the bottle of Wray's. Patrick took the warning and fled the Conference. He walked home looking over his shoulder, the devil to his back, Percy Twig in his mind.

That night he couldn't sleep, anticipating Sheldon coming to his house, with malice, to silence him for good. Sleep finally caught him unawares, and surprisingly enough he never dreamt a damn thing that night.

~

The next day brought with it grey clouds and cold. Patrick woke to soft raindrops on his window and his fellow lodger, Hanna, calling from the bottom of the stairs.

"Patriiick!"

Patrick sat up and looked at the clock on his bedside table, which read 1 pm. He rubbed his face with both palms, shocked he had slept for so long.

"Patriiick!"

He slowly rose to sit, and his belly purred with hunger. His mouth was sour, his uniform still on from yesterday.

"Yeaaah?" Patrick replied.

"The phone!"

"Okay!"

He stood up, surprised he had a call. He stretched, rubbed his eyes and made his way out to the ground floor where the phone was situated.

He walked down three flights of stairs, past nine sets of rooms, full of fellow lodgers, unable to afford much more. The phone lay on its side on a small hallway table. He picked it up and looked around. Hanna was nowhere to be seen, and neither was anyone else. He placed it to his ear and spoke.

"Hello?"

"Patwick!"

"Mr Ting?"

A smile crept across Patrick's face.

"Patwick, I need favour."

Both listened to the silence for a second.

"What is it?"

I hope he doesn't want me to aid and abet him in a robbery or a murder, Patrick thought.

"One of my dwivers pull out for VVIP client, Mona Range … You know her?"

"Nah, can't say I do."

"Anyway, not impawtant, I need you ta dwive, I pay twiple."

"Triple! Tell me where and when."

Mr Ting filled him in on the details and Patrick was set for the evening. He was due to pick Mona up at 7 pm from the Hilton in Paddington. Mindful of the time, he decided he had to be at Mr Ting's by 5 pm at the latest in order to get debriefed, check the car over and, more importantly, arrange and finalise his fee and when exactly he would get it. Although Mr Ting was generally okay when it came to making payments, he had been known to be tricky at times and had been assaulted on more than one occasion for trying to short-change drivers who had done extra work for him. By 4 pm the night was so eager to come that a faint moon had arrived and occupied its space before the sun could fall.

Patrick stood holding the overhead bus rail by the entrance of the number 260. People got on and looked at him; his immense height, dressed like a penguin, his cabbie hat tucked under his free arm.

Patrick stepped off the bus and walked down past Harlesden Tube station, past the infamous Stonebridge estate, past people ending their working day while he began his. He walked into Mr Ting's yard and was met with a cream Mercedes-Benz limousine, its wheels beautifully clean, its bodywork waxed and shining under the moon and glare of the yard's floodlights.

It stood in the middle flanked and faced by several other limos, parked in rows on either side. The reception light shone through the window revealing Mr Ting, who paced up and down, a cigarette hung in between his fingers, his face wearing its usual look of worry.

Patrick walked towards reception to put him out of his misery; Mr Ting spotted him, went to the door and yanked it open.

"Shit! Patwick, you fucking cut it close, it 5.05 pm already."

He stood aside and let Patrick walk in. Patrick walked to the customer counter and leaned against it. Mr Ting began shooting out a million and one words at once. Patrick noticed his ability to speak English diminished incredibly when pressured.

"Wight, wight, wight, the keys … You know Hilton address, wight?"

Mr Ting pointed at Patrick, with two fingers, the cigarette between them, its head nearly burned down to the filter. Patrick forced a flummoxed look.

"Patwick, you know or not?"

A smile crept across Patrick's face and he nodded, Mr Ting held his chest as if it was about to implode, then the cigarette finally burned down. He yelped, threw it down and danced on it on the spot.

"Shit!"

Patrick laughed out loud. Mr Ting sucked on his fingers and spoke.

"Stop fucking about, Patwick."

Mr Ting grabbed the limo keys from his pocket and gave them to Patrick.

"Hurry up."

Patrick grabbed the keys and went to ask about payment. Mr Ting anticipated this.

"Pay, tommowow, 11 pm. Yes!"

They looked at each other and smiled. Patrick moved past him, walked out of the office and Mr Ting stood on the step, observing his attire.

"Ahhh! Patwick, where ya hat?"

Patrick continued to walk, raised his hand with the hat in it, and placed it on his head. Mr Ting lit another cigarette and Patrick started the engine, clipped his seatbelt in and pulled out of the yard, bound for Paddington.

~

Friday-night traffic was generally a nightmare in London, but Patrick's drive towards the hotel was relatively smooth. He was going against the tide, the majority of commuters going in the opposite direction, heading back from London based offices or school runs towards Wembley, Harrow, Sudbury and various other suburban areas.

By 5.45 pm the night had truly set in, bringing with it a further plunge in temperature. The radio DJ gave the temperature as five degrees; Patrick reached across and switched the heating to warm.

By 6.01 pm he had manoeuvred through the many one-way roads and avoided several pedestrians who had a death wish. This part of London was always like that; fast and abrupt, pedestrian or vehicle, they seemed to appear from nowhere, hell-bent on reaching their destination swiftly at all costs.

By 6.10 pm Patrick was just pulling into the main passenger pick-up bay of the Hilton. "Hilton London Metropole, 225 Edgware Road, London W2 1JU," Patrick whispered to himself, amazed by its immaculate beauty. Soft spotlights shone from the floor. A large marble wall had the hotel's name carved into it, written in gold. From overhead the hulking building came out far and provided shelter for guests coming out to cars. By the entrance were large potted trees shaped and pruned to perfection.

A well-dressed man in white gloves, top hat and tails walked out from his standing position and held his hand out from the kerb, signalling for Patrick to stop and pull in. The man bent down to speak to him. Patrick reached for the knob to wind the windows down but couldn't find one. He looked down then remembered he wasn't driving the 'shit brick' and pressed the orange illuminated arrow pointing south. The man talked through a smile at his expense.

"Mona Range?" the door attendant asked.

"Yes."

Knowing he was too early, he anticipated he may have to park elsewhere and come back when she was ready.

"Okay. You can wait right here, she'll be out by 18.55."

Patrick counted back two and translated the time to 6.55 pm, then looked at the time on the car clock, which read 6.13 pm. Patrick smiled at the man, who smiled back. He stood straight, turned and went back to his initial position by the entrance. Patrick wound up the window and sighed, feeling a little nervous. Mona Range began to feel like a big deal.

He looked at the clock: *6.15 – forty minutes*. Patrick looked around the car to pass the time. The car was pure luxury on wheels. He had never seen this model. Mr Ting must have kept this one for VVIPs. Climate control, cruise control and, below the tape slot, another slot that read CD by it. He wondered what it was used for, as he ran his finger against its opening and eventually decided it was where the climate control exited. *Climate dump,* he thought to himself.

Six forty-five: ten minutes. Patrick was really and truly bored now. Hardly anyone had come and gone, a few cars had pulled up in front of and behind the limo, the drivers appearing to have a problem with not accessing the main bay, the attendant swiftly sorting them and their attitudes out. *Mona must be a huge deal,* Patrick thought, and she was. Two Oscars the year before for best supporting actress and best female actress had sky-rocketed her to stardom. She was wanted by every film director and had suddenly begun to win every award on earth; the latest was her reason for being in the UK – a Bafta for her role in the film Smooth Mumba that had won her the two Oscars.

Out of what seemed like nowhere a cameraman appeared at the entrance. The door attendant asked him to step back, and when he didn't he called for hotel security. Two stocky guys came out almost immediately and began to chat with him; they appeared to be arguing.

The Hilton didn't expect what was to follow. Out of nowhere five more cameramen appeared. Cameras hung from their necks, the lenses as long as rulers. This wasn't meant to happen; there had been no press release about where Mona was staying. The hotel had been informed that there would be no media circus to disturb the other guests, who had paid big money for their stay. Unfortunately for them, the media had sent out scouts to all top hotels in London, finding and paying a small fortune to crooked hotel supervisors to inform them if Mona Range was on their books.

Security began to get more forceful, pushing the cameramen back out of the entrance. One of them had clocked on that Patrick's limo must've been Mona's, and tapped on the window, a fistful of notes whispering through the closed glass so the rest wouldn't hear.

"A hundred and fifty to let me in; come on, a hundred and fifty."

Patrick ignored him and looked over at the entrance. The guy struck the window with his fist and Patrick felt anger boil in his belly. He almost got out and placed his hands on him.

He looked down at the clock. A minute past seven. *Where is she? I want to get out of here before this gets any worse.* And it did. Patrick counted at least twenty cameramen and stragglers who stopped to see what the big fuss was all about.

Security and the doorman went inside and emerged with two more massive security guards, who pushed and pulled guys back from the entrance, throwing cameramen into a sea of cameramen. It had got real crazy; beyond a circus, more like a rally.

Then the doors opened and, like a squadron of fireflies, cameras suddenly burst into life. Click, click, click, click, click; the sound deafening. From Patrick's position he could see who he assumed was Mona Range making her way towards the limo, hotel security creating space around her, a tall white guy to her right and a black guy just behind her. On closer inspection of the black guy's face, Patrick's blood began to curdle, his palms began to sweat and his face burned.

"Red Wayne …what the fuck?" he said to himself.

Red Wayne was called that because his skin was a light brown that verged on the cusp of red at times. His eyes were green, his hair black when cut low, but with growth had a brown hue to it. He was short with a medium athletic build, born to an English mother and a Bajan father.

Patrick's mind ran to Leroy, Sheldon and that gun; a brown and silver handle, tucked into Sheldon's waistband; a life-taker and possession-negotiator. Patrick pulled his cap low over his eyes to make it harder to recognise him, then stepped out and looked across the ocean of people trying to get a piece of Mona. He looked for the pair, impossible to miss in an all-white crowd. He scanned left then right, then left again and right again, but he couldn't see anything but cameramen and the general public.

She neared with her manager and Red Wayne still in tow, security still throwing people back and forth beside and behind them. Patrick looked away from Wayne. He opened the door and allowed Mona to get in, camera lenses coming this way and that, security doing just enough to keep the masses held back. With them both seated, Patrick attempted to close the door. Security men had formed a four-man semicircle around her door, their backs to the limo, but Wayne held the handle, resisting its closure.

Patrick looked at him, while Wayne looked around and behind himself, biding his time for Leroy, Sheldon and the gun, no doubt. A horrible feeling of impending doom swirled around Patrick's body. Everything went silent and time slowed down. He raised his hand and brought it down with force into Wayne's forearm, making him recoil. Wayne looked to his right, holding his throbbing arm, but Patrick had closed Mona's door and had got in himself, preventing Wayne from getting a look at his face.

He looked in the rear-view mirror and within two seconds had trapped her image: pale-skinned, busty, her hair dark auburn. She was much prettier than Julia Roberts, and that was saying something. She wore a figure-hugging red dress and of course she had on that necklace: big, bright, shiny and worth an estimated £80,000.

Her manager was thin and tall. He wore a black suit with a bow tie, his blond hair parted down one side.

Patrick looked away from the driver's window. Wayne hunched over and glared through it in an attempt to see the driver's face. Patrick kept his hat low and his face angled awkwardly. He clipped his seatbelt in and took Mona's screamed advice to "Drive!"

The car sped off, Patrick breathing hard, Mona and her manager Max laughing and giggling, totally unaware they had come close to having a gun pushed in their face and £80,000 worth of jewels taken.

At the first set of traffic lights, a small nail-varnished hand rested upon Patrick's shoulder. He turned and came face to face with a double Oscar-winning superstar, her face even more beautiful up close. Her eyes were glazed, as if she was in love or on dope, her nose scarlet as if she had been crying or had a cold.

"Ya did real good back there, real good," she joked.

From behind, Max burst out laughing and flung himself about the seat in fits. Mona fell back and rolled with him. Patrick looked into the rear-view mirror. Just then, the lights turned green and traffic began to move, but he couldn't – as through the tinted back window he was able to see the inhabitants of the car behind them. The driver was unknown, but the passenger was Sheldon Johnson.

The car didn't beep or draw attention to itself. The two giggling idiots in the back hadn't even realised they hadn't moved until cars behind Sheldon's began to beep furiously as they drove round it and besides the limo, gesturing rudely.

"Hey! Why aren't we moving, buddy?" she asked.

"Yeah man, light's real mean green – let's go to the show!" said Max.

Both broke out laughing. Patrick put his foot down, searching his brain for how to deal with the tail they had gained.

They passed North Westminster School on their left, heading towards the Harrow Road, bound for Wembley arena. Patrick drove steadily, trying not to let nerves and anxiety take hold fully. He looked into his rear-view mirror once more and still they remained; resilient, baleful, slow but sure.

They stopped at another set of traffic lights by Kensal Green graveyard.

"Yo! How big's ya dick?" Mona Range yelled.

Patrick spun round and frowned at her, shaking his head. In the three years he had driven for Mr Ting, he had never had passengers of such high calibre and he had never been made to double-take and blush. They both broke out laughing again. Under normal circumstances he may have bantered, but he was busy trying to keep the devils off their back and that chain around her little neck.

The lights flipped green and Patrick consulted his rear-view mirror once more. The fuckers were gone, replaced by a man on a motorbike and beyond him a lorry. He sighed. *Maybe they've given up?*

They drove down the Harrow Road through to Harlesden. Patrick became ultra-alert when they reached there, aware they had stepped into the wolves' lair, Sheldon and Leroy's turf. He had a feeling he would not leave Harlesden without incident. Traffic was bad but moving; the few people out on that cold night were stopping and staring at the limo, a rarity in NW10.

The pair in the back had discovered the champagne and were sipping, talking and giggling. The light turned green and only a handful of cars went through. The rest in front of them crawled, then stopped. Patrick's heart began to beat a little faster; he felt something was coming. He looked all around the outside of the car but saw nothing untoward. The light changed again and a few more cars went through. It was their turn next and Patrick prayed it came quickly.

Max's hand came up and rested upon his shoulder.

"How much longer, bud?" Max asked.

"About fifteen more minutes, sir."

Max patted his shoulder.

"Good man."

He sat back down.

The light turned green again, but the car in front didn't budge. Patrick observed one guy in the back, another up front, and the driver made three. The guy in the back pulled something over his head. The guy who got out of the passenger-side door had already done this and was walking towards the limo, balaclava on, pistol by his side. The eyes belonged to Sheldon. Leroy jumped out as well, pistol in hand, held low, walking slowly towards the limo. Vapour escaped from their covered mouths in the cold air. Patrick pulled his hat lower and, without thought, revved that engine so high that it sounded like the car was a rocket ready to explode into the stratosphere.

Patrick put his foot down and the limo spun out and jerked diagonally to the left in Sheldon's direction. From the right a loud flash commanded everybody's attention; a flash that struck the wing mirror and shattered it.

Max and Mona fell silent then both began to scream. Patrick floored the pedal and sped towards Sheldon, who shot through the windscreen, shattering it. The screams in the car gained in volume, and the people on the street joined in, running this way and that like wild gazelle in the presence of predators.

Sheldon jumped out of the way and fell on his side, letting off another shot that missed and shattered a shop window on the limo's right. Patrick moved forward in Sheldon's direction and Sheldon rolled out of the way. By now, the driver of their car had begun to reverse, trying to stop the limo squeezing past. It almost succeeded, but Patrick moved further left. As Patrick did his best to get around the car and not crush Sheldon on the ground, Leroy was already on the back passenger door besides Mona, who moved over and squashed in against Max on her left. Sheldon stood up and was walking, gun out front, towards the side Mona and Max were bunched up on.

The car in front was now trying to manoeuvre so as to cut off any chance of escape. Patrick floored the pedal and sped through the diminishing gap, partially crushing Sheldon against street railings and the right side of the car against the car trying to block them. The sound of metal on metal was like pulling nails down a blackboard. They were away and moving. A flash bled into the night behind them and faded, Leroy letting off one last shot before the police would arrive to find

Sheldon holding his stomach, his legs the wrong way, his entrails hanging out, his eyes open, waiting to be closed, for pennies to be placed.

The next day, the police found Leroy and the driver in Birmingham, hiding in someone's attic; Leroy got a jail sentence of twenty years, and the driver ten. The community sighed in relief that Sheldon, who had terrorised the town, was dead.

Mona never made it to the awards show; she went to hospital with Max, where the police questioned them about the whole thing. Patrick said what he was obliged to. The case was closed, but the circus began.

"Mona nearly killed in dramatic shoot-out in crime-ravaged Harlesden."

"Attempted robbery, one dead and one in jail – and one Hollywood superstar! Read inside for more details."

"Heroic driver saves Mona Range from certain death at the hands of Yardie gangsters."

The world was served pictures of the mangled limo and shot-out windscreen with Mona and Max sitting in the back seat. Mr Ting even took the opportunity to take several pictures with the limo, a shameless plug for business.

Out of fear of reprisal, Patrick refused to sign a release for his pictures. Not one came out; journalists were forced to silhouette and question-mark his face. Business at Mr Ting's shot up. Undercover reporters were hiring limos left, right and centre in an attempt to try and get an exclusive with the mysterious driver, and offering other drivers humungous amounts to try to lure Patrick out to talk to the nation and sign a release.

The top drivers were kissing his ass, trying to strike deals with him to talk, acting as agents for the media. Patrick held firm, the glare of the camera too bright for a man like him: he didn't like all that attention and fuss. The fact that Mr Ting had doubled his wages to stay on was more than enough for him – he was happy with that. He gave some written interviews – no photos – and earned a small fortune for them. He sent a large portion of the money to his aunt Edith in Jamaica and used the remaining amount as a deposit for a small mortgage on a neat little studio flat in Kilburn.

Mona made no further contact with him personally but she had her agent send him a bottle of something he couldn't pronounce and a bouquet of flowers. She recommended Mr Ting's in every interview she gave, happy to be alive to do so.

When the story died out, it left a nice mark on the company. Businessmen and women, celebrities and politicians began hiring Mr Ting's limos at an alarming rate: they were so popular that he found it hard to cope. They moved to bigger premises, hired more drivers and bought more vehicles.

Years flew by and Patrick's heroics were long forgotten by most, but never by Mr Ting, who said, "No matter what, Patwick, you'll always have a job here." Business began to die down in 2008, forcing Mr Ting to create another sideline to his company, a sort of glorified cab service with luxury cars, aimed at clients who wanted something a little less conspicuous.

On 5th October 2010, Mr Ting received a call from Valda's PA Claire, requesting a driver. Mr Ting sent Patrick. Patrick arrived at the address provided: 495 Brittle Street, WC1 2NP. The road was slap-bang in the heart of the City, surrounded by hulking grey buildings that were huge and imposing. Buildings that were at least a hundred years old, with ugly gargoyles and weird symbols at the top, only noticeable if you stood and looked for long enough. Workers in this part of town earned an average of £50,000 per year. If the horde baying for blood hadn't been there, there would've been people in grey and black suits, both male and female, scurrying around the streets like ants over sugar cubes. Instead, they stayed in their offices peering through blinds at the mob below.

When Patrick arrived he was met by a scene reminiscent of that terrible night twenty odd years ago – the night he saved Mona (who tragically died in 2006 of a drug overdose), Max and himself from harm or death. Paparazzi, animal rights protesters and conspiracy theorists were everywhere, tussling with the police and security, outnumbering them three to one, threatening to go inside and deal out justice of their own. The owners of the building had gone into red alert and locked down all entrances and exits.

Valda was inside at a conference with other major business players, having their annual meeting chaired by Winfred Alfred Isaac Cuthbert (WAIC), which conspiracy theorist swore stood for We Are In Charge. They theorised that these annual meetings were held by a bunch of devil worshippers, hell-bent on controlling the world through fashion, media and food. In actual fact, they were just a bunch of very rich businesspeople who were trying to make more money by networking, siphoning ideas and learning how to pay everybody less.

Patrick approached and stopped a small distance away. He called Claire and alerted her to the situation, informing her that even if Valda could leave via the main entrance she would surely be accosted by the mob.

Claire seemed frantic. The meeting had ended an hour ago and all attendees were trapped. Valda had called Claire to ask her to work out a solution. The first thing she did was call Mr Ting for a car, with no idea of how she would get Valda to it.

Claire had told him that all the exits had been shut and she had no idea when this thing was going to blow over, so he was to stay put until it did. Patrick didn't fancy that, and began to think about getting her out, then it struck him. He looked up, all around the building, and saw open, reflective windows a couple of floors up. They were the type that only opened a certain amount to prevent people slipping out, or people getting in. Above the large windows were rectangular ones, a metre and a half across, which appeared to open out fully, enough for a child or petite women to manoeuvre through. Patrick got out of the car and shaded his eyes with his hand and looked at the windows glowing under a full September sun.

The mass of people swelled and pushed. The police were attempting to form a ring around them; this only aggravated the mob further, who consequently turned their attention from getting into the building to getting at the police. Small skirmishes flared up; rocks and bottles deflected off police helmets, shields and armour. Patrick felt this was the right time to go, as law and disorder were distracted by each other.

He figured if he could drive down the side road to the back of the building unnoticed, he could get Valda to climb out of a downstairs window and be away with her.

He called Claire and pitched his idea. She was over the moon. *A solution,* she thought. She asked him to remain where he was, while she called Valda to run it by her.

The street fight raged on. More police units arrived and joined the fray. Things were looking nasty; protesters lobbed objects at the building's windows and police, who used their shields to block the onslaught and charge when appropriate. A news van rushed past Patrick and parked just in front of his car. A reporter and full crew jumped out and started to set up their equipment on the pavement besides him.

Patrick's phone jumped into life.

"Do it! She's had a look out the back and it's all clear round there. I'll text you her number. Call her when you get round there and she'll climb out … Oh, and one last thing? Make sure this works, or your ass and mine are for the chop."

"The chop?"

"Trust me, you don't know this woman."

They both fell silent. Patrick cleared his throat.

"Okay."

He got out and stood on the pavement, shading his eyes with his hand, to see more clearly. He began to plan his approach. Driving up the road and simply taking a left past the building was near impossible on account of the crowd's erratic nature; calm one minute, then fighting across both road lanes the next.

Patrick calculated that the turn on the other side came just shy of the crowd. He decided he would approach from that way, making the left turning his right.

He stepped back into the car, turned and drove around the block. His mind ran back to the night Sheldon had been killed. He remembered he had not screamed or made a noise as he rolled between car and railings, hands held high, trying to make himself small. *Bad to the last,* he thought. *The man was bad to the last.* He remembered how Red Wayne moved out of the area and never returned after it was rumoured that Sheldon's people began to say Red Wayne had set up Leroy and Sheldon, tipping off the actress. *An eye for an eye.* Patrick thought they wanted his blood, and had he stayed, they would have had it.

As he drove down the other side of Brittle Street he wondered what Valda would look like, whether she would look as alluring as Mona had. He continued down the road and the protest approached, looking like a horde of ants, faces, arms and legs merged together, going every way. Luckily, a large section of the crowd had moved away from the building towards where he had parked earlier. The police and protesters were going at it hammer and tongs. Behind him came more blue lights, the noise of the sirens deafening. Two more police vans hurtled past, surely stacking the odds in the police's favour.

He slowed to the turn and simply took it, with no resistance from police men or protester. He took the next immediate left and was behind the building.

He parked up on the pavement, as close as he could get, and looked around for trouble. Content that it was safe, he looked through his phone for Claire's text, opened it and was just about to call Valda, when he heard someone shout out from a ground-floor window twenty metres to his left. He looked over and saw a hand waving from inside. He jumped out of the car and walked towards it.

"Cab?" Valda shouted.

Patrick stood a few feet away, looking up into its diagonal slant.

"Yeah! Are you Valda?"

"Yes."

A loud bang echoed from within the building, the sound of the strong resistant window being non-resistant. They both froze for a second, then proceeded.

"I haven't got much time – help me get out."

"Okay, swin—"

Before he could complete his sentence, one leg was already out of the window. Attached to it was a very expensive high-heeled stiletto. Then came another leg, her skirt riding up. Patrick was so nervous about touching her bare legs that his hands danced back and forth inches around them.

From inside came another bang followed by another. Valda's legs swung from side to side, her skirt pushed right up to her waist, revealing a thong lodged between her tanned buttocks.

"For fuck's sake, hold my legs and get me down."

Patrick snapped to it, grabbed and held her legs, allowing her to push the rest of herself out. Once out, he stumbled around and she wobbled in his arms. He set her down and she made herself neat then stepped quickly towards his car.

"Come on!" she commanded.

He followed her. Both jumped in the car and Patrick drove away. Neither of them said a word until they were clear. She looked over as they turned away from what could only now be described as a riot and saw people and policemen jumping through shattered windows; the building breeched.

She sighed quietly, not even sparing a thought for the other attendees who had barricaded themselves into the conference room, waiting for the law to save them, unaware that Valda's excuse of going to the toilet was actually her great escape.

Patrick looked up into the rear-view mirror, the indicator clicking to turn right at the lights. She met his gaze there.

"Whose idea was it?"

Patrick paused for two seconds, considering the angle of the question. Thanks to her tone, so deadpan, he couldn't tell if she was pissed off or pleased. Either or, her question required an answer, and he gave a truthful one.

"Mine."

The light changed and Patrick pulled out. He glanced back into the mirror; she looked deep in thought, looking out of her window. The high sun bleached her face with its smudging light.

"You're quite resourceful, aren't you?"

Question or comment? he thought, unsure. He played it safe and said nothing.

"How much do you earn?" she asked.

A nervous chuckle escaped him. "Not enough."

"I'm looking for—"

Before she could finish, he cut in. "Sorry, I don't do this often. I think you think I'm more than I am," Patrick made clear.

She fell silent, then spoke again.

"I'm looking for a personal driver – an instinctive, intuitive full-time driver; I'll triple your current salary."

His thoughts cut into her proposal.

"Can I have some time to think ab—" he asked.

"Think about it, you have my number. Call me tomorrow."

The odd job had created an audacious job proposal that Patrick couldn't and wouldn't turn down, spelling the end of his time at Mr Ting's and the beginning of his life with Valda.

Infans

24th December 2013
11.30 pm
St Mary's Hospital

Nurse Rosita Webb leaves the delivery room, citing giddiness. Her chubby fingers hold on to the hallway wall for balance, preventing her short plump frame from falling over. Her plimsolls slap against the polished floor. Sweat beads off her back, chest and arms; her white uniform clings to her; she is so hot she wishes she could tear the damn thing off.

She takes a right past two young doctors on their way home who are forced to slow and stop as she approaches and passes them, watching her move like a woman possessed. Rosita makes a right at the corridor and slams into a disabled toilet; the door swings open and closes in one motion. The lights click on automatically and she slips down to her backside and leans against the door, her breathing laboured, her dark black hair stuck to her brow, dripping with perspiration.

She begins to unbutton her uniform, button by button, dragging the sleeves down, leaving her top half exposed. A sudden thirst grips her, an extreme thirst like no other, so bad it forces her to her knees and she begins to crawl towards the sink, every ounce of her body hurting.

She begins to moan and groan in pain. Tears roll down her cheeks and she begins to pray to God. Her thoughts are a hot mess, rushing around her head, colliding, none of them able to gain prominence.

She reaches to pull herself up onto the sink, but her arms feel like lead weights and they hover just over the basin, before falling to her side in defeat. Unable to even consider a second attempt, she does what she would have deemed unthinkable an hour ago and slips her hand under the toilet seat, down into the bowl, cupping water to drink.

Hung between her brown breasts is a baby-blue rosary. She grabs hold of it with her free hand and rips it off, throwing the beads, crucifix and string to the floor. The plastic is melted. The chain's links have left small white boils, sores and disturbed skin around her neck where it lay.

~

A dressing gown hangs separated at her rear, revealing her bum and vagina. Valda growls in a sedated pain, her legs spread, her hands dug into the mat beneath her. Alex is on bended knee, rubbing her back softly, trying to soothe her discomfort. He whispers constantly, "You're doing well, you're doing well," while thinking the two doctors who have retreated to the back of the room and the nurse who has just bolted through the door would say otherwise.

Her mind is an unclear muddle of confused thoughts and colours, whites and reds, both vibrant and pristine. She flashes back to her childhood flat, with no one but her there. She looks at the walls, which are ash black, as if the house had been painted by Goths. Pain injects a purple in front of her mind's eye, a matt purple with speckles of flickering white, bringing her back to her present. She asks for more gas and Alex quickly hands her the nozzle. She sucks in deeply then removes it from her mouth and whispers, "I can't do this."

Alex replies, "You can, you're doing really well," continuously looking over at the doctors. An assistant midwife is standing right behind Alex, her hands on her waist, her face cracked by a routine smile that says: *It's Christmas Eve and this is the tenth birth I've had to deal with in the last twenty-four hours. Get on with it.*

Alex looks to the nurse for more help. She kneels down beside him.

"Her cervix isn't dilating; they're considering going for a caesarean section," she whispers.

Valda asks for more gas and Alex hands her the nozzle.

Alex looks up at the doctors, then over at Valda, her head slumped, the nozzle in her hand. He thinks how exhausted she looks; he feels for her and wishes he could take away her pain.

"It's been twenty-two hours and her progress is a little slow. Don't worry, it's routine. You guys have paid for the best, and those two are brilliant."

Alex lets out a sigh, his hand moving over Valda's back like a windscreen cleaner. The nurse draws her hand over his to comfort him.

He looks at her again. "Where's Rosita gone?"

The midwife looks at the door, then back at him. "I really don't know, but I'm sure she has her reasons."

~

The pain easing, Rosita manages to stand up, her calves and forearms shaking uncontrollably. She looks into the mirror; her neck and chest are inflamed and raw, so raised that it looks as though she has had acid poured over her. She gasps and her eyes water at the sight.

The crucifix has burned its shape where it lay. Rosita raises one hand to it and gently moves her fingers across the pus-filled sores. Her hand trembles with panic; she looks down at the rosary pieces, which are becoming discoloured, fading to a pitch black before her eyes.

Fret ties Rosita's insides and makes her vomit into the sink. She raises her head afterwards and looks at herself again, her eyes red with exploded blood vessels. An immense feeling of doom fills her and erect hairs rash her skin. *That baby, that baby.* Her belly cramps, she bends to appease it and then stands back up.

"He's … he's here … th-the … opposition."

The toilet lights begin to flicker, stunting her thoughts and speech, the darkness creating a strobe effect, slowing time. Rosita looks into the mirror and pushes her fingers into her eyes, shutting the effect out.

In her darkened mind, she thinks of her children, Maria and Leandro, how beautiful they are and how much they will suffer with her gone.

"It must be done."

Rosita splashes her face with water, fixes her hair and gingerly pulls up her nurse's dress, mindful of her neck. She hobbles out of the cubicle towards Valda's birthing room, the world's salvation in mind.

~

Patrick wades through a crowded street in the centre of London. Everyone is dressed in business attire, their faces replaced by a smudge of colour. The buildings are so tall they touch the tips of the sky. A huge sun burns above, so close that, if it were real, the Earth would be dust. Cars pull up and disappear in the same instance. A dog barks but makes no sound. *This place has no sound,* he says to himself in thought.

He wades further through the crowd of clones who all appear to be walking symmetrically; suddenly they part like a school of fish moving in wondrous unison, leaving a woman standing at the opposite side of the street, her hands on both hips. They appear to fear her, they huddle up in bunches on either side away from her. She stares at Patrick directly. She is short and plump with olive skin. She is dressed in an ancient white tunic, pinned at the shoulder. She wears sandals with a thong separating her big toe from the rest.

She says nothing, but stares. Patrick takes his eyes off her and pans around his surroundings. To his amazement, the city and its people have gone; now just he and she stand alone, on a bed of black nothingness that stretches as far as his eyes can see. He looks up to the heavens, at a daytime sky with jet-black clouds. He tries to react, but finds his capacity for emotional expression limited in this version of Earth.

I am Core.

Patrick looks over at the woman wondering how he had heard her voice without his ears.

I am one of many, the many who bring the word, and you must listen.

Patrick attempts to form a response, but is unable to think straight, let alone form dialogue.

Valda will die tonight; she has been summoned. She has been compromised and corrupted and is now one of Earth's liabilities. Someone will come to stop our process: you must not aid them. This is your free will, free will, free will, free will, free wiiilll!

The woman's arms leave her hips and side, stretching out horizontally like the Angel of the North. Wings emerge from behind her, great dove-like wings, and the ground begins to shake as if the world was about to explode. Energy resonates through his legs and body, bringing him to his knees.

Patrick looks up and Core's eyes and mouth are bright white light. Her wings begin to vibrate, the light from her face intensifies, so bright he has to look between criss-crossed fingers. Her wings flap once and she shoots off into the heavens in a single stream of stretched light. Patrick watches her ascent until everything fades to black.

Patrick wakes to tapping on his window. The hospital car park is rammed, with cars tail to nose. Patrick rubs his eyes to clear his vision and looks to his right. A hospital security man is bent over, looking into the car. He gestures for Patrick to wind down the window. Patrick rubs his face once more and presses the illuminated arrow facing down.

"You Patrick?"

Patrick nods.

"Valda's asked me to come and get ya."

Patrick looks at the ID hanging from his neck.

Stuart Cromwell.

"She wants me?"

"Yeah mate, sounded kinda urgent."

They look at each other and share a second's pause.

"Okay," Patrick replies.

"She's in the Cambridge private wing, room four," the security guard informs him.

"Okay, got it."

Stuart smiles, his dark pupils large in the absence of light, his coffee-stained teeth giving away his age.

Stuart steps back from the window. Patrick winds the window up and Stuart steps aside to allow him to get out. Patrick slides out and begins to move towards the entrance. After a few paces, he turns around, expecting Stuart to be behind him. Instead he could see Stuart walking off in the opposite direction, left from the Bentley. Patrick watches him move until he is out of sight.

They wheel Valda to operating room four, the Cambridge wing. Rosita waits by the lifts. Patrick walks up and stands besides her. Patrick looks over at her, her thoughts are obviously somewhere else. He begins to think about his dream.

The surgeons glove up and prepare their tools for the caesarean section. Alex paces up and down outside the room.

Patrick allows Rosita to leave the lift first, Patrick sees Alex up ahead and is assured he's on the right floor.

Rosita walks up ahead, acknowledges Alex and walks into the surgery room.

Patrick walks up to Alex, who has a look of bewilderment at his being there. The pair begin to talk.

"How's it going?" Patrick asked.

Alex draws a breath in and exhales.

"Well, she's had a problem with the whole natural thing, so they've suggested she has a caesarean section."

"I see."

They pause, looking at each other.

"So, it was you who sent for me?"

Alex looks at him, his face mystified.

"No."

Patrick squints, his eyes slithering from side to side.

"A security guard came to the car and said Valda wanted to see me."

Alex shook his head.

"That's impossible; she can barely speak, let alone send requests."

Suddenly Patrick's eyes widen and he darts over to the surgery room doors, yanks them open and bolts in. Alex stands in shock for a second, and then runs in after him.

Upon entry, he finds Patrick and two surgeons pinning Rosita to the ground. The four are wrestling in splotches of blood. A third female surgeon is screaming down a phone in the corner of the room. Valda is sat up in bed with a pipe hanging from her mouth, her eyes wild and unhinged, watching the fracas, giggling as if it were the greatest show on earth.

Rosita screams inaudible nonsense. Her strength is beyond her body size; she fidgets and writhes around, both her arms barely able to be held in place by the surgeon and Patrick. Her legs kick and lash out at the surgeon holding them.

The head surgeon aiding Patrick shouts towards Alex, who looks like a deer caught in headlights.

"Get me that fucking syringe!"

The head surgeon points under the operating bed. Alex walks quickly towards it, kneels down and retrieves it. The female surgeon on the phone screams at security to hurry, she abandons the call when she realises Valda has begun to slide out of the bed with laughter. She leaps over, grabs her and pulls her back to a sitting position.

Alex hands the syringe to the surgeon and stands back. Rosita stops moving and becomes calm in an instant. She looks directly at Alex, her eyes so desperate, so convincing, her quick change of behaviour is like something out of a horror movie. She begins to talk through exhausted, shallow breaths.

"Don't … da … d-d-don't inject me, you don't under … understand. The child is … satanas – the child is …. satanas."

The surgeon plunges the needle into her arm and she lets out a bloodcurdling scream. Her eyes grow so wide it's as if they are about to pop out. The female surgeon holding Valda pulls her closer to block her from seeing what is going on.

Rosita begins to fight again, giving everything she has left, throwing her arms this way and that, kicking with both legs, almost shrugging off both Patrick and the surgeons. A scream emits from the pit of her stomach, then she begins to ramble.

"Diyos matulungan kaming lahat … diyos matulungan kaming lahat … diyos matulungan kaming lahaaaaaaaaaaaa…"

Her muscles begin to relax. Her motions begin to slow. Dribble and bubbles form between her lips. She shudders once more then her arms and legs relax.

Everyone remains still, barely breathing.

The head surgeon on Rosita's arm reaches over and opens one of her eyelids. The eyeball is rolled back into her head. Satisfied, he releases her arm and stands, and the surgeon at her feet follows. Patrick looks between the two, over at Alex then back to Rosita. He gets to his feet and stands, freckled with blood.

The head surgeon removes his gloves and mask and draws his hand down his face. Everyone looks to him, waiting for words, but he says none. The doors burst open and two burly security guards step in. Everyone looks at them and they look back. The room is completely quiet.

The head surgeon takes a deep breath, looks at security then down at Rosita, and shakes his head.

"There's a baby to deliver. Get this woman out of here," the head surgeon commands.

The security guard speaks. "The police are on their way. Shouldn't we just wait for them?"

"No. She can be placed in one of the small triage rooms downstairs," the head surgeon replies.

The security guy goes for a wheelchair and returns.

The taller security guard looks at the floor and the surgeon's clothes.

"Is … is she all right? Isn't she bleeding? I mean, I don't wanna catch anything."

The head surgeon shows his badly lacerated palm to the guards.

"She isn't cut, it's me."

They pick Rosita up, place her in the chair and wheel her out.

Valda begins to moan in pain. Alex walks over to her and pulls her towards him.

The female surgeon talks. "Should I call for another team to come up to complete the CS?"

"Absolutely. In the meantime, give Valda some more pain relief. I need to go and sort my hand out," the head surgeon replies.

The head surgeon turns to Patrick,

"Thank you for your assistance. I appreciate it."

The junior surgeon pulls his mask down and speaks. "Sorry, can I be relieved? I don't think I'm—"

"You're both relieved but, Victoria, please wait here until the other team arrives."

"Okay," she replies.

Victoria turns and dials for another team. The head surgeon turns to Alex.

"Please accept my apologies for this."

The head surgeon gives a small fabricated smile, the junior surgeon holds the door open and the head walks out, one hand cradling the other, and the junior follows.

Victoria speaks on the phone, her back to the room. Alex places the gas nozzle in Valda's mouth and looks at Patrick, who is standing facing him.

"How did you know?"

Patrick shakes his head subtly.

"I didn't."

Alex and Patrick look at each other.

"But you came up."

"I know. Like I said, a security guard came to the car and told me Valda wanted me."

Alex squints.

"One of those guys?" Alex asked.

"No, this guy was a lot thinner than either of them. I don't know; it's all a bit strange."

Alex doesn't reply. They both begin to wonder about a reasonable explanation for what has just happened. Victoria turns and talks.

"A team is on the way up. Do you mind if I go to the loo? I'll be back in a sec."

Alex replies, "Of course, no problem."

"Okay, you're doing the right thing, by the way; just keep giving her the gas if she needs it."

Victoria walks towards the doors and leaves. Alex talks to the room.

"She was saying 'satanas, satanas'. What does that mean?"

Patrick looks to the ground at the scalpel the head surgeon dragged out of Rosita's hand by the blade. That action has ended his career; he has severed nerves in his hand which will mean he can never operate again. Patrick looks at the blade, dyed dark red, then looks up at Alex. Their eyes fill with concern and trepidation, and Patrick speaks 'Satan.'

~

25th December 2013
03:00am
St Mary's Hospital
Triage room ground floor

One police constable stands at the head surgeon's bedside, notepad in hand, taking his statement. The surgeon's hand has been sewn up. His name is Gregory Hines and he has worked in St Mary's as a consultant obstetrician for twenty-five years. His hair is grey, his eyes a remarkable blue. His face is drawn in by a perfect diet of fruits, nuts, vegetables and fish.

His once-steady hand shakes uncontrollably. He is much more disturbed by the incident than he lets on.

"She came in as we were prepping for the caesarean section," Gregory explains. "She came in and stood by the prep unit where Clinton was standing. I thought it was weird she was there but she was a senior midwife, and the patient …"

"Sorry, the patient's name is?" asks the PC.

"That's confidential, I'm afraid."

"She'll have to be questioned anyway."

"Well, I'll let you deal with that, but I certainly won't be revealing any confidential information."

The officer sighs.

"Okay, proceed."

"Well, I thought maybe the patient had requested her presence. After all, they pay a fortune to have things done their way privately. We've had dogs present …"

The officer sighs and rolls his eyes.

"Sorry, I digress. Anyway, only after I had turned to properly acknowledge her did I realise the state she was in. Her clothes were damp and her neck had sores all over it. I was just about to ask her about her appearance when I realised she was talking – but nobody was there. Her eyes were on the patient. She looked angered and distant. Concerned, I walked towards her, and then realised she was holding a scalpel. She said a jumble of words then ran towards the bed. Luckily, I grabbed her by the arm and yanked her back. It all got rather messy after that. She tried to slice at me with the scalpel, Clinton grabbed her waist and I went for her wrist, but misjudged it and ended up grabbing the blade. In rushed …"

The PC stands, attention focused, as if he was a child around a camp fire.

"Who rushed in?" the PC asks.

Gregory brings his good hand to his chin and gives it a thoughtful rub.

"I didn't catch his name; in fact, I don't even know what he was doing there, but I'm grateful he was. If not for him, she could have reached the patient and we might have been having a different type of conve—"

Another PC walks in and disrupts the flow of conversation. He whispers in the first PC's ear and the first PC nods and looks back at Gregory. The other PC leaves.

"Valda Payne has had the baby and is now recovering. Rosita is on her way to the station," the PC states.

He scrolls through his notes to pick up where they left off.

"What happened when the black guy – Valda's driver – walked in?"

"He's her driver?" Gregory questions.

"Yep, according to my colleague."

"Well, he came in, grabbed her other hand, which she was trying to gouge my eyes out with, and he helped bring her to the ground. It was all rather messy. We knocked over the prep tray, and syringes and tools flew everywhere. By then, Victoria—"

"Victoria? Who's that?"

"A junior surgeon. She called for security… We struggled with Rosita, she was so strong, it was as if she was a man – she pushed and pulled us as if we were mere children …"

Gregory stares at a spot on the floor and pauses.

"You Okay?" the PC asks.

"Yeah, I'm fine, it's just … she fought with so much conviction and was so completely coherent at times that I …"

They both sit in silence.

"I … I'm not a religious man by any stretch of the imagination, but … she said things that bother me somewhat. She seemed to believe Valda's child was …"

Gregory shakes his head slightly, as if he is debating whether to further elaborate.

"Some sort of … demon. Yes, that's what she said, she said the child was a demon, or something to that effect. She looked like she really believed this … I've known Rosita, not known her personally, but have worked with her for years, and she is by far one of the best midwives I have ever worked with. To see her like that was disturbing and I've seen a whole host of horrors. I was on the ground at 7/7."

"She's a devout Catholic, isn't she?" the PC asks.

"Is she? I really don't know. Like I said, I only worked with her and knew her on a professional level. Her personal life, I don't know anything about."

"Well, she is. You know, sometimes these fanatics can get an idea and run with it."

Gregory shakes his head.

"Rosita was no fanatic, my friend, she was as balanced as they come."

The PC sighs.

"Well, the baby has been born and I've yet to get a report of it having a pitchfork and horns, so I'll put it down to her being a religious nut, and leave it at that," he jokes.

Gregory crumples his lips and shakes his head again. "You had to have been there."

"So what happened next?"

"Well, we injected her with a sedative and she began to mumble words in her native tongue. I can't remember what she said before she went down, maybe the others will … Anyway, security came and now you're here."

"She's obviously got one or two screws loose," the PC remarks, before closing his book and slipping it back into his shirt pocket. "Thank you for your time, doctor, we'll be in touch. Merry Christmas."

Gregory stares at him, the PC tips his hat, walks out of the door and leaves him alone with his thoughts. Gregory drops his gaze to a spot on the floor, his logical mind replaying what Rosita said, replaying the scene.

~

The sky cried with unexpected rain, and spectacular gun-metal grey clouds rolled across the heavens, suppressing the daylight. The clouds lit internally like Chinese lanterns hung high. Lightning jumped from above and kissed the earth. The sound that followed was like a million mustangs revved at once.

Alex held his daughter to his chest. She weighed an ideal 6lbs 8ounces. Her little fists were curled; her eyes appeared to be permanently sealed shut. He came away from the window and looked out of the one-way glass at the two security guards standing outside. He panned around the massive private recovery room, with all its luxuries: a leather couch, trendy beanbags, massive flat-screen TV, drinks machine and food on tap, and thought how much he would have given for a standard NHS suite, filled with gushing grandparents, family and friends. But they had none: no guidance, no concern, just those that said yes and no to Valda when asked. Those whose advice was available as long as they were paid.

It's a sad state of affairs when the closest thing you have to family is your personal driver. He, Valda and baby made three: they were really and truly alone in the world. Alex hadn't spoken to his parents in over five years and couldn't even remember what had happened to all his friends: Geoff, Mel, Steve, Katy, Donald, Lewis, Gavin … His love for Valda had killed off all his other relationships, one by one, like a corrosive disease.

He looked at Valda asleep and felt a scornful love for her. A feeling he tried with all his might to dismiss, but couldn't. She had hunted his people and past to extinction, making ghost stories of his back story. She had separated him from his pride with the promise of paradise; she was a lonely, rogue creature, used to the dark, at comfort with solitude, despair, fear and hate.

Maybe Valda was the devil she spoke of; maybe she had dragged the sanity out of Rosita, he thought, watching her take shallow breaths. Maybe Rosita had sensed what everyone else who had come into contact with her had; perhaps it had tipped her over the edge.

Thunder roared across an ebony sky and his daughter shuddered in his arms. He brought her closer and she relaxed again. He loved her and, he knew with every fibre of his body that she loved and felt secure with him.

There was a knock on the door and Patrick peered through the tinted glass. Alex walked over and let him in. He had to duck his head to enter. The doors swung shut behind him, and security went back to securing.

They stood in the middle of the room.

"Shall we sit?" Alex asked.

Patrick nodded.

They took a seat on the large leather sofa. Patrick ran his calloused hand down the baby's back so gently it was as if he hadn't touched her. They both smiled. Then Alex's smile faded and Patrick noticed.

"So what happened? What did they ask you?" Alex questioned.

"Well, they wanted my account of …"

"Got that, but did they tell you anything about her, or why she did what she did?"

Patrick shook his head. "No."

Alex pushed his fingers into both corners of his mouth and his eyes moved from left to right, thinking.

"What do you think happened?" Alex asked.

Alex looked Patrick in the eye and he looked back and exhaled.

"I spoke to Victoria, and she said Rosita had been on duty for almost twenty-four hours for the third time this week. She thinks she had a breakdown," Patrick replied.

Alex continued to look him in the eye. "You believe that?"

Patrick fidgeted on the sofa. "Well, what else is there to believe?"

There was a pause as they silently dared each other to bring the unthinkable to the table and make the monsters in the movies real. Alex felt there was something his past self wasn't telling his present self; something that offered a little opposition to Rosita's new status as barmy. He couldn't place it, no matter how hard he tried. It was at the edge of his conscious mind and, if he could think more clearly, he would have remembered the bracelet he had questioned Valda about at Riku's, the night she had told him she was pregnant. The bracelet she denied knowing anything about, all thirteen pieces of it. The bracelet he had put away for further analysis and had completely forgotten about; it had faded from his memory.

"He slimed me, ha!"

Both Patrick and Alex turned to look at Valda, whose eyes were shut, a big smile on her face.

"Ghostbusters … her favourite," Alex chuffed.

They both watched for any more dialogue, but there was none.

"Well, at least someone's happy…" Alex commented.

"Yeah …"

Patrick slapped the arm of the sofa, exhaled and stood. "I'd better be going. When did they say you'll be out?"

Alex looked up at Patrick, adjusting himself for the elements outside.

"Three days."

"Okay … call me when you're ready."

Alex held out his hand and Patrick took it, gripping firmly.

"Thanks, Patrick, thanks for being there for her. Besides me, she only has you."

"No problem, no problem at all – jus make sure you look after both of them."

Alex smiled. "I will."

They held each other's stare. Patrick ran his hand down his face, turned and walked away, his hands in his coat pocket, his head dipped in anticipation of the door frame. Patrick didn't look back as Alex expected he would, and he knew why; it was the same reason he couldn't enjoy this life-changing moment: something wasn't right.

Patrick drifted along the hallway like algae at sea, with no rhythm or reason. He passed several illuminated exit arrows and signs that he could have taken, but didn't, his thoughts still on the incident. He moved past wards with Christmas lights and decorations twinkling and gleaming, that dark rainy Christmas morning. He passed families carrying presents, some in tears of sadness or joy. He walked around, subconsciously hoping to see the security guard who had sent him up to the ward, to ask him who had sent him. He walked for at least an hour, his dream replaying over and over in his mind, Core's wings outstretched, her words circling round his mind.

Valda will die tonight. She will be summoned, she has been compromised and corrupted and is now Earth's liability. Someone will come to stop our process, and you must not aid them. Free will, free will, free will, free will, free wiiilll

The more he thought about the dream, the more it worried him. The more he thought about it, the further it moved away from a mere coincidence. Patrick left that day under angry black clouds and returned after three days for Alex, Valda and Heaven, under a beautiful clear sky.

Exspectata

"Hello."

Alex held his finger to the intercom button and watched Tricia in the little security screen. She looked directly at him, as if she knew exactly where the hidden camera was.

"How can I help you?"

"I'm the maternity nurse. Is this the Payne residence?"

"Yes … Ah, yes it is. I'll buzz you through."

He pressed down on the entrance button and the gate pulled apart, letting her and her pedal bike in.

He watched her approaching the door.

"Who is it?" Valda hollered from above.

"The nanny!"

Valda didn't reply, but made her way to the staircase to descend. Alex pressed the button to switch camera to the one above the front door. The nanny's face stretched in it, comically long, as if she were in a fish bowl.

Valda appeared behind him and looked over his shoulder.

"Ask her for ID," Valda whispered.

"Ah … sorry, could you show us some ID?"

Tricia looked at the camera for a split second. "Of course," she replied. She went to her satchel, removed an ID badge and showed it to the camera.

"Tricia Hungerford," they both said in unison.

They looked at each other and smiled.

"Happy?" he whispered to Valda.

"Yeah, she seems okay, I like Tricias."

Alex opened the door to both her and the cold clear winter's day. She stood at the doorstep and looked from one parent to the other, their faces bright and overtly excited. Alex stood aside for her to enter.

"Sorry … my bike?" Tricia asked.

"Don't worry, just leave it there. No one can get through the gates," Alex replied.

"Thanks."

Tricia walked in past Alex and Valda. She had curly jet-black hair. Her skin was a light shade of brown, her nose straight. Her face athletically thin, she wore a black dress with black tights and white trainers. The scent of vanilla followed her in; she was tremendously beautiful and slender.

Alex walked her to a seat on the long sofa facing the TV. Alex sat on the single and Valda sat beside her. She looked around from her seated position, while removing paperwork from her satchel.

"Your home is beautiful. I love the statues. Are they Greek or Roman?"

"Both," Valda replied.

"I see."

"You must have worked in loads of beautiful houses?" Alex questioned.

"I have, but this is by far one of the nicest."

Tricia placed all paperwork on the table including her ID; Valda looked at it once again. She looked a lot older in the picture. Valda looked up and met her stare; her eyes were a mixture of green and brown. *Bizarre,* Valda thought.

"Sorry about the whole ID thing. It's just that we had a little trouble at the hospital when we had Heaven and obviously we are somewhat known to the world," Alex said with all sincerity.

"Oh, don't worry about that, I completely understand. We specialise in working with clients of your calibre, so we totally understand the importance of total security and secrecy … Loved you in Beat The Boss, by the way."

Alex laughed; Valda smiled.

"I assure you, we're completely different from that in real life."

Alex looked to Valda for a co-sign but got a frosty stare.

Alex cleared his throat and rose to his feet. "Can I get you a drink or anything before we start?"

"Oh, that would be great," Tricia replied.
"What would you like?"
"Got any tea?"
"Yep, one tea. Sugar, milk?"
"Two sugars and a little milk, please."
"V?"
"Water," Valda replied.

Alex walked across the room through to the kitchen. Tricia watched the doors for two seconds then turned back to Valda.

"He seems really nice; I bet he's happy to be a daddy?"

"We're both happy to be parents," Valda replied, then cleared her throat. "So let's talk numbers, hours, roles and responsibilities."

Tricia pointed her thumb sideways towards the kitchen door. "Should we wait for-?"

"Don't worry; I wear the trousers in this house."

Tricia let out a small laugh, as did Valda.

"I see … Okay. Well, most people call me a nanny, but I'm not, I'm actually a maternity nurse and my role is to help new parents get to know their newborns. I'll do feeds, nappy changes, stimulation and whatever else you require for mother and baby – within reason."

Alex kicked open the door, holding a tray with two steaming mugs of tea and one glass of water. He walked around the table and laid the tray down, placing their cups in front of them.

"What'd I miss?" he asked.

"Nothing, we've just started," Valda replied.

"Okay."

"Like I was saying to Valda, I'm not a nanny, I'm a maternity nurse. A maternity nurse can be a great comfort to mothers who do not have family or friends close by to help them."

"Well, that's exactly what we're looking for," Alex said.

"Neither of us have parents locally," Valda added.

"Sorry to hear that."

"Don't be. We want for nothing," Valda replied.

"Okay. My prices are flat and very fair. We charge £800 a week, which includes feeding, changing, washing and playing with baby; walks, talks and anything else within the parameters of childcare. I might add, I am not a housekeeper."

Tricia looked at Alex and smiled.

"I won't be fetching beers, picking up dirty washing or cooking for the boys during the Arsenal game on Saturday."

Alex smiled back, and Tricia turned and looked at Valda.

"However, I can and will assist Mum with light day-to-day chores if needs be, which may include getting meals for Mum, helping with laundry and anything else geared towards Mum's wellbeing. How does that sound?"

Valda looked over at Alex and they both nodded.

"Sounds great to me. When can you start?" Alex asked.

Tricia took a sip of her tea and placed it down. "Well, I like to leave a twenty-four-hour cooling-off period to ensure you guys are sure about me. I'll leave you some pamphlets with personal testimonials, my price plan and list of my roles, responsibilities and FAQs. I'll return tomorrow and, hopefully, get to meet the princess if you guys say yes. Gosh, it just struck me – where is the princess?"

Valda pointed upstairs. "She's sleeping."

"We have her baby monitor plugged into a sound system that operates in every room, including the bathroom and kitchen," Alex added.

"Superb. That's what I like to see – parents making sure the child's safety is paramount."

Tricia took a long sip of her tea, her eyes half-closed as if it were pleasure in a mug. She places it down and pats her mouth with the tips of her fingers.

"Well, if you don't mind I'll be off now."

"Thanks for coming," Alex responds.

All three stood, Valda more slowly than the other two. Tricia bent over to spread her paperwork across the table neatly.

"Sorry, I really am anti-mess and disorder."

All three smiled again. Tricia made her way to the front door, flanked by Alex and Valda. Valda had looked for any faults in Tricia, but couldn't find a chink in her armour, aesthetically or personality-wise.

The door opened and a cheeky winter chill rushed in, making them shudder. Tricia stepped out and looked up at the clear winter's sky. Alex and Valda stood beside each other, looking at her from the entrance.

"May I ask you a question?" Tricia said.

"Of course," Valda replied.

"You said there was trouble at the baby's birth. What happened?"

Valda and Alex looked at each other, then back at Tricia. "Sorry, we'd rather not talk about it," Alex replied.

All parties froze in the moment's awkwardness. Tricia held her hand to her chest.

"So sorry, I didn't mean to pry. It's just that I like to know all angles of a situation before I get involved in one. I didn't mean to overstep my boundary."

"Don't worry, I'd probably have asked as well," Valda responded.

Tricia smiled and stepped off the step onto the gravel.

"Well, I'd better be on my way. They say it's going to snow this week; I'd better get back in the car."

She looked at them both, grinned and pulled her bike towards her.

"Ah, what time should we call you with our answer?" asked Valda.

"Around this time should be fine," Tricia replied

"Great, we'll be in contact. Thanks for coming."

"No problem."

Tricia turned and walked her bike down the driveway to the gates. Alex placed his finger on the button beside the door and opened them for her to leave. The bitter cold forced Valda to cross her arms. The gate opened and Tricia slipped out. Valda closed the door and stood facing Alex.

"What did you think?" Alex asked.

"Emmm … she comes across well."

Alex laughed and walked over to the sofas, Valda shuffling behind him.

"Why do you do that?"

"Do what?"

"That whole standoffish sort of thing you do … everything in life isn't a multi-million-pound business deal. Either you like her or you don't: she's the sixth one we've seen. What are you looking for?"

They both sit down. Alex clicked on the TV and lay along the sofa, his hands behind his head. Valda took a seat on the single.

"Well, if you hadn't noticed, this is a little bit more important than a frigging business deal. This is the care of our child, and I want the best … besides, if you had let me elaborate, I would have gone on to tell you I'm actually interested in her."

Alex placed his palms together and pretended to pray.

"Thank God for that."

Valda sighed and shook her head. "Anyway, are you ready for your new role?" she asked.

He turned on his side to face her fully.

"Well, seeing as I've never been a CEO of a major company, I would say … no."

"I wouldn't worry too much about it. All you have to do is be there, sit on your ass and look threatening all the time. The business runs itself, each department has a manager."

Alex frowned. "Me … look mean?"

"Well, you'd better, you're the only one who can be there. I can't trust anyone else. I need you on the ground, or the mice will play. The staff had that party, and Claire's been telling me all sorts."

"I hear that, but I know fuck all about business, so you'd better make sure you're calling every day to ensure things are moving the way they're supposed to."

"That goes without sa—"

The sound system hissed, drawing Valda and Alex's attention. From the speakers came a gurgle, a pause, then all-out crying. Heaven had sounded her call for care. Alex and Valda shot up; Valda recoiled in pain and sat back down as Alex sprinted upstairs.

~

With the TV their only source of light, volume turned down low, Alex had fallen asleep on the sofa. Valda sat with Heaven at rest in her Moses basket. Valda stared at her, fascinated by her. She lay so still, Valda felt she had to place her hand on her back to make sure she was still alive. Heaven moved in reaction, adjusted her position and licked her little lips, chewing on nothing, the way old people and babies do.

She looked over at Alex and back at Heaven, her own little family unit, and felt a tainted happiness. She felt like someone who had discovered her lottery numbers had come up, but who had realised they hadn't played that day; all too aware of how close they had been to financial freedom. A life without limits, in her mind Valda was happy, but in reality her quest remained unfulfilled.

She pulled her sleeve up and looked at the bracelet: phase one was complete. She explored it, knowing iniquity had a stake in her paradise. Although she had decided to go along with everything months ago, she still sat on edge nightly; waiting, praying that wearing the bracelet, fulfilling her end of the agreement, would keep those terrifying nightmares, visions and encounters out of her life. She covered the bracelet once more and looked at Alex, asleep, the television's images jumping around on his face and chest. She looked down at Heaven, leaned forward and kissed her on the side of her bald head, then swung her legs up onto the sofa and looked into the kitchen's dark glass, her eyes heavy, closing … closing … closing until the TV was the only thing still conscious, projecting its images out to a captive audience. It watched them until its timer ran out and its screen blinked black, leaving a solitary red standby dot at the end of a pitch-black room. It slept and they slept.

BBL

In Valda's absence, BBL's headquarters had become a fun place to work. She had left no direct leader in charge of the business, opting for all departments to be run by their managers, who would amalgamate, gather figures, issues and ideas together on a weekly basis, to be emailed over to Valda via Claire.

With the sudden change in BBL's climate, Valda expected figures and work rates to plummet at least a little. Instead, things seemed to improve. The designs coming out of Gibb's department were fantastic, bordering on groundbreaking.

Gibbs sent a suggestion to Valda centred on expansion into all facets of retail. He proposed that they design and make women's dresses, skirts, tops, coats and more. Boldly, he had had a few prototype pieces made and sent to Valda for approval; something he wouldn't have done a year ago. But it appeared in the absence of authority creative minds had room to create.

He called it the GB range. Valda liked it and gave Good Bitch the breath of life. She ordered that Gibbs be given a section of shop space in their flagship store on Oxford Street on a trial bases. Glowing reports came back; the stock had sold out in three days and the public wanted more.

The Cog ran the headline:

"Who needs Braga when you've got dresses, thongs and a Bad B%*ch running the show? BBL expands into full retail, but what does this mean for Britain's leading lingerie brand?"

Word got back to Valda that all departments had a massive party, to celebrate GB being a success. This was partially true, but if you asked any attendee individually, they would have told you they drank mostly to the creation of more work and greater job security.

Valda wasn't amused, to say the least. An unauthorised party, with alcohol, drugs and drunken sex, was not something

Valda wanted happening on her premises. It smacked of disrespect and needed a swift response.

Valda ordered each of her managers to a video conference call in order to explain themselves. Each one denied it had taken place. Fearing she was losing control, she decided to place a man on the ground, someone she could trust. Alex.

~

Valda and Tricia sat around the island in the middle of Valda's kitchen. Two cups of tea and a saucer of biscuits sat in front of them. Valda pointed at the last name on her list of testimonies. Tricia looked over at where her finger hovered.

"Oh, Mariah Wray. Yes, I worked for her before she—"

Tricia stopped abruptly and paused, her facial expression sombre. "Sorry," she whispered.

Valda stared at her. "What is it?"

"Do you know her?" Tricia replied.

"Not personally, but I have met her at business events and parties."

Tricia shook her head and exhaled.

"What's the problem?" Valda asked.

"If I tell you, will you give me your word that you'll not repeat it?"

"Of course."

"I mean it; I could be in big trouble if it got out."

"You have my word."

Tricia looked around, making sure they were alone. "Well, when I first started there she was lovely – a little bossy, but a wonderful mother to her daughter. Her husband had to be away on business often, so she sought me out to assist her with the day-to-day stuff, sort of like here. The first few months were brilliant. I taught her and she listened; she sucked it in like a sponge. Fast-forward three months, and things weren't so good."

Tricia picked up her mug of tea and sipped. Valda watched her every motion, her expression intense. She cleared her throat and proceeds.

"I first suspected something was wrong when she misplaced a bracelet she seemed to be extremely attached to. She went ballistic and tore that house apart as if her life depended on it. When she couldn't find it, she ordered back all the rubbish that had been taken away from her street that day and made them dump it in her driveway. If you had ever … I mean, bundles of black bin liners lined up besides her car. She ran up and down the bags, as I held Lilly, standing on her doorstep. Up and down the bags she went like a roach, tearing bags open, sifting through dirty nappies, rotting food and God knows what else."

Valda picked up her tea. Her hand shook like the last autumn leaf on a tree. Tricia watched the tea go to her lips and back down to the island's matt granite worktop.

"You okay?"

"Fine, I just caught a little chill. Carry on."

The pair paused.

"You sure?" Tricia asked.

"Seriously …"

"Okay. After about two hours, she came back in, I was attending to Lilly. She walked past muttering to herself, words I couldn't make out. She went right upstairs her clothes and face a mess. I had just finished feeding Lilly when she came down and ordered I leave that instant. I told her I had an hour left of my shift, but she screamed at me to leave, and I wasn't to come back. I didn't argue – I didn't dare, I felt like I was being blamed or something. Anyway, I reported back to the agency and informed them of her behaviour, asking them to maybe contact child services for Lilly's sake, but they declined my suggestion, not wanting to rock the boat with such a wealthy client … Can you imagine?"

Tricia picked up a biscuit, broke it in half and placed the other piece back in the saucer. Valda looked at the halved biscuit, then up at Tricia, who ate it in two bites then dusted off her lips.

"Well, they were soon to understand why I was so concerned. Within a week, rubbish men had found the body of little Lilly, burned to a crisp, wrapped in newspaper and sellotape, chucked in with the rest of the rubbish."

Valda gasped and held her hands to her mouth.

"Oh my God …"

"I know … unbelievable."

Valda shook her head. "What drives a person to do such a thing?"

Tricia stared at a spot on the table and ran her tongue in between her lips.

"I really don't know."

"How haven't I heard about this?" Valda asked.

"The Chuggfords must have paid millions to stop it getting out. Can you imagine the only heir to their estate being shown up as a child killer?"

The pair sat in silence.

"One thing I can say is that everything changed the day I left there, the day she lost that bracelet. Losing it seemed to be the catalyst."

Valda shook her head and crossed her left hand over her right, feeling for her bracelet, and feeling a bizarre sense of relief, happy in a selfish way that Mariah's unfortunate situation had shed light on the consequences of defaulting, further reinforcing her need to see things through.

Valda drew a breath. "Think I've heard enough …"

"Sorry if I …"

Valda touched her arm. "It's fine; I asked."

Valda looked at her looking into her mug of tea, and for a split second thought Tricia was suppressing a smirk. After a second glance, she realised it was a look of discomfort.

A sudden crackle made them both jump, and Heaven's cries blared out from above both of them. Valda shot up off the stool, stood and immediately curled up in agony. Tricia rose quickly and held her around the shoulders.

"Careful, you're not ready for sudden movement like that. Take a seat, I'll go to her."

Valda lowered herself back to her stool, feeling helpless. She could hear Tricia shushing and talking to her daughter over the speaker system. Heaven calmed almost immediately.

Through the speakers, Tricia spoke.

"She's hungry. I'm gonna bring her down."

Valda waited a minute and Tricia walked through the kitchen doors with Heaven held close to her chest. She walked over to Valda and handed Heaven over, her little eyes moving around, her arms outstretched, her hands opening and clenching. She opened and closed her mouth, rooting for a nipple.

"Are you breastfeeding?"

Valda steadied Heaven, who was thrashing about, smiling and gurgling.

"Yeah, but I've also pumped some and stored it in the fridge for you and Alex to use, if I'm not up to it."

"Excellent, you really are a good mum."

Tricia went to the fridge and retrieved a plastic bag of Valda's milk, which she poured into a bottle and warmed before handing it to Valda.

"How'd you know I wanted to give her a bottle?"

Tricia tapped her forehead with her middle fingers. "Experience."

Valda smiled and Tricia smiled back.

~

Valda was sitting up in her dim bedroom, propped up by pillows. Alex walked in. Valda looked at him over her tablet.

"She was hungry?" she questioned.

"Yeah."

Alex inhaled and lets out a lion-sized yawn before collapsing on the bed, his hands behind his head.

"So how was she?" Alex asks.

Valda goes back to the website she was looking at. "Good."

Alex looked at her sideways. "Just good?"
Valda turned and looked down at Alex.
"Well, it's nice having someone to talk to and help out, so, yeah, she was good."
Alex inhaled. "How was she with Heaven?"
"She takes half the time to calm her than I do, so I think she really likes her."
Alex fell quiet.
"Alex …"
"Yeah?"
"Oh … I thought you'd fallen asleep on me."
He inhaled again.
"I tell you what, doing nothing is bloody tiring …"
"You're not doing nothing – you're making sure these people don't turn BBL headquarters into Glastonbury."
"I really don't know what you're going on about. I've seen nothing that indicates that would happen."
"That's because you're there."
Alex rolled over. "Well, if that's true, then fair enough."
They spoke for a little while longer then Alex went to sleep and Valda read until she fell asleep too.

Heaven

Wherever God erects a house of prayer, The Devil always builds a chapel there; And 'twill be found, upon examination, the latter has the largest congregation.
(Daniel Defoe)

They say Church Road is haunted; they say when the estate was built they disturbed the sleeping contingent, buried six feet under. Those they couldn't excavate they simply built over; no roses or tulips for the dead, just schedules and demands for housing.

I have seen them. I have seen the ones below, above, glowing like the Northern Lights, wearing clothes from centuries ago.

He moved with no malice or malevolence, just a curiosity that we both seemed to share. He crept towards me and we both froze. As it became too much for my young mind to comprehend, I felt my knees buckle and my body slip from the window ledge. Upon a surge of courage, I stood once more to look for him, but he was gone. Everyone there has a story or two to tell. A friend of mine claimed he was once kept awake by a sprite making music on his squeaky staircase. Others profess to have seen men and women walk into the cemetery by St Mary's church, lie down on their respective graves and vanish.

-Exert from a Church Road resident's diary.

Valda had never seen a ghost, but she lived with the devil and that was surely enough. As in her adult life, her childhood world was incredibly small, with no aunts, uncles, cousins or grandparents; just her, her tormentor and his passive accomplice. At school she and her brother were weird loners who walked by themselves, barely speaking to each other, let alone the world.

Leon spent much of his silence thinking of ways to make his sister small so she wouldn't be disturbed that evening.

Valda's childhood home had become a thing of urban legend. People on the estate told anyone who would listen that Valda's mother, possessed by a disgruntled ghost, had set upon her happy family with meat cleaver and hammer, bludgeoning and cutting them to death. The legend states that the little girl was never found and her ghost still haunts the flat, searching for peace.

Little did they know, the little girl lived and was still living. A real-life rags-to-riches story.

Valda wanted so much to go to church. She missed sitting in the back of a service while Father David's voice bellowed with bass and theatrical conviction throughout. She missed how he would address the topic of the day and always point out where Christian teachings and values could have been applied to an incident or situation, rendering better results than those achieved.

She wanted so much to be whisked away with her fellow sinners, to that building trapped in time. That place where candles as long as your arms burned, standing straight on oak tables, adorned with various other gold ornaments, symbols of the faith. That place that smelled like years lost, with that sweet, rustic smell of incense; that place you pictured, not in black and white but caramel-brown sepia.

But, wearing the bracelet, Valda could barely muster a prayer, let alone tread holy ground, and for this she was sad.

~

Days passed quickly and, before she knew it, it had been four weeks since Heaven had been born and Rosita had attempted to prevent that happening. Valda asked Alex about it once and he replied, refining the story for her own good, so he didn't upset her, so much so that if you had actually been there, you would have believed he were describing something totally unrelated.

January became February and winter really set in. The days were so cold that your fingers lost sensation after five minutes of exposure. Tricia had completed a full three weeks of work. Valda had grown to like her a lot. She was helpful and a true master of child rearing. She had taught Valda to suck boogers out of her daughter's nose when bunged up, how to distinguish between various cries, and calmed Valda when Heaven caught a terrible cold that Valda was convinced would kill her.

Tricia suggested certain foods and beverages that she would prepare for Valda, to aid in her recovery. Gradually, Valda began to feel stronger, almost fully recovered from her caesarean. Tricia quickly suggested she breastfeed full-time from now on, as it was best for baby's health, strength and brain development. Valda listened not only to that but virtually every word that fell from her lips.

When Dr Ryan came to see Valda, he was astonished at how fast she had healed. He scratched his head and said to both Tricia and Valda he had never seen someone so mobile and able after such a short period of time. Valda put it down to the brilliant care Tricia was providing for both her and Heaven. Dr Ryan had no choice but to agree.

Tricia and Dr Ryan seemed to get on well, and Valda thought at one stage she sensed a spark between the two, but nothing came of it. Three more weeks passed and Valda began to notice her weight dropping. The long-sleeved tops she used to conceal the bracelet from the world also hid protruding ribs which, when she raised her arm , were clearly visible. She consulted Tricia. Tricia said it was normal to lose weight quickly while breastfeeding, and not to worry.

After five weeks, Alex had begun to take the role of BBL CEO seriously. He barely reported back to Valda, opting to handle internal situations by himself. She noticed his lack of communication, but felt uncharacteristically unbothered by it. She knew her money was his money and he would do his best by them both – and if he really got stuck, he would ask.

Besides, she liked the roles they occupied now. He was the breadwinner and she the homemaker. Even if it was a fictitious situation, she loved it so much she asked Tricia her opinion on allowing Alex to continue in the role after Heaven had reached the age she could attend nursery. Tricia thought it an excellent idea, saying the longer a child had their mother at home, the better.

Tricia was staunchly against children being left in the care of strangers unnecessarily, providing horrible examples of children, especially ones who were too young to talk, being abused and neglected for months at the hands of those meant to care for them. Valda shuddered and her mind was made up. Tricia had a good few home tutors she could recommend; she had an answer for everything.

By now Alex was going in to the office early – sometimes so early Valda barely had time to communicate with him – and coming home late. He had become nothing more than a presence that occupied bed space beside her at night. From a man who would wake if Heaven so much as scratched her nose, to snoring through her cries. He sneaked into bed while Valda slept, and was on his way out by the time she rose.

One Monday morning in mid-February, Valda made a point of waking early. She rose at 6.30am, and walked towards the garden, through the conservatory, where she opened the back door and stood on the step. Alex turned and looked over at her, his coffee in mid-air. A triangle of toast sat on his plate. The pair looked at each other like long-lost siblings. Heaven slept above.

"I'm concerned about my weight loss."

He looked her up and down, thinking how much she actually had lost and he hadn't even noticed.

"What's Tricia had to say about it?"

"She's gonna start me on some special shakes … is something wrong?"

"With me?" he replied.

"Yeah. Is everything okay?"

"Absolutely."

"Sure?"

"Yes! Why so concerned all of a sudden?"

"You seem distant, that's all."

Alex paused. "Don't know what you're on about. I'm going to work. Of course we're gonna see each other less."

"I know, but are you happy?"

Alex cracked a smile; his thoughts were hijacked by Heaven's birth, and he internally sighed. Even awake, he was occasionally plagued by the nightmare of that day. The incident played over and over in his mind, marring what should have been the happiest day of both their lives. Within that instant he explored her question: *Are you happy? Are you?* Within that split second it became obvious to him. If he was being completely honest, he wasn't.

He had a lot of questions that festered and could not be asked or answered without someone suggesting he sought professional help. Rosita, although giving the appearance of insanity, had a powerful uncompromising belief in her cause. That made him, and he suspected everyone else of sound mind in the room, uncomfortable. Her words had not been slurred or tainted by madness, alcohol or drugs. He remembered all their faces, faces flushed with fear – including Patrick's – who spoke about everything but that day on their daily commute. The topic was waiting to surface whenever silence fell between them.

If he was being honest, he would have told Valda that Heaven split him emotionally. On one hand, he loved her with everything he had. On the other, there was something about her, something that made him uneasy whenever they were left alone. Feelings he couldn't explain to himself, or anyone else. If he was being honest he would have said that most nights he hears her crying but acts like he's sleeping so he won't have to enter her nursery in the dead of the night. Maybe he was traumatised by the incident. Maybe he needed professional help. He didn't feel manic or crazy, just scared: scared for no apparent reason.

"Of course I'm happy. I'm just getting into the swing of things at the office, that's all."

"Well, I want you to take some time off so we can spend time as a family."

Alex nodded and smiled. "Sounds good to—"

Alex paused, his wide eyes narrowed as he watched Tricia appear from behind Valda. Valda observed his gaze wander and fix on something, and she turned and jumped, startled by Tricia's early, unannounced showing. Her hair drooped. The skin surrounding her normally seductive eyes was puffy. Black mascara ran down her cheeks. She looked like shit. Alex stood as she neared.

Valda looked back at Alex, his fists clenched, his eyes fixated on Tricia. In that moment she saw the father from McDonald's in him. The man who stood when he felt Clover could be a threat to his loved ones. He stood, protective, rough and ready.

She turned back to Tricia, who was now within reaching distance, sobbing hard. Valda opened her arms, wrapped them round her and drew her close. Alex looked on and stood awkwardly like a third party to a romancing couple.

No one said a word. Not even the morning birds sang. Alex knew he should have felt something for her. But his only thought in that slice of time was *How the fuck did she get in?*

~

Valda and Tricia sat on the sofa facing the TV, which was showing morning programmes. Heaven had woken in the hour since Tricia's arrival but had fallen asleep once more in her Moses basket. Alex stood above them, watching the three of them from the landing. He caught some man's name through Tricia's sobbed words – 'Gary' – and pieced the rest of the story together from there.

The doorbell sounded and Alex moved downstairs. The women were so engrossed in their conversation that neither of them even looked over to see who it was. Alex looked at the security screen at Patrick. Alex opened the door and looked back at Valda. She stared so intensely at Tricia; it looked like she was an unhinged lovestruck teenager. He went to say goodbye, but Tricia went into meltdown mode and started to bawl her eyes out. Valda pulled her close, and rubbed her back. Alex hated awkward silences, moments and people; and this set-up ticked all but one of those boxes. He slid out and left them to it.

He and Patrick sat in silence. The radio on, they stopped at lights. Patrick looked up at the traffic light, which went from red to amber to green, then red once more with little to no movement of traffic. He turned to look left and met Alex looking at his profile. They held each other's gaze for a little longer than normal, then Alex spoke.

"Have you met Tricia properly?"

Patrick looked thoughtful.

"I wouldn't say properly … introduced, yes, but I haven't spoken with her since. Why'd you ask?"

Alex shook his head. "Nothing major. Tell me something – has Valda ever given you a key to the house?"

Patrick looked at him, flummoxed. The sound of the car behind beeping drew his attention and Patrick realised the space in front of them was so wide the neighbouring lane of traffic had started to filter in. Patrick got moving.

"Never. Why, is something wrong?"

Alex sighed and lied.

"Nah, not really. It's just that … Tricia let herself in this morning and I wasn't aware she had a key."

"Well, she is helping out with the baby, and right after the birth Valda couldn't get about very easily. It would make sense that Tricia can get in and out freely …"

Patrick glanced left at Alex, while braking at another set of traffic lights. Alex nodded, knowing he had made a valid point but feeling uneasy all the same.

"I suppose so …"

Patrick looked at him.

"You sure anything else isn't bothering you?" he asked, knowing they shared a subject that bothered both of them; Patrick wanted Alex to bring up the subject.

"Not really. How about you?" Alex said, placing the ball back in his court.

They both fell silent, neither wanting to go any further with things until the other showed their hand. They both had thoughts and feelings, feelings and doubts, and if you had spoken to the surgeons present that day, they would have said the same thing. Some things happen and disappear from your mind, but some things happen with such intensity that they are difficult to comprehend. They stay with you like a horror film you see late at night, on some obscure channel, that is so disturbing it crawls under your skin and attaches itself to your thought, feelings and dreams, making them nightmares. Your mind's eye plays the scenes over and over; trying to make sense of fiction, hoping reality had no stake in its making.

They left the conversation there, returning to silence and their own thoughts.

~

With BBL under Alex's watch, things had changed so much, the place was virtually unrecognisable. When he first arrived, he had noticed how everyone moved around, jaded, like children in a Victorian orphanage.

Valda created this ethos, he thought in disgust, watching them move, afraid of their own shadows; afraid that if they made a mistake they would never work in fashion again. Although Valda had changed for the better towards the end of her time at BBL, they were still wary. They believed that if they had took her too lightly, they could forget themselves and end up like so many that had fallen at her hands, expelled from the world of fashion for good.

Valda was extremely powerful and influential in the industry. She had been known to fire people who decided to talk back to her; unaware that Valda's roots ran deep and, when she fired you, you stayed fired from fashion – period.

The first thing Alex did was call a meeting with the heads of departments. Charlie Gibbs, design manager, Drew, head of PR, Keisha Patel, the new head of marketing, Selen, head of accounts and his PA Claire. He explained he wanted an open-door policy while he was there. He wanted people to feel free to express any concerns or ideas they may have, without fear of being berated or browbeaten. He asked to meet every single staff member, one by one in his office, so he could get to know every cog in the wheel that was BBL – and now GB.

Change was slow, but by the third week of being there, he enjoyed it more than being at home. He met some really cool people during his one-to-ones; people with amazing pasts and plenty of potential. A seamstress from Venezuela called Raquel, who had survived a plane crash; Abdi, who had escaped war-torn Somalia aged eight years old, but sat before Alex aged twenty-five, one of the company's junior accountants; Becky, a BBL PR assistant from Bethnal Green, and the grand-daughter of ex-British heavyweight boxing champion, Sledgehammer Sam; Robert, part of the marketing team, who at sixteen was almost picked to swim in the Olympic team.

Alex could have listened to those people all day, fascinated by how their lives had led them to this point and their conversation.

He was slowly but surely beating the boss, changing the culture of the business, making it an environment he and others wanted to work in. Slowly but surely department doors opened, and music and good vibes drifted out. People communicated with him and each other. Production didn't suffer, as Valda would have argued; in fact, production increased, ideas flowing for GB, demand high for their new brand, which included neat little dresses, tops and trousers, which sold out faster than they could manufacture them.

Alex, fascinated by GB's impressive start, called the marketing department to find out why the BBL range was now playing second fiddle to GB. Keisha, a chubby, dark-skinned Indian girl with a short bob, came up to Valda's office and explained that a new girl group called Pandora who had just won X-Factor were championing the brand, mentioning GB in interviews, on Facebook and Twitter. She explained that their fans were sucking it up and were flocking to stores and online to buy pieces worn by the girls.

"Should we make contact with them and see how we can capitalise on this further?" Alex asked.

Keisha shook her head.

"I wouldn't advise we do that. The moment we make contact, we have to get into endorsement deals with management – contracts, red tape and blah, blah, blah. Let's just go along for the ride and see what happens with it."

"Okay, you know what you're doing. Keep me posted."

"Will do … by the way, you're doing a great job, everyone really loves your approach."

Alex smiled. "Thank you. That means a lot."

She left and he spun his chair around and looked out at the lights across London. The notion of going home threatened. The thought lowered his mood instantly. He looked at the clock on the desk phone. 18.00. Patrick would be there by 19.00. He slumped in the chair and chilled until home time.

At 18.55 Alex made his way downstairs past various employees going home. He said his goodbyes, stopped at reception and leaned on the pod.

"Anything for me?" he asked.

Veronica shuffled and placed a few letters on the desktop.

"Not for you, but Valda …"

Alex swept them off the top and smiled.

"Thanks … Claire told me it's your thirtieth birthday tomorrow. Is that right?"

Veronica nodded and looked at him cautiously. "Yeah."

"Take it off, and the day after."

"But—"

"Don't worry about it; just enjoy your day. It only comes once."

Veronica's face went from happy to contemplative. "Thanks, but I can't afford to miss out on two days' pay and I've used up my annual leave."

Alex laughed.

"Don't be silly. I'm giving the days to you, fully paid. Now take them before I change my mind."

Her jaw dropped, her eyes widened, she shot up out of her swivel chair, flung her arms around him before jigging up and down with excitement. Alex smiled and laughed.

"Oh my God, thank you sooo much!" she screeched.

"Don't mention it."

She sat back down, her face so young and full of energy it made him feel alive. He walked towards the exit. He looked back over his shoulder and could see her bubbling, her phone to her ear. Phoning friends, no doubt; telling them the good news; the security guard gave him a thumbs-up as he passed and he gave one back. He met Patrick outside and they set off home.

As they neared his gate he looked for Tricia's car, but it wasn't there. Patrick touched the gate key against the sensor. It slowly swung open and they entered. Alex got out, stood in the open car door and bent to look in at Patrick.

"See you tomorrow."

The pair said their goodnights. Alex walked to the door and Patrick reversed. Alex stood on the doorstep and watched him disappear out of the gate. Prior to the last five weeks and besides the Rosita incident, Alex had never really had much contact with Patrick; the thought of using a chauffeur to drive him to work had made him cringe and think of his parents shaking their heads in disgust. However, Patrick needed the work and Alex liked their morning and evening chats, so everyone won.

Alex opened the front door. Warmth and a beautiful smell of food hit him. Spices and seasoning that he had never associated with their abode. He took off his shoes and coat, walked in and stood in the middle of the living room. The TV was playing. He looked towards the kitchen's frosted glass doors; a black figure moved behind them. He looked down at the table at one of the pamphlets Tricia had left.

Past employers:
Amanda Brace
Jane Heckles
Anita Klein
Audra Henley
Mariah Wray

Alex placed it back on the table and moved towards the kitchen. He opened the door. Valda hadn't noticed his arrival. The island was set for dinner, with a basket of homemade bread still steaming, and a bowl of salad with feta cheese squares dropped in it. Golden-brown chicken wings gleamed, glazed with honey. The aromas were out of this world; they forced a growl from his belly.

Valda knelt, placing dishes in the dishwasher. He walked over and crouched beside her. She jumped and he smiled. They both stood and Valda smacked his arm.

"Don't do that, Alex, you almost gave me a heart attack."

"Sorry."

Alex turned and pointed towards the island. "What's all this?"

"Food for us. Tricia made it before she left."

"Oh."

"Oh? What's the 'oh' for?"

"Nothing; I just thought you'd made it."

"Come on, businesswoman I am, but domestic goddess I'm not."

Alex smiled.

"Heaven's upstairs" Valda said.

Alex went up reluctantly. He looked in from the nursery doorway, the light from the hallway diluting her darkened room a little. He looked at the gigantic teddies sitting in both far corners and at her overhead carousel with moons, stars and clouds attached, which hung, motionless. The moonlight shone through her window, making the room feel ghostly. A shiver ran up his back and he felt he wasn't alone – as if something was watching him watching her. He closed the door, stood behind it and shook his head. Rosita's face injected itself into his mind; her eyes clear, truthful and honest in her belief. It was at that moment he decided he would accredit the bizarre feeling to that day, and decided he should see someone about it.

He walked back downstairs, not looking back.

Valda sat at one end of the island and he sat down at the other, his plate already set.

"How is she?" she gushed.

He wished he could enjoy Heaven the way she did.

"Asleep; she's so adorable," he lied.

"I know, I know."

The lie tightened his stomach and almost cost him his appetite. But he continued.

"I swear she almost said Mama today – ask Tricia."

Alex forced a smile and chose a chicken wing.

"Babies don't talk at five weeks. Besides, she'd say dada first."

Valda smiled.

"You wish."

Alex selected some bread and spoke through a mouthful.

"This is really good."

"I know, she's a phenomenal … phenomenal – I don't know. Phenomenal everything."

Alex laughed. "Wow. Calm down, lovestruck."

Valda giggled and Alex went to the wine.

"But seriously, if I was a man I'd snap her up … that's not for you to get any ideas."

"Well, they do say once you go black you don't go back," Alex replied.

They both laughed.

"She's mixed-race, so that only applies to half," Valda joked.

They laughed again

"We haven't done this in a long time, have we?" Valda asked.

They smiled. Alex took some olive oil and dribbled it over his salad.

"How are things at BBL?"

"Everything's under control," he replied.

"See, I told you all they need is a presence."

Alex didn't agree, but would never have dreamed of saying a thing.

"Tell me something, what was up with Tricia this morning?" Alex asked.

Valda speared a bunch of salad leaves with her fork and stopped just short from her mouth; the fork hovered.

"Oh, she's having some issues with her boyfriend."

"Gary?"

"Yeah – how'd you know his name?"

"I overheard."

Valda placed her fork back down. "He's some controlling asshole, who likes to have his cake and eat it."

Alex nodded; Valda picked up the fork and ate. Alex reached for a chicken wing and the pair ate in silence for a few seconds. He placed the bones on a plate, grabbed a piece of kitchen towel and wiped his hands.

"I see … I was shocked when she came in; I never knew she had a key."

"Of course she has a key; I can't keep getting up and down," she said.

"I figured."

Valda bit into her bread and Alex took another sip of wine.

"Tell me something: did you know Mariah Wray was one of her past clients?" Alex asked.

Valda spoke through a mouthful of sweet bread.

"Hrmmm, she … I … asked about her a few weeks ago when I saw her name on the leaflet she left."

"Spoken to her lately?" Alex asked.

Valda pinched her bottom lip between her fingers and sighed.

"That wouldn't have been possible." Valda replied.

"Why?"

"She's been sectioned."

Alex leaned forward, his eyes narrowed.

"For what?"

"I don't know if you want to know."

"Of course I want to know. Tell me …"

"She killed her own child."

Alex reeled back in horror.

"What the fuck? But the last time we saw her she was so excited, they both were; her and Ian. She said she was seeing someone about getting pregnant and everything."

They embraced the silence created by the revelation. Then Alex spoke.

"Can't believe it," he said, shaking his head.

"I know, it's crazy. Tricia said the family was devastated. You know, she was set to inherit the Chuggford Chocolate Company from her father, which would have made her the wealthiest woman in the UK," Valda replied.

"No, I didn't know."

"Yeah, she would have been valued at two billion."

"Wow! When did this all happen?"

"Last year, 2012."

"The Olympics kept it out of the press, I expect," Alex questioned.

"No, apparently the family paid a fortune to have it kept out of the media and her out of jail."

Alex rubbed his jaw.

"Cra-zy. I wonder what could have driven her to do that."

Valda's gaze left his and she looked down at her plate. He registered her look of guilt and attached a question he would never ask. *Why do you look responsible?*

"I don't know, maybe postnatal depression or … I don't know," she answered.

"Well, if you ever feel like—"

Her brow dipped deep and her lips trembled with anger.
"Don't you dare …! I love Heaven to death! I'd kill for her! I'd never let anyone hurt her. How—" she barked.

She paused and a lonely tear rolled down her cheek and fell from her jaw to the table. Alex lowered his gaze. She stood and walked towards the living room. Alex watched her go by, in shock at how strongly she had reacted. With the mood soured, the rest of the evening was spent separately, in silence, Valda upstairs, Alex below. The house slept for another night.

Tricia

Thursday 7th February 2013
Dr Ryan's office

"I just don't feel the way I should about her."

"And you don't think the situation at her birth has anything to do with it?"

Alex shook his head. "I really couldn't tell you. I'm not going to say it didn't affect me, because it still plays over in my head every other day."

Dr Ryan paused, then wrote in his notebook.

"I think you're suffering from postnatal depression," Dr Ryan suggested.

"Me?"

Dr Ryan let out a small laugh and looked over the top of his spectacles at Alex.

"Depression doesn't discriminate."

Alex drew a deep breath

"I don't think you understand. I'm afraid of her … afraid to be in her room by myself," Alex confessed.

"You feel you may harm her? This is common in postnatal depression."

Alex looked him in the eye and, although not completely convinced by the diagnosis, he felt Dr Ryan could have a point. Maybe, just as shell-shocked soldiers who have seen too much on the battlefield go a little crazy, the Rosita situation was his own small trauma, enough to unhinge him.

"I'm going to prescribe you some medication and literature to read over. Let's see how that goes. If they don't work, like it or not, I'll be forced to refer you. You can't live like this … do you agree?"

Alex sighed and rubbed his jaw. "Fair enough."

Alex left the surgery feeling a little more optimistic. At least he had symptoms of something that could be attributed to a condition other men had suffered from. He walked down the steps with his prescription and reading literature tucked away in his jacket pocket. He stood at the bottom of the steps and took in the day.

The sun shone, but it was an illusion of warmth. The temperature was five degrees. He pulled his hat low and the lapels of his jacket up to cover his ears. He decided he wouldn't head back to the house yet; he wanted a rest from everything Valda and Heaven. Today he was single and childless. He'd take the bus and possibly the Tube, destination undecided. It really didn't matter: he had a black credit card that could take him to the moon and back twice, if he wanted.

He moved left towards the high road, people walking around in a selfish daze, with a unifying quest; knowingly or subconsciously searching for relief from monetary restraint, a non-issue for him. His quest was now for something much more important: his sanity and peace of mind which, funnily enough, were two of the things no amount of money on earth could buy.

The high road was littered with retail chains, coffee shops and fast-food restaurants. Alex walked into a large chemist to collect his medication. The store was painted in clinical white. The staff wore white jackets with blue trimmings, and navy-blue trousers. He approached and asked a lady called Lisa where the pharmacy was and she pointed towards an escalator going up.

Alex thanked her, but she held his gaze a little longer than he was comfortable with. He was rarely recognised in public without Valda, but he still got his fair share of celeb chasers who knew everyone's face, probably from some trashy magazine that had run an article on the top ten sexy celeb partners in the absence of real news; those magazines that removed their readers from their reality and made them more concerned with the lives of others.

Alex moved quickly from her. He looked over his shoulder and noticed her squinting in thought, a look he knew too well. He stood on the escalator, looked back once more and was relived she hadn't followed.

At the top, a queue started for the pharmacy counter, ten deep. He joined it, rummaged in his pocket for his prescription, unfolded and held it. He kept his head low, not wanting any more attention. Three people were seen and left, and his mind began to wander, thinking about life before Valda, about whether he were happier then or now. A familiar voice drew his attention back to the present, from up at the counter. He looked around the queue and noticed it was Tricia.

He leaned around the person in front and watched her talking to the counter staff. She suddenly turned; the way a person does when they feel they're being watched. Alex fell in behind a broad man in front of him and peeked slyly. She looked for another second, and then turned back to the counter.

With her items she walked past the remaining customers in the queue, scrutinising each of their faces as she passed them. She would have seen Alex had he not moved to the far end of an aisle, where he watched her from a distance. It looked as if she would pass, but she stopped at the other end and looked down the aisle directly at him. He dipped his head and began to examine a box of vitamins. He watched her feet move towards him, stop for two seconds, then turn and walk away.

He looked up and watched her descend the escalator. A voyeuristic urge and urgency gripped him, so powerful he couldn't even comprehend it. The voice in his head said *Follow her*. He walked quickly down the aisle, the vitamins still in hand. He hopped on the escalator and reached the bottom just in time to see her back exiting the store.

He hurried and was just about to leave when Lisa jumped out of nowhere in front of him, her fingers pointed.

"Beat the Boss, and now you're with Valda Payne!"

Alex let out a nervous smile but kept his eyes on Tricia, who was walking quickly down the road.

"Ahhh …. yeah," he replied

"Oh my God! Valda, like, owns the shop down the road."

"Yeah, erm, I'm sorry; in a little bit of a hurry."

He moved around Lisa who observed the vitamins, unpaid for.

"Hey! Aren't you going to pay for those?" she asked.

Alex slowed, turned and shoved his hand in his pocket, grabbing two crushed-up fifty-pound notes and placing them in her open palm.

"Keep the change."

Outside he walked in the direction Tricia had, and came back to the road he had emerged from earlier. He stopped and looked straight up the high street, but couldn't see her black coat and woolly hat. Then he looked left and saw her walking down the road towards Dr Ryan's surgery. Alex started after her, making sure to stay at a distance. She slowed as she neared Dr Ryan's surgery; then she ascended the steps. Alex stopped at a pedestrian crossing, one hundred metres away. He watched her enter the doctor's building.

The green man glowed and he crossed over to the other side. He walked a few paces then stopped; the voice, that voice that had told him to follow, now wanted him to stop. "Stop … stop now," it said, so clearly that he felt he was going insane. His chest tightened and he clutched it. He took two deep, deep breaths. "Go home," it came again. "Get home now."

He shuffled over to a building wall on his right and leaned against it for a second. People passed, looked and said nothing, even though his face was awash with distress. This was the nature of big cities: everyone was so focused on their lives that they didn't want trouble, or to be troubled. To them a perfectly normal man in distress became a crack fiend who probably deserved everything that was happening to him.

He pulled his hand down his face. His vision split, came together and cleared. His breathing normalised, he shook his head and leaned away from the wall slowly. He looked down the road towards Dr Ryan's surgery then turned and walked back up to the high street, homeward bound.

The cab pulled up two roads away, as he and Valda usually requested it did whenever they took one, their address anonymity always at the forefront of their minds. He took a bunch of notes – purple, red and blue – and literally threw the bunch at the driver, who sat there, his face flummoxed.

"My God!" the cab man hollered.

Alex slammed his door shut without reply and began to jog around the corner. His jog suddenly became a full-on run, fuelled by an urgency he still couldn't understand. He stopped just in front of his gate, applied the gate card and it opened. He walked into the centre of the driveway and stood in the middle, did a 360 and looked up at the evergreen trees within the walls of the driveway their pines looking sparse; he looked down at the ground by their base and noticed heaps of them laid there. Three birds sprang out of the trees, clapped their wings and circled above him like vultures waiting for dead flesh to fall from a corpse. He watched them until they flew away, out of sight.

He walked onwards towards the door, expecting the worst inside. Extreme feelings he couldn't make sense of. Rosita's face appeared spontaneously among the muddle and jumble of thoughts, her eyes clear and sane, unbefitting of a person who was meant to have lost their mind. Her belief in her actions was justified; justified to harm, or possibly kill Valda, Heaven or both. *Maybe it should have been*, he heard himself say.

With the level of empathy for Rosita's actions so great, in that moment he realised why he felt so uncomfortable. His legs went to jelly under the thought, so heavy and frightening; he held his hands over his head and shook it to disperse it. He felt he couldn't trust himself now; he felt he could harm them the way Mariah had harmed her own.

"But why? Why shouldn't they be here?" he whispered. "Why … Why … Why?" Alex walked back towards the gate, wanting to leave and never return. The voice came again. "Go home …" it whispered, delicate but authoritative. The voice cleared his mind and brought him back to the world. He brought his hands down his face. *Get a fucking grip, man, you're losing it here*. He took a deep breath and walked towards the front door.

He inserted his key into the lock and pushed the door. It swung open and he stood on the step. Valda and Tricia looked over from the sofa, where they sat next to each other like the best friends they had become; Tricia sat as if she had been there the whole morning. His stomach turned and he was almost sick. Those few seconds felt like hours.

Valda shot up. Her face looked distorted and smudged through his tears that had gathered on the cusp of his lower eyelids, waiting to be full enough to stream down his cheeks. She rushed towards him and pulled his head down onto her shoulder.

He looked from over her and saw Tricia standing with Heaven, smiling, a horrible impious smile, then he blinked and looked again and she wasn't any more; in fact, she looked as distressed as he felt and Heaven was curled into her chest sleeping.

"I ne-ne-need h-h-help," Alex sobbed.

Valda rubbed the back of his head and comforted him. Tricia stood looking on.

~

From below, Dr Ryan's voice translated into inaudible muffle upstairs. Alex lay on his side, his eyes wide open and dry. He stared and listened to them talk about him as if he were among the dead.

"Postnatal depression?" He heard Valda repeat, shocked.

"Yes," Dr Ryan replied with a chuckle. "Why do people seem to believe men are not susceptible to a human condition?"

The rest of the conversation was so low he could barely hear it. For this he was happy. He exhaled; the sleeping pills had begun to slow his mind. His eyelids became heavy and in an instant the blackness had taken him.

Patrick

Friday 16th February 2013
8pm

The TV played with no sound. Patrick sat on the edge of his bed watching the moon, its platinum light painting his room a romantic silvery-blue. His little studio flat had begun to feel unusually lonely. With his job being on hold for the last week and daily adult interaction at a bare minimum, an uncharacteristic melancholy had begun to set in.

He sighed, stood and walked over to the window and looked out of it, left towards Kilburn High Road. Cars, bikes and buses whizzed up and down. Girls and guys were out in force, cruising for whatever the night could feed their primal desires.

Patrick wasn't the type of man to make new friends easily. He was often private and at times he spoke little to anyone he didn't know well, usually opting to let a conversation ignite, burn and die out due to his lack of input. This made people uncomfortable, especially females. He didn't care much for courting or attracting potential partners.

Now in his fifties, his time for rearing children had come and gone. If he wanted sexual pleasure, he'd pay for it, which he massively preferred: no headache, no obligations or unrealistic expectations on either part.

The friends he had had in the past had either gone back to Jamaica (either willingly or deported), got married (some for a passport) or simply disappeared, scattering around the UK in search of work.

Patrick looked up at the moon and thought back to the day he had driven Valda to visit to that woman, Lilif. He had connected the dots and was almost sure that visit had sparked off the catalogue of misfortune Valda's household was experiencing. He wished he could rewind time and stop her ever going.

Patrick stepped away from the window, pulled on his trousers, top and overcoat. He switched off his TV and left, bound for bright lights and possible human interaction. He walked up the high road, past girls queuing to get into nightclubs; their faces heavily made-up. Others wore tans so deep their ethnicity was ambidextrous. He strolled past guys who queued up behind females, their chests pumped out, trying to look bigger than they felt.

Patrick walked into the Horse and Snake, a local wine bar where you could find an old familiar face if you were lucky. The ownership had changed hands over the years but the clientele stayed the same. That's the way old people were; they stick to what they know and it keeps them safe. He ordered a beer and took a seat at the bar, which over the years had evolved from one of wood to a clear plastic, with bright glowing neon lights within it, which faded from pink to purple to blue. The music was low but the sound of crowd murmur more intense.

He sat watching the TVs above and behind the two bar staff whizzing up and down, serving drinks as if the world were about to end. He sipped his beer and felt a hand settle on his shoulder, firm and steady. Patrick looked around and saw Dermot Connor standing there, his bright blue eyes still, piercing, and as old as the sea. His head completely bald, his nose crooked. His once handsome face made rough by life's everyday motion.

"Fancy meeting ya 'ere, laddie."

Thirty years in England had robbed the passion and at times ferocity from his proud Irish accent.

"Dermot!" Patrick said, raising his voice above all other sounds.

Patrick was happy to see him, happy to have someone to share the evening with. Maybe they would talk about old times and modern politics, or women. Dermot loved to talk about women: women with huge breasts, blonde with blue eyes, the way he liked them.

Patrick tapped two fingers on the stool next to him.

"Sit down, man; let me get you a beer."

Dermot hopped on to the stool. The strong smell of leather and cigarettes hovered around him. Patrick raised his hand for service and was acknowledged.

"You sure people still do this?"

Patrick looked at him, puzzled. "Do what?"

Dermot laughed.

"Sit at the fecking bar – whatdya tink this is, 1975?"

Dermot laughed and smacked Patrick's back, making him jolt forward. Patrick smiled and shook his head.

The pair had met while they were in between jobs in the 1970s. Dermot was a trained chef looking for work in his field and Patrick was desperate for anything. They worked on a building site run by Errol Smith. Dermot had never come into close contact with a black person before he had met Patrick and, from what he saw and heard of them, he never really wanted much to do with them either. Unfortunately for him, due to politics at the time and the IRA's various campaigns, the two were thrown together. The Irish were right up there with the blacks on the national hate chart.

Smith sensed their desperation, employed them and treated the pair of them like shit. He made them do all the horrible jobs on site: heavy labouring, guttering and work on the sewer pipes, while the English workers were given light duties, often laughing about Patrick and Dermot's misfortune. He wanted to break them so that when they left he could walk around calling Patrick a lazy black bastard and Dermot a filthy murdering Irish bum. At first they didn't speak, accepting their joint persecution individually.

Within a month they had begun to really get pissed off with their treatment. Instead of leaving, they came together and plotted about ways to get him back. They pissed in the tea Smith would order them to get for the rest, scratched the paintwork on his Jag, and fucked up jobs the others were on while they were away at lunch.

After five months, things had calmed a little and weren't so bad. One day the pair were working on a wall in a driveway when Tracey Smith arrived on site. Errol Smith's daughter was blonde, with huge breasts, wore stilettos and was daddy's little treasure. Dermot watched her pass by and she looked back at him with warmth. Patrick tapped him and advised him not to even think about it, but Dermot had seen an opportunity Patrick hadn't: an opportunity to really get up Errol's nose.

Dermot waited until she left and walked up behind her, gave her his phone number – and that was it. He began seeing her, taking great joy in being treated like shit by Errol, knowing his daughter had fallen for his Irish charm and was getting the living hell fucked out of her after work, normally on Errol's bed.

The secret remained hidden for a further six months until one day Errol stormed on site, his cheeks puffing, his face glowing red like heated coal. He grabbed Patrick, who was mixing some cement at the time, and demanded if he had known about Dermot and Tracey. Patrick denied it, but Errol was having none of it: he fired Patrick on the spot, calling him every name under the sun.

Dermot's act had cost them their jobs, but Patrick wasn't too bothered. He would have paid a thousand pounds to witness one minute of Errol going through hell, and here he had it for free.

Dermot and Patrick kept in contact for a few more years after that, until Dermot got a chef's job in Cork and their promises to stay in contact fizzled out.

They moved their unexpected meeting to a booth in the back of the pub, with a bottle of scotch. The wine bar had begun to fill up. It was the type of place young people came to for cheap drinks before heading to nearby clubs or the West End.

"So tell me, how's life been treating ya?" Dermot asked.

"Can't complain; I jus get on with tings."

"Kids? Married?"

"No sa. You?"
"Married, divorced, married, again divorced, I 'ave two boys who live wid they mam."
Patrick looked at his eyes, scanning him from left to right. There was something he had to say, something beyond idle chit-chat.
"How's the chef work?" Patrick asked.
"Ah, that's on hold for a bit. Had a little bit of a holiday, if you know what I mean." Dermot smiled but he wasn't happy about it.
"How long did you get?" Patrick asked.
"Got ten years, did five. Good behaviour, ya know?"
Patrick nodded and rubbed his face, and in that instance thought back to that night in the Conference Club when Leroy and Sheldon had planned to make him an accomplice to their crime. Dermot's eyes had that same look; that probing stare that wanted to know if he were made of the right stuff.
"You still drive for fat cats?"
This was a good question given his current situation. He wasn't sure if he would still have a job, since there was no need for him. The line of questioning brought a strange sense of déjà vu; so similar to that night in the Conference that he expected Dermot to ask him if he was desperate enough for money to help him rob a bank or, worse yet, kill someone. Patrick waited to hear what his eyes wanted to say.
"Yeah, I'm working for a family now. Have been for a good couple of years."
Dermot nodded, poured himself a drink and raised his glass. Patrick raised his in accordance with tradition.
"Cheers to the old times, when it was cool to sit at the fecking bar eating nuts and drinking beer."
Patrick nodded and they both put their drinks down.
They sat in silence for a few minutes, taking in the night. Then Dermot spoke.
"I've been coming to this area every week for the last month to see if I could catch ya."

At that moment, Patrick wished Dermot would shut up and drink in silence.

"I'm gonna cut to the chase. I don't want this to turn out funny or nuttin, but I've been dreaming about ya … Every night." Dermot looked deeply at him and shook his head, as if he didn't believe it himself.

"A serious dream that stays wid me … The same one, over and over and over, it's terrifying …"

The pair paused and it was as if the contents of the bar had evaporated into thin air – people, furniture, smells and sound – leaving just them. The pair tuned into each other.

"Go on," Patrick said.

Dermot looked over his shoulder and around him to make sure he wasn't being listened to, the collar of his leather jacket unintentionally flicked up like the Fonz from *Happy Days*. He leaned over the table towards Patrick, and Patrick did the same.

"No bullshitting. You and I are running, running for our fecking lives, running in London, but it's not London. It's a … a version of London you'd see in a disaster film – the dead and dying are everywhere, lying on the ground, begging for help, reaching up towards us … it's so fecking vivid, Patrick, so vivid. You can see everything burning, cars turned over, crumbling buildings, fire reaching out from beneath the pavement. So hot I can feel it in my sleep; flesh hanging from people's faces and hands, their eyeballs hanging out. The sky as black as tar, fire swimming along it like tides of water … it really and truly looks like hell on earth. We run and I turn to look at what we're running from. No word of a fecking lie, we are running from an angel, a huge angel. Her wings are golden with light so bright you can't see beyond her; she floats behind us, fast. I look back ahead … .And I swear it happens in the same way every night I dream it. I look back over at you, and you've left my side and jumped on top of an overturned car. But you have been joined by two people: a woman and a man. They're faceless, but her name is Valda and the man's name is Alex. I don't know how I know, but I know. I look back at the angel again and she is bigger, grander, her wings seem to stretch for an eternity, her eyes are now circles of blinding bright lights, sucking in particles, growing. No bullshitting … I cross my hands in front of my face, the light so hot and bright I can't see, but I can feel the heat, heat so hot my skin begins to melt from my hands. I look back at you, and you are … you are a fecking demon – all three of you, your tongues as long as dogs' tails, your skin like lizards', black and scaly. Valda whoever that is, is holding a baby – a human baby, then comes this blinding light from behind me, eating everything and everyone in its path, me included. Then everything is white, but it's like I'm still there, conscious… Yeah, I know. After that I can hear voices, upset, distressed like, loads of voices mixed together as if the world was talking at once. So many voices that I feel like ma head's gonna explode, Patrick, explode with madness … and then this voice comes that overrides them all. It's so powerful the rest just melt away into the background … it says three words: 'Heaven must die.' Then I wake up sweating, sweating like a fecking pig."

Patrick looks at him as if he's in a trance.

"On my kids' lives, Patrick, I swear to ya … I've been having the same dream for the past four weeks, exactly the same … I'm not gonna lie; I feel like I'm losing my fecking marbles. You been in any trouble or, I don't know, anything? Is there anyting you could say about it: do you know an Alex or Valda?"

Patrick rubbed his face and made his decision.

"Nah, can't say I know anyone by those names," Patrick lied.

The hope in Dermot's eyes dwindled; he looked totally deflated, his last hope of finding answers to his nightly torment dashed by a lie. They discussed it further. Patrick, wanting to get off the subject, suggested Dermot see someone who could help him with recurring dreams, knowing that yesterday's dream would be Dermot's last one: his role in whatever Patrick was involved in was complete; the message sent loud and scarily clear.

They drank the last of the whisky, exchanged numbers and said their goodbyes for the last time. Patrick walked home slowly. He sat on his bed, watching the moon once more, thinking about Rosita and how honest her belief was in her cause. He thought about Dermot's dream, all mounting signs pointing to the fact that something wanted Valda's baby dead.

Valda's visit to Lilif had done more than bring a child forth; it had brought something into this world that wasn't meant to be. This he was sure of now, but what was he to do: fight or run?

~

"Maybe he should go in if you feel he isn't improving …" Tricia whispered.

Valda kissed Heaven's head and her eyes became watery.

"Look at him. I don't want him around Heaven in that state. I called Dr Ryan and he said it's the medication he's on, but maybe you're right, maybe he should be observed more closely by professionals …"

They both looked out into the garden, where Alex stood barefoot and in a bathrobe, looking up at the sky, as if it spoke to him. He turned and began walking back towards the house. He walked into the kitchen and passed the pair of them, looking straight ahead, ignoring them.

Tricia turned to Valda.

"I see what you mean. He's totally out of it … Maybe he has had a breakdown. There's no way you can deal with him and Heaven, especially with going back to BBL again. Being sectioned for a couple of weeks could be beneficial for everyone."

"But I feel so awful."

Valda began to well up. Tricia rubbed her shoulder.

"It's not your fault; mental illness is nothing to be scared or ashamed of. If you want, I can call Dr Ryan and get things rolling for his admission. You have enough on your plate."

"Thanks. I don't know what I'd do without you; you are truly a Godsend. Oh, while you're on to him, tell him I need an appointment for myself."

Tricia looked at her. "Why, what's wrong?"

"Nothing serious; it's the weight thing and the constant tiredness …"

Tricia laughed.

"Oh, first-world parenting issues …"

The frosted kitchen door banged. They spun around and looked at it. Alex was standing there, looking through it towards them.

"He's starting to—"

"Scare you? Me as well," Tricia finished.

They looked at each other than back at the smudged silhouette he made. Bobbing up and down slowly, he paused, turned and walked away.

Valda slept on the sofa, Heaven in her Moses basket. She woke to her shoulder being pushed gently. When she opened her eyes, Alex was standing there in a T-shirt and underpants. He stood over her the same way her father had when he'd hurt her, his fists clenched, angry knuckles protruding. In that instant she thought Alex was going to kill her and Heaven. He swayed, stabilised, then spoke.

"The garden is dying; the birds no longer come … the trees are shedding …"

She sat up. "Ah—"

Alex raised his finger to his lips and she froze. "She may hear you."

Valda paused. "Who?"

"The old lady… The one who watches over Heaven."

~

Patrick pulled up in the Bentley and parked on the gravelled driveway. Valda stepped out of the door, kissed Heaven and handed her over to Tricia. She walked towards the car, her hair pulled back in a bun; her tights jet-black, matching her black skirt and blazer suit.

The only things that marred her threatening look were her emaciated face and the fact that her clothes looked one size too big. Valda was checking in on things at BBL, but Patrick felt she should be checking into hospital.

If anybody had taken the way Alex was currently behaving, or Valda's unexplainable appearance, at face value, they would have sworn they were a pair of junkies on the verge of death. Things were really and truly falling apart at the Payne residence.

Valda stepped into the car accompanied by a smell which could only be described as expensive perfume masking damp rot. She smelled so bad that Patrick thought she was a corpse and had to double-check in the rear-view mirror that she wasn't a walking zombie.

Jesus! He thought.

"It's been a long time…" Valda said, opening her bag.

Patrick forced a grin in response to her genuine smile. "Indeed."

Valda rummaged around in her bag and Patrick reversed out of the gates. Tricia stood on the doorstep, watching. Patrick looked back in the rear-view mirror. She watched them leave, her face grave as she turned and closed the door. A chill ran through him and, at that moment, Patrick felt groundless, somehow; as if Tricia wasn't who she professed to be.

Patrick expected them to talk about everything. He expected her to open up to him about all the bizarre things happening at home, giving him a segue in to Rosita, his dream and Dermot's. But she didn't and couldn't. She had fallen asleep, her head leaning right back on the headrest. So uncouth, so un-Valda; her shine had disappeared. Her previous glare of power had dwindled away to a rudimental flicker.

Alex stood at the top of the stairs, looking down. Tricia walked out of the kitchen, bottle in hand, up the opposite set of stairs and paused, having noticed him there. She looked across. Their eyes met. The house was silent; they were silent.

She continued up the stairs and looked back at him when she reached the landing. He kept his gaze on her until she entered Heaven's room, closing the door firmly.

Alex paused for a few seconds then moved downstairs, went to the kitchen, opened the drawer closest to the kitchen door, and retrieved the leaflets Tricia had left when she first came. He walked back through the living room, up the stairs and back into his room, closing the door behind him.

~

"It's spelt L-i-l-i-t-h and the section you need is RE; Religious Education." The librarian pointed towards the far end towards the right. Patrick thanked her and moved in the direction she had instructed. Westminster Library was grand and old. At eye level, everything was modern: the tables, chairs, plug sockets, the computers with flat screens and the people sitting at them; all modern, new age and fast. But if you looked up, you would have realised the things below were mere illusions, removable fixtures placed into an ancient building. Dark-brown rafters created a ribcage across the roof, holding it firmly. The windows were as old as sin and as thin as sheets of paper. The smell of old books grew, the deeper you walked in, musty and dry.

Patrick turned into the aisle he had been told to and began looking through the titles to find information on Valda's fertility specialist's namesake. He found a book titled *The Fabled Creatures* and opened it. He looked at the index, scrolled down to the Ls and her name didn't appear. He moved across again and found a book called *Women of Religious Texts.* He opened it and scrolled down to the Ls – and there she was: Lilith. He froze, looking at the name and the pages her story occupied. He closed the book and went in search of somewhere to sit with it.

Back at home, Alex sat with his back on the bed's headboard, Valda's tablet in his lap. He touched the screen and it came to life. He took the literature he had obtained from the drawer and tapped the search bar. The cursor flicked on and off, waiting for his input. He looked at the list of people Tricia had formerly worked for, and typed in the first one.

Patrick found a seat in a far corner of the library against a stone wall, far away from the youth, who were loud and there more to socialise than study. Light rain began to pelt the thin windows above, creating a soothing sound that radiated all around the building. He opened the book and began to read.

Amanda Brace. Born 1969, died 2001. Alex clicked on the top link provided by starnow.com and began to read.

Oscar-winning actress Amanda Brace was found dead in her house last night following a house fire that blazed out of control. Her newborn baby daughter Korea and her husband director Morgan Brace also died in the fire. Her family's tragic demise concludes a bizarre year for the actress. Reports from people close to her said they believed she was displaying signs of having a mental breakdown in the latter stages of her life. Some speculated that she may have been suffering from drug addiction as she lost so much weight. All this happened after she celebrated the birth of her daughter. Ex-husband Jason Gunn said they had tried for years to have a child, but had been unsuccessful. He blamed this factor for their split. Her best friend and nanny to Korea, Tricia, said Amanda was so happy when Korea was born. She had always wanted a baby and was over the moon. However, she went on to say that, half way through Korea's first year, Amanda had confided in Tricia her concern that her own baby was trying to kill her. Worried about the state of Amanda's mind, Tricia reportedly contacted Morgan and told him to get her help, but things deteriorated. Morgan agreed with Amanda. Tricia said she suspected the pair were using drugs, although the couple had never been known for their drink and drug abuse. Co-actor in many of Amanda's films, James Post echoed Tricia's observation when he spoke about her terrible Grammy appearance: "She rocked up there looking like she'd walked off the set of George Romaro's latest zombie film." And let's not forget the interview she gave us, which she cried throughout and spoke about being watched by devils and demons who were trying to rule the world. Fortunately, her friend Tricia survived the fire after escaping through an upstairs window.

Patrick opened the book at page 106 and read.

Lilith as Adam's First Wife

A modern spin on Lilith is that she is at constant war with God, an ally to Lucifer, and is trying to establish a following on Earth, made up of the wealthy, powerful and those who have influence over others. She offers the person the one thing they want the most: fame, riches, whatever else it may be, and in exchange they submit their children to her teachings for one year. This must all be done of the patron's free will, and the deal consummated by the wearing of a bracelet or piece of jewellery given at the meeting, rendering God virtually powerless to stop it. She uses her previous offspring to watch over the ones coming up; they usually come in the guise of carers or friends, and they gain trust and entry to the homes of those who have entered into a deal with Lilith, to ensure the baby is well cared for and subject to their teachings. Her other agenda to isolate these women from friends and family as their babies suck the life force from their mothers, eventually leading to their death. Lilith's ultimate goal is to destroy all Adam's sons, Eve's daughters and eventually God's earth, in revenge for her bitter demise.

Usually come in the guise of carers or friends, usually come in the guise of carers or friends ... they gain trust and entry to the homes of those who have entered into a deal with Lilith, and ensure the baby is well cared for and subject to their teachings. Isolate from friends and family ...

"Tricia," Patrick whispered. "Tricia ..."

Thunder rumbled outside. Patrick and Alex looked up at the windows above them, the clouds grumpy and black, threatening heavier rain. Alex put down the tablet and Patrick closed the book, got up and walked towards the exit with it. Alex placed his ear up against the bedroom door. Patrick pulled his coat collar up. Alex continued to listen. Patrick borrowed the book and walked quickly back to the car. Alex heard Tricia breathing outside. Patrick got in. Alex moved back from the door. Patrick drove like a bat out of hell. Her shadow stretched underneath the bottom of the door; Alex paused. Patrick drove on. Alex turned and walked back to the bed and looked for it. *For what? The Bible. Whose Bible? Valda's. Oh, she got rid of that. Who got rid of it? Tricia.* Lightning flashed and the rain came. The flash curved crevices in Patricks face. Patrick passed a green light, the rain heavy now. Alex looked back over at the bedroom door and saw the shadow had gone from beneath. Heaven had begun to cry, echoing out of the house's speakers, then came the sound of Tricia soothing her, singing a lullaby. Alex froze. Her voice was so haunting that he felt like jumping through the window to escape it. Patrick drove closer and closer at speeds the Bentley had never before reached. People ran for cover everywhere, huddling in shop doorways, under bus shelters and under futile umbrellas to escape the torrential downpour. Tricia's singing grew louder and Heaven began to laugh. Alex brought his hands to his ears and fell face-down on the bed; her voice seemed like it acknowledged no boundaries, perforating through his hands, which were flat against his head, louder and louder, driving him insane. Patrick drove faster and faster, two minutes from Alex now; the rain came harder, visibility due to the weather so bad he was virtually sightless. Tricia stopped and Alex sobbed, his ears ringing, her voice still echoing in his mind. The realms of reality seemed blurred now Alex pushed himself up, exiting the house in his mind. He stumbled all over the room as if drunk, and collapsed into the wardrobe and dresser. The bedroom door swung open, and there stood Dr Ryan, Tricia and two burly men dressed in white. The final light before Alex's house burned red. Patrick felt something against his neck; it felt like someone breathing against it with cold breaths. He looked up into the rear-view mirror and was met by a pair of crayon-green eyes, a smiling mouth full of decaying teeth surrounded by vampire-pale skin. His heart jumped and his lungs paused. Leaning forward and pressing his foot down on the accelerator, he shot out through the red light into the path of oncoming cars, the first one missed him but the second ploughed straight into his side. The Bentley spun anti-clockwise, sending water spraying up from beneath its wheels. The driver of the other car went through the windscreen and ended up on his own bonnet and other cars behind piled up; screeching brakes and car horns rang out. Patrick's airbag inflated, but the side impact had caused his neck to snap sideways so violently that it broke. As he sat there dying, his mind ran through his whole life and earthly existence. Blood trickled from his lips. There was a man stood on the bonnet peering in, a woman was at his shattered window, with others on the passenger side, conferring about ways to help him, unaware it was too late. He could feel their spirit – that beautiful human spirit that forgets prejudices, nationality or sexuality – that human spirit he knew people always had. He felt tired now; he felt no pain, just tired. He closed his eyes and he heard people coax him to keep them open, their voices a distant echo. His eyes shut and he heard his last breath, and then came a rumble, an almighty rumble all around him, followed by magnificent, pristine white light. A figure walked into focus, his aunt Edith – but not the old version, the young one who had taken him in when he was left alone. From behind her came his parents, Patricia and Marcus Williams, dressed so elegantly, his father in his favourite two–piece suit, his mother in her best dress, and from behind them came a quartet of grandparents he had only seen pictures of. From behind them came people he had never met, some dressed in rags, the majority in fine brightly-coloured cottons and silks, the women with their heads wrapped, adorned with gold jewellery, their feet dressed in golden sandals. They didn't speak, but they smiled; they all smiled and he went to them.

Patrick passed away at 1.30 pm. At 1.30 pm Tricia had arranged for Alex to be sectioned. This hurt Valda like hell. She sat at her desk in tears, imagining Alex being restrained, barefoot, pleading for his freedom. Begging for it like a child. Being held by his arms and ankles, and pulled this way and that, from the house. There was no way she could have been present for that; no way she could hear him in pain and not want to call it off. Tricia was right – it was best she handle it.

At 1.31 pm Dr Ryan stood in the middle of Alex's room, the muscular help flanking him. Tricia stood with Heaven in the corridor looking in. Alex stood at the far end besides the bed, cornered, his hands held out open-palmed.

"I won't resist, just let me get a few things ..."

The help looked at Dr Ryan, waiting for his answer to Alex's request. Dr Ryan nodded for Alex to proceed. Tricia stepped into the room and watched Alex move from one end to the other, gathering his belongings; socks, bathrobe, baseball cap and some books.

Alex walked towards the side of the bed, bent down and picked up the jeans he had worn on the day he had seen Tricia going to see Dr Ryan. He pulled off his shorts and slipped on his jeans. He felt the pocket to make sure his black credit card and keys were still there; satisfied, he stood looking on at his uninvited entourage.

Alex looked at Tricia, smiled and spoke.

"I saw you going to Ryan's; I followed you from the chemist."

She didn't reply. Alex looked at Ryan.

"After I left you, I saw her going to see you, and somehow she got back here before me. What business do you have together? How'd you reach here before me, Tricia?"

Dr Ryan shook his head.

"Alex, you're not well. Tricia has never visited my surgery," Dr Ryan replied.

Alex took a deep breath and took a step forward. The orderlies took two steps, and their brows deepened.

"Amanda Brace and Mariah Wray … you've been a nanny for both. One is dead and the other killed her own child and is now locked up. Something's not right with her, Dr Ryan something's not right with either her or Heaven."

Alex walked back towards the bed and picked up Tricia's list of testimonials and pointed at the names.

"I bet you Jane Heckles, another former employer of Tricia's, has also met some form of misfortune … let me Google…"

He heard himself and even he had to admit he sounded like he'd been smoking the good stuff. Dr Ryan shook his head.

"Enough! It's time to go, please don't resist."

Alex stared at Dr Ryan then at Tricia, who kissed Heaven's crown and walked out of the room. Alex paused, knowing his time for debating was up. He exhaled, gathered his things, hung his head in defeat and walked towards Dr Ryan. The help grabbed each arm gently and walked him out of the room. Tricia stood by the nursery entrance patting Heaven's back and watching Alex leave. He looked back over his shoulder and she smiled, so gently, so inoffensively, that he almost smiled back out of habit. But her eyes sang a different song; so focused and baleful it made the hairs all over his body stand to attention.

Dr Ryan stood by the front door, which wide open, light rain making the floor wet inside. Alex slowed besides him.

"I hope Valda knows …" Alex began.

"Don't be absurd; she's the one who set this up. You mustn't worry, Alex, she has paid for the best treatment for you, and you'll be fine in no time, I promise," Dr Ryan replied.

Although he should have known Valda was responsible, it hurt to hear Dr Ryan say it. He had his head dipped as he entered the car. One of the orderlies sat on his left, the other on his right, squeezing him in the middle. The driver turned and looked at him then straight ahead. Dr Ryan stood on the doorstep talking to Tricia. They finished what they were saying and Dr Ryan jogged back to the car and got in the front. He turned around and spoke to Alex.

"I sincerely mean it – you'll be okay."

Alex looked at him and grinned, giving the illusion of compliance. In his head he was plotting to escape and return to this house, to rescue Valda from whomever or whatever Tricia was.

Alex

At 2 pm Valda's office phone rang. Valda wiped her eyes, blew her nose and reached for the phone.

"Valda … I know you said you weren't to be disturbed, but the police are here."

They listened to each other breathe.

"Okay."

Valda began to feel sick.

"Shall I—" Claire began.

"Send them up," Valda cut in.

"Okay."

She hung up, but Valda still held the phone to her ear as if the silence could offer comfort. She placed the handset down, stood and looked out of her grand window overlooking the city. The clouds had now dispersed but it still rained. The droplets running down the window made the city look like a gothic painting from the mental depths of a manic artist.

She went over the possible scenarios that could have transpired between Alex and Dr Ryan's people that could warrant the police having to come see her. *Maybe he killed one, or maybe they killed him ... Oh, Alex, what have I done?*

The clock in her head estimated they would be there in thirty seconds. She could see them leaving the lift at the top of her corridor, spearheaded by Claire. She could see everybody watching from their offices. She could hear them whispering, talking, speculating.

Tears streamed down her face and gathered on regretful lips. She caught her reflection in the window and saw how her face had hollowed out, how her cheekbones protruded either side of her face, her neck so thin within her blazer and long-sleeved jumper that she barely recognises herself. Her reflection was an appalling sight. She looked away, stood behind her desk, wiped both eyes and awaited the knock, which came within seconds.

"Come in, it's open."

The door opened. Claire stood aside and let the two officers walk in ahead of her, signalling to Valda she was going back down. Claire left and the door shut.

They wore long police rain macs, wet in appearance. Valda remained standing, and gestured for them to take a seat at her desk.

"Please," she said, pointing to the seats opposite her.

They both mumbled a thank you and sat. Valda did the same.

"Ms Valda Payne, I'm PC Blake and this is PC Cunningham. Are you the owner of a Bentley Continental GT V8, registration HX59 PLQ?"

Valda's eyes widened: she didn't expect to be asked about her car. Her mind ran to Patrick, and her legs began to shake uncontrollably.

"Yes, that's my car, what's the problem?"

"I'm afraid it's been involved in a collision—"

Valda lurched forward, her hands brought together over her mouth. She looked at PC Cunningham's eyes and although the officer tried to hide it they gave it away and Valda knew he was dead.

"Oh no … Oh God, no! What about Patrick, what about the driver?"

Blake shook his head.

"I'm sorry; he didn't survive."

Valda shot up from her seat and stood looking down at the pair, on the verge of hyperventilating.

"This has to be a mistake. I just left him a few hours ago; he's due to pick me up. He's due to be here for six … Are you sure it's my car? Are you sure it's him?"

PC Blake compressed his lips and looked her directly in the eye.

"Sorry …"

Her mind ran riot, her legs went to jelly and she fell back into her chair. Blake jumped up and grabbed her arms, easing her down. Valda sat, her mouth ajar, eyes wide, shaking her head in disbelief. She stared at the pair of them, from one to the other. PC Cunningham touched his arm and PC Blake spoke up.

"I'm sorry, but we have to go. We'll leave these with you; they're a few counselling numbers if you wish to get help with dealing with this. His body is being taken to Kensal Rise morgue for official identification. We managed to retrieve some items from the car, and they are being held at Queens Park police station for you when you're ready to collect them. The car will be placed in the compound. Once again, we're sorry to have to break this to you. We wish you all the best."

The pair stood up, gave her a routine sympathy look and left. The door closed and Valda began to feel tremendously small, vulnerable and scared. Her world was spinning off its axis, crumbling at the edges – and she knew why.

She closed her eyes and tears squeezed out from where her eyelids met. She thought of every idle conversation they ever had. She thought of every business decision he had inadvertently aided her in making. She thought about every time she had shut him down when they both knew he was right; that uncomfortable silence that would follow that he was so comfortable in. She thought about every time he had picked her up, slightly worse for wear, and she had been delivered home safely knowing her life was safe in his hands, with no newspaper headlines or pictures to worry about. Every secret he carried for her. She thought of how distant they had become and how wrong she had been to let that happen, giving him the impression he played a lesser role in her life than the one he really did. He was like a father to her; a great man who wanted nothing but the best for her – and now he was gone.

Tears ran her face ragged, and her mind's eye conjured him, tall, dark and lean, his smile so comforting.

He is dead, and so am I, she thought.

She walked the office a few times to gather herself as best she could. She buzzed for Claire to call her a cab. She sat waiting and looked at the bracelet and knew she was being punished, but when would the damnation end?

And when the thousand years are ended, Satan will be released from his prison and will come out to deceive the nations that are at the four corners of the earth, Gog and Magog, to gather them for battle; their number is like the sand of the sea. And they marched up over the broad plain of the earth and surrounded the camp of the saints and the beloved city, but fire came down from heaven and consumed them, and the devil who had deceived them was thrown into the lake of fire and sulphur where the beast and the false prophet were, and they will be tormented day and night forever and ever.

Revelation 20:7-10

~

Alex walked through two sets of security doors, spearheaded by Dr Ryan and his henchmen. The place looked more like a hotel than anything else. He expected there to be people screaming and running around, talking to themselves. Instead he passed rooms of people who looked like they had simply had a rough time and needed a break from reality. This place was no run-of-the-mill NHS mental health hospital; this place was for people who had money.

Dr Ryan sat to his left and the manager of the unit sat in front of them, his glasses lens thick, black and stylish. He wore civilian clothes; a blue fitted jumper, his hair parted down the side, his face a little chubby and his moustaches shaped and curled as if he were Phileas Fogg. He leaned across the desk with a Cheshire cat grin. Alex looked down beneath his pile of paperwork and saw the edge of a celeb gossip mag peeking out. In that moment he had summed him up.

"My name is Stuart. Welcome to the Life clinic. If you haven't been told, the Life clinic is for all sorts of people in all sorts of conditions – people in rehab, some recovering from drug-induced psychosis, some from mild breakdowns. Let's face it, we all need a little help with life from time to time. We offer one-to-one counselling and treatment, including CBT, medication, and so on. You won't find better treatment anywhere in the country."

He pushed his spectacles back up the bridge of his nose and smiled. He looked as though he loved the finer things in life, Alex thought. The type of man who saved up all his wages to eat in places like Riku's, kept the receipt and accidently let it fall out of his pocket in front of people he wanted to impress; the types who shopped in Harrods for a pair of socks, but demanded a large bag. He moved with trends, obsessed with celebrities and stars; his ridiculous moustache would be gone as soon as Beckham or some other celebrity cut his. He probably sought work in the Life clinic to get closer to rich and wealthy celebrities, sane or not. He was a victim. He was irritating, but he was perfect for Alex.

Valda had phoned ahead to Queens Park police station, informing them she would be coming to collect the things from the car and instructing them to have them ready. She sat, teary–eyed, for the whole journey; the cabbie kept his eyes on the road after being forewarned by his manager that she was a high-calibre client and he was by no means to make conversation with her, only speak when spoken to. He would have kept quiet anyway; her smell was so strong that if he opened his mouth he would have swallowed the rancid scent and probably been sick. They pulled up at the station and she hopped out, the pavement and air damp from the rain earlier. She walked up the steps and entered through large double doors. An officer recognised her and pulled out a plastic bag from under the counter, tagged at its neck like a bag won from a funfair, containing a goldfish.

There wasn't much there: a hairbrush, an old magazine, a few packets of half-eaten chewing gum, nail varnish, lipstick and a book – a book she didn't recognise at all. She signed for the things and left.

She slung the bag on the back seat of the cab and slid in herself. She spent the rest of the journey in a psychedelic trance, her eyes moist, her lips glued together. The journey home was quick. The cab man turned to tell her the fare, but was beaten to it by a crisp fifty-pound note being brandished in front of him.

"Keep the change," she insisted.

"Thanks".

She opened the door, dragged her plastic bag out and began to walk home two roads away. She looked up and the moon seemed non-existent, the clouds so thick they engulfed the sky, smothering the stars and Luna's rock. The damp smell the day had carried bled into the night. *It will rain again,* she thought.

Alex's room was painted cream with polished dark flooring. Within the room was a long cream leather sofa, a flat-screen television attached to the wall, a fridge fully stocked with the order he had made earlier, and a telephone for twenty-four-hour patient service. Alex lay awake in the most non-typical crazy room he had ever envisaged. He laughed to himself; this is ridiculous, even rich mad folk get treated better than average people. They get called 'eccentric' or people say they're 'going through a rough patch' and get placed in a room like this. He sniggered and his thoughts moved back to where they were before digressing. He thought about tomorrow; thought about escaping and getting home. Then a thought struck him: *Mariah! She said Mariah had been sectioned. Maybe she's here, maybe I can speak with her?*

Valda walked in and closed the door behind her. Tricia stood up from the sofa and looked at her. They both stood in their positions. Valda bent her head and began to sob like a child. Tricia walked around the sofa and threw her arms around her, pulling her close.

"You mustn't cry. He was fine, Dr Ryan made sure of that," Tricia said.

Valda drew a deep breath.
"No, no, no, no … you don't understand…"
Tricia pulled back from her. "Understand what?"
"Patrick was in an accident this afternoon and died."
Tricia gasped and held a hand to her chest. "Oh my …"
Valda began to cry harder. "I-I-I know, I just… just can't believe it."

Tricia drew her closer.
"All of this in one day. No wonder you're so upset, you poor thing."
Tricia stroked her hair gently.

~

Valda came down the stairs from seeing Heaven. Tricia stood at the bottom by the door, slipping on her coat, scarf and hat. Valda stopped on the last step.
"Where're you going?"
Tricia slowed the tying of her scarf and looked up at Valda.
"Home."
The pair paused.
"I-I-I was hoping you could stay. I'll pay you extra."
Tricia stood frozen, her expression a manifestation of her thoughts on the proposal. "You don't have to pay. We're friends; if you need me, I'm here."
Valda smiled.
"I wouldn't have asked, but with Alex gone and Patrick's dead, I just don't know how I'll cope in the night when she wakes."
"You don't need to worry about that; it's sorted. I've left you your shake and some food in the kitchen. Shall we eat?"
Valda winced. "I'm not hungry. I think I'm gonna get to bed; I've got a lot on tomorrow."
Tricia looked at her and smiled. "I know you're tired, but you should at least get something down you."
"Honestly, I'm not up to it, I just want some sleep."

Tricia sighed. "Fair enough."

Valda looked down at the plastic bag containing the things from the car she had brought in. It sat by the front door. She looked at the book inside and thought about getting it to bring upstairs, but everything felt like an effort, even the thought of reading. She decided to uncover its mystery tomorrow. She said goodnight to Tricia, who walked towards the sofa, taking off her coat, then plumped herself down in front of the TV, turning it on.

Valda went to Heaven's room and kissed her forehead and cheek. She moved in response and Valda smiled, yawned then whispered, "This time next year, you'll be all mine."

Valda cried into her pillow until sleep took her to where Alex was. At 5 am, she sat up straight, breathing hard. She rubbed her eyes, raised to her knees and looked out of the window above and behind her. The sky was bright blue. The sun washed her room golden. She normally heard her gardens birds bringing the daylight in, but they didn't sing that morning; not a squeal or squawk, nothing at all. She thought it odd but paid it no mind.

She stood and stretched; her body felt brilliant. No pain or discomfort that she had become accustomed to since having Heaven. She walked around the bed to the wardrobe door and looked into the mirror; even her cheeks seemed rosier and plumper, as if the unbroken sleep had breathed life back into her. She looked more closely at them, and a horrible smell reflected off the mirror, making her sniff into the air, eventually tracking the horrendous odour to herself.

Oh my God, I smell like that?

She grabbed a towel and walked out of her room towards the bathroom. She looked in on Heaven, who was still sleeping. She carried on, washed, dressed and walked downstairs.

Tricia had fallen asleep with the TV on, curled up with a blanket. Valda tiptoed in, making sure not to wake her, and went to the front door to retrieve the bag, but it wasn't there. She looked all about the entrance but could see no sign of it. She looked behind the sofa Tricia lay on.

She moved it, why? Valda thought.

With it too early to call Alex, she had planned on turning off the baby monitor, taking some food upstairs and sitting in with Heaven to see what the book from the car was all about.

Maybe it's in the kitchen.

She no longer crept, but she walked lightly to the kitchen, gently opened the door and went in. Upon entry, her sense of smell was overwhelmed by that same rancid smell she had smelled on herself earlier. She sniffed around and her nose brought her to the blender containing the shake she was meant to have drunk last night. She lifted the lid and was forced back by the stench, she felt like heaving. She held her nose and looked into it and immediately knew she wouldn't be drinking that stuff again. She walked towards the sink, flushed it down the drain, ran hot water into the blender, poured bleach and disinfectant in and left it to stand.

She looked around the island at the rest of the food from last night, covered by pieces of kitchen towel, foil and clingfilm. She went to the bread, lifted the towel off and noticed it didn't smell right. It didn't stink, but it didn't smell like normal bread either. It smelled like thyme mixed with garlic and another smell she couldn't identify; either way, she wasn't keen on eating it. She stood and looked at the rest and in an instant decided she would tell Tricia to stop cooking for her.

The lack of sound from the garden drew her attention. Valda looked out into the garden and noticed the weeds had begun to grow wild around beautiful flowers that had shrivelled. Her evergreens had begun to shed needles. She walked through the conservatory, opened the back door and walked out into the garden barefooted, the grass damp, the beautiful sunlight a mere illusion, her every breath making a puff of vapour in the cool air.

She looked up at the trees and sky like Alex had, that day both she and Tricia had watched him, hinting he was losing his mind. The day she had decided that his silent, bizarre ways were becoming too much and he had to be treated professionally.

No birds, not even a pigeon...

She walked towards the feeding podium and noticed it was still full. She shook her head and walked on, deeper into the garden, where she found more fallen pine needles and bare dry branches. More weeds, some of them with thorns she had never seen before, she watched where she stepped. She stood at the end of her once glorious garden and realised it was dying – everything was dying. She looked up at the sky once more and still there was no birdlife; no life in or above her garden. Something was wrong – something was *really wrong.*

Alex picked up his phone and dialled the front desk, which was manned by a team of six whose job it was to wait hand and foot on their important clients.

"Good morning, Minka speaking, how I may help you?"

Alex sniggered. *Help?*

"Please tell Stuart the moment he arrives I want to see him."

"Ahhh ... Okay, no problem, anything else?"

"Hash browns, eggs, baked beans and a glass of grapefruit juice please."

"Okay, so that's hash browns, eggs, baked beans and a glass of grapefruit juice."

"That's it, thank you," Alex said, ending the call.

On Valda's approach to the kitchen, she looked out beyond her garden and realised the trees in neighbouring gardens were still healthy. She walked back into the kitchen; this time it smelled like a swimming pool and she preferred that. She looked around the kitchen, looking for the bag, but couldn't see it. She looked in the cupboards, drawers and on the stools surrounding the island and on the floor. It just wasn't there.

Alex lounged on his sofa, remote in hand, watching the morning news, but not really concentrating on it. His mind was on other things, thinking about how different his life could have been had he only stayed with his parents or at least in Goa. He began to feel sorry for himself. The selfish part of him told him to get on the first plane heading to Goa and leave Valda and that child to their fate. But his heart wouldn't let him: he loved her too much, and had only realised the true extent of his feelings now they were in serious trouble.

There was a knock on the door. Alex stood and walked towards it. He opened to Minka, a skinny white girl with her hair pulled back into a ponytail. She held his breakfast selection in a plastic tray accompanied by plastic cutlery. Alex accepted the tray with a smile. She smiled back and stood in the doorway. Alex invited her in but she declined.

"Why not?" He asked.

"Rules and regulations."

"Rules and regulations? So, tell me this, how come you're allowed to come to my room by yourself if I pose that much of a threat?"

"You don't. This is A wing."

Alex laughed. "Well, what types of people are on A wing?"

"People who are a little run down; people who are normal but going through a tough time and need to be out of life's circle under supervision in case they go D wing on us," she replied.

"D wing? What type of person is on D wing?"

"The people who are really, really gone. People who have done serious things to themselves or others."

She looked around, then lowered her voice. "Put it this way, if their families didn't have money, they would be in prison or a prison psychiatric ward … Money can make the press, judges and people in power see, yet not see, if you see what I'm saying?"

Alex nodded. *That's where she'll be if she's here,* he thought.

"Yeah … yeah, I get you. Okay, thank you. Please make sure Stuart comes to see me as soon as he arrives."

She nodded and Alex closed the door.

Valda went back upstairs and looked in on Heaven again. She then went to her room, picked up the tablet and sat on the edge of her bed. She touched the screen and it came to life, displaying the website starnow.com. Jane Heckles' name was still in its search bar, waiting for Enter to be pressed so it could reveal her story. She had come upstairs to Google the book in Patrick's bag, but this name intrigued her more. *What had Alex been looking at her for?*

~

Stuart tapped on Alex's door. Alex stood and went to it.

"Hi, Minka said you wanted to see me?"

"Yes, I have to ask you something. Will you come in?"

Stuart paused in deliberation, then moved forward. "I really shouldn't. We have ru—"

"Rules and regulations, I know."

Alex walked ahead and sat on the bed, and Stuart stood awkwardly in the middle of the room, they both paused.

"I'm gonna cut to the chase with this. I'm looking for someone who may be here … an old friend," Alex explained.

Stuart's face went from cautionary to confused, in need of elaboration.

"Her name is Mariah Wray," Alex continued.

Stuart eyes narrowed so slightly that if Alex hadn't been looking for a reaction he would have missed it.

"Wa—"

"Before you answer me, I can make it worth your while."

Alex was never good at negotiations of any sort, but the one thing Valda had taught him was that money is king, and the prospect of gaining vast amounts can make the sturdiest of men buckle in their morals, or forget rules and regulations.

Stuart's eyes moved to the corners of the room; he looked at the door, then back at Alex. He took a seat next to him on the bed so they could talk more intimately.

"What are we talking about here?" Stuart asked.

"I need some time with Mariah, an hour or so, I also need to get out of here today."

Stuart laughed.

"Are you mad? My job would be gone in an instant. Sorry. No ca—"

Alex cut in. "How much is your mortgage?"

"What? My mortgage? Ok, I think this conversation has run its course."

Stuart attempted to stand.

"Hear me out. I have a black credit card. I can move as much as £500,000 around in one day. How much is your mortgage?"

Stuart paused. "What are you suggesting?" he asked.

"I will pay your mortgage off if you can do the two things I require."

Stuart's eyes blinked rapidly, his mind running over the figures, exploring the grand possibilities attached to being mortgage free.

"Wh-wh ...wow. I mean, are you being serious?" his voice melted to a whisper.

"One hundred per cent. I will pay half the amount into your account now, and the rest after the deal is complete."

He got to his feet and nibbled on his bottom lip.

"Okay, okay, okay, let's do it."

"Good man I need you to get me to her and give me as much time as possible."

"Have the day if you want – fuck, have the week," Stuart said with gusto.

Alex smiled.

"After that I want to leave, but I want people to believe I'm still here, for as long as possible," Alex requested.

"That won't be an issue; I'll say you were feeling stressed so I gave you a sedative that knocked you out and no one will disturb you."

"Okay, that sounds like a plan. Get me a phone and I'll get my bank to transfer the amount into your account."

Stuart shot up, almost stumbling in his haste to get to the door.

"Brilliant, that's erm… £100,000. Oh, and some, you said and some."

Alex smiled at him, disgusted at the ease with which the man had given up his 'rules and regulations' for money – an act that plays out all over the world, on every scale, mostly at the expense of life, liberty and justice. You could kill a priest and get away with it if the price was right; *money is king,* Alex thought, *emperor of all men, an enemy of God, an ally to Satan.* He watched how Stuart practically ran out the room and felt filthy at flexing his monetary might. He exhaled, pulling his legs up on to the bed, knowing it was a necessary evil to achieve a greater good.

When Valda hit Enter, starnow.com returned no search results, so she went to Google and searched for her name there. The search returned with several pages for Jane Heckles. Valda hit the first one and a picture came up showing her holding a Grammy award and wearing a beautiful blue satin dress. Her lips full and fleshy, her hair red, cut into a bob, her hourglass figure perfectly detailed by her dress. Valda scrolled down and began to read about her. She was a double Grammy award-winning recording artist who had won Best Female Artist awards on two occasions, in 2006 and 2008, for her albums “Take me away” and “Running”. Beneath that section was an embedded video of the red carpet walk and interview.

Valda watched it then scrolled further down to another picture; it was one of those normally unflattering pictures the paparazzi take while a celeb is entering or leaving a car. A camera flash covered her, bright white, immortalised with the image, but it wasn’t Jane who caught her attention – it was the person on the other side of her waiting to get out. It was Tricia, caught in motion sliding across the seat behind her.

Valda looked at the picture and confusion set in. *If Tricia had been a nanny for her, how come she wasn’t at home looking after her child?* Tricia appeared to have transcended her duties and appeared to be closer to Jane than her job role. Valda thought of her relationship with Patrick. *Would he have been my choice to accompany me to a Grammy awards show? No.* She scrolled down further and came to a story.

Death of a songbird and controversy

On December 28th 2010 Jane Heckles, daughter of the legendary actor Burt Humphrey Heckles, was found dead in her home from unknown causes. Pathologists can only confirm her heart, lungs and other organs had all failed suddenly. Reports from her nanny turned best friend, Tricia, stated that towards the end of her life she had suspected Jane had become addicted to hard drugs, because she displayed bizarre behaviour patterns. She went on to say that during her last days Jane would lock herself in her room for days on end, neglecting her role as mother to her newborn child, Cole. One of the strangest public displays of her sudden eccentricities was when she called a live radio show and told listeners she suspected something was trying to kill her and her child. She said she needed help from a holy man, then began singing some of her greatest songs terribly, and screaming a whole lot of bizarre ramblings before slamming the phone down. Reports say her husband, Ruben Smith of the band The Braxxx, left the family house and their marriage four months before she met her demise, citing irreparable differences. Bizarrely, he refused to look after his son, offering to pay for his upkeep but saying he didn't feel responsible enough to look after him by himself. Cole was eventually adopted by persons unknown, and stands to inherit his mother's estate when he reaches the age of eighteen.

~

Stuart came back from checking his account, a bounce in his step, the biggest smile drawn across his face, unable to contain his happiness at seeing his account in such a healthy state.

Stuart stood in Alex's doorway, rocking from foot to foot and looking from left to right.

"All there?" Alex asked with an arched eyebrow.

"Yep, but you're gonna put the rest in when—"

"We are finished…" Alex completed.

They paused for a second.

"Okay. Okay," Stuart repeated.

Alex stood and left the room with Stuart. They moved through A wing, then B wing, the level of security visibly increasing. The doors got thicker. Glass panes in doors were reinforced with wire, the size of the windows getting smaller. They moved from open doors to shut ones, to ones with digital locks then they reached D wing, which had its own security desk. The receptionists were no longer pretty, young and cute; two huge beefy-looking men and one woman without a visible neck manned the desk.

Stuart told Alex to stand back while he spoke to the receptionists, then came back, and nodded for him to walk with him. A guard left the desk and walked around to the huge door that opened out into D wing's corridor, with rooms on either side.

He unlocked the doors with a code and stood aside to let them pass. Stuart walked through first, followed by Alex, then the receptionist. Once through, he closed the door behind them. Alex passed doors to patients' rooms, their ghostly eyes peering through small windows, following him like an old picture in a haunted house.

He passed rooms where people walked around in circles, their lips moving, talking to whoever they imagined was there. These were the children, fathers, brothers, mothers and sisters of the mega-rich, people who wanted their family's weakest links hidden from the world, out of public view. Alex wondered how close he had got to being in D wing, that maddening feeling he got when Tricia appeared to be in one place but wasn't really; his feelings towards his daughter; his unmentioned and disgraced sympathy for Rosita when he should have felt pure unrefined hatred for her. He knew something was up, and in the back of his head he knew his feelings had a root. *That night in Riku's* he thought, *that night she had told him she was pregnant, there was something they had debated, something he just couldn't remember.* He would ask her.

They slowed on approach to cell 1408. Stuart stopped abruptly. The receptionist walked round from behind them and pulled a bunch of cards attached to a chain from his top. He sifted through them, located the card needed and slotted it into the card slot. He tapped a pass code into the keypad. The light above the door flashed green three times and the huge bars that slotted across the door made a clumsy clunking sound.

The guard looked through the glass then back at Stuart and nodded. He pushed open the door and went in first, then Stuart second. Stuart looked back at Alex and nodded for him to walk in. Alex walked gingerly into the room, which smelled of Savlon antiseptic. The walls white and padded and the floor bouncy, the bed frame was attached to the ground, made of rounded plastic, and a large window let beautiful daylight in.

The window overlooked a lake surrounded by a well-kept garden. Mariah sat in front of the window, wearing an all-white gown. Her hair was cut short and she sat awkwardly in the chair. The receptionist stood in the middle of the room, his hands held out in front of him. Stuart stood beside Alex and whispered, "Good luck; she hardly says anything that makes sense."

Alex looked at him. The sly bastard hadn't mentioned that when they had struck the deal, but Alex was in no position to argue with him about it. Alex whispered back, "I need to be alone with her."

"Alone?" Stuart replied.

"Yes."

Stuart's eyes darted around and he nibbled on his lip again.

"Okay, but we'll stand guard out here, watching. If you try to harm her, Heinz will be forced to restrain you and you won't like it, I promise you that."

The pair eyeballed each other and Alex nodded.

Stuart walked over to Heinz and whispered in his ear; Heinz tilted his head to one side and nodded with whatever Stuart had instructed. They turned and walked towards the cell door. Alex looked back at them as the door shut, then turned towards Mariah.

~

It was 8 am. Valda clicked to a previous tab Alex had explored, Amanda Brace, then scrolled down and read the snapshots of her life and tragic death, burned alive along with her daughter and husband.

Mariah, Amanda and Jane ... Mariah, Amanda and Jane ... Mariah, Amanda and Jane ... and Tricia. Tricia. What the hell is going on?

That instant, a horrible feeling surged through her body, a feeling so powerful, it made her belly feel as though it was full of lead. Her mind cluttered and foggy, she stood up, walked out of her room towards the banister and looked over it down into the living room below.

Tricia still slept. Valda walked into the nursery and went to the cot, her mind goading her to seize Heaven and leave the house. She paused.

This is ridiculous; she heard her inner voice say. *Tricia has been wonderful, nothing but helpful to me – us. They must have been on drugs; you know these types, Valda ... the types you've always shied away from. But Mariah? What about Mariah? What about her? She fucked up, she defaulted on the deal. That had nothing to do with anyone else; let's put the rest down to coincidence, that's all, pure coincidence. Really? Yes, really? Why, what would you suggest? Maybe Tricia has a connection to Lilith, but you can only be certain that, out of the women she has worked for, only Mariah has been to Lilif... Exactly. It's obvious Tricia would have tended to the top celebs – she works for one of the most prestigious nanny services in the country. Stop that nonsense – you know what you have to do, and if you don't, you know there will be penalties. Mariah found out the hard way. But where's the book that was in the car? That book, I think you should find it ...*

Alex knelt in front of Mariah and looked into her eyes, her look so vacant he wondered if she was even alive. Her lips were crusted with worn skin, her face dry, almost dehydrated. She blinked twice slowly, and Alex knew she was there.

"Mariah, I know you can hear me … I need you to help me."

She continued to stare out onto the garden below.

"I have a woman called Tricia in my home. You knew her as well."

Still she stared.

"I know something isn't right with her, and I know you know something."

She blinked again slowly and continued to stare.

Alex exhaled and ran his hands over his cheeks.

"Please, I need to know if I'm right about this."

She continued to stare beyond him. Alex stood, contemplating defeat. He looked at her and remembered how beautiful she once was, tall and imposing like the capital's skyline; destined for everything, her life planned out from birth, but derailed by destiny, a mean twist of hand, sending her on a trajectory no one would have foreseen.

Here she sat, one of the richest women on Earth, a mad child-killer spared jail by her father's purse.

Alex believed he would receive nothing from her. Her mind was probably a maze of madness, and somewhere in the middle of it stood Mariah Wray, unable to find her way back to her promised reality. He looked over at the cell's small window. Stuart glanced in, then went back to talking to Heinz.

He looked down at her, shook his head and began to walk back towards the door. After only two paces, he heard what he could only describe as a low growl and gurgle. Alex slowed to a stop and turned back. Mariah now sat straight up, and turned her head and shoulders as if the rest of her body couldn't move, and stared directly into his eyes, her stare so piercing and haunted it stayed his breath. She parted her cracked, dehydrated lips and two single tears ran down her pale cheeks.

Her mouth quivered but her speech was plain and clear.

"Kill-That-Bitch."

She paused and the pair held their breath. She closed her eyes tightly and more tears escaped. She turned her head back and sat lopsided in the chair again, looking out over the gardens once more. Alex froze, staring at the back of her head, her murderous instruction swirling and swimming among his thoughts. He kept his eyes on her and began to walk backwards until his back touched the cell door. He heard a clink and felt it give way behind him. He stumbled out. Stuart looked at him and held him steady around both shoulders. Heinz went to lock the door and Stuart whispered, “You okay?”

Alex looked him in the eye and replied, “I need to get home.”

~

Valda moved down the stairs, paused half way and noticed Tricia was no longer on the sofa. She panned from left to right, and continued down the stairs. At the bottom she walked to the spare bathroom, then to the kitchen. She wasn’t there either. She walked back out and was about to walk up the stairs to check the spare rooms and main bathroom, when she felt a breeze. She looked back and saw that the front door was ajar. She had begun to walk towards it when Heaven stirred above.

She paused and listened to see if she would wake fully. She counted to ten and when Heaven had made no more noise, Valda went to the doorstep and noticed the driveway gate was open as well.

After no more than a second, Tricia came walking around the gate from the pavement. Valda watched her walking back towards the house. Tricia looked up and saw Valda was there. She smiled and waved. Valda forced a wave, but inside she was frowning, questions still in abundance.

Valda made way for her to come in.

“What you doing up so early?” Tricia asked.

Valda closed the door behind them.

“I’ve been up for a while.”

Tricia took off her shoes by the sofa and placed them just behind it. Valda stared at her. Tricia paused and looked back at Valda. "You okay?"

"I'm fine. Where'd you go?" Valda replied.

"Oh, I went to put the rubbish out. It's Friday, remember? You sure you're okay? You look a little lost."

Valda was about to ask her where the bag at the door had gone, when an inner voice told her not to.

"Friday…" Valda whispered.

Tricia walked over to her and wrapped her arms around her

"You poor thing, the whole Alex and Patrick business must be really hard to deal with. You know I'm here for you if you need me."

Valda hugged her back, buried her head in her shoulder and sniffed. She didn't know why, but she did, and she realised Tricia carried no scent at all – nothing. Tricia released her and held her round the shoulders, her hands so cold.

"Well, at least you'll see Alex today."

Where's Patrick's book, Tricia? In the bin? Why? What happened with Mariah, Amanda and Jane? Coincidence? Or is there something you don't want me to know about you? Valda thought.

Valda smiled.

"Well! I'd better get set for the day. I'm gonna get something to eat. What can I get you?" Tricia said with energy.

"I'm fine."

"Come on, you didn't eat at all last night."

Valda paused in thought. "Okay, I'll have something."

Tricia's face lit up. "Good choice."

Tricia walked towards the kitchen, humming like Valda's father would, which made Valda uncomfortable. She watched her disappear through the doors, heard the beep of the rubbish van, then the beeping recede.

Heaven woke with her usual cry. Valda turned for the stairs, and Tricia popped her head out of the kitchen and watched her walk up. When she entered her nursery Heaven was bawling her little lungs out. *Hungry no doubt.*

She lifted her out and kissed her rosy cheeks, walked over to the wicker chair in the corner and sat with her in her lap. She pulled her top up and her breast fell free, her nipple erect and dripping. She squeezed the nipple in between her fingers and tried to insert it in between Heaven's suckling lips, but as soon as a drop touched her mouth she turned away to reject it and continued to cry. Valda tried again, but she turned away once more. Valda looked down, baffled, then to her left at the door, her attention drawn by the sound of footsteps. Tricia popped her head around the door, a glass of smoothie in one hand and the bag in the other. Valda looked at it hanging from her arm, all Patrick's possessions present. Valda felt a little sense of shame that she had thought Tricia had got rid of it. Tricia walked in, knelt down beside Valda and placed the bag beside the chair. Valda looked down at it. Tricia looked at her.

"What's wrong? She won't feed?" Tricia asked.

"Yeah, I don't know why."

"It's because you haven't drunk any of the smoothies in the last two days. Your milk probably tastes unusual now; babies are very funny creatures."

Heaven began to ease up.

"Just get back on them and she'll come back around to you. For now, I can give her some of the milk you pumped, if you want. I know you're pressed for time," Tricia said.

"What time is it?" Valda asked.

"Nine thirty."

Valda exhaled. "I suppose you're right."

You're always right...

Tricia took Heaven off her lap and she stopped crying and started to gurgle. Tricia left the room with Heaven to get the milk. Valda waited until she heard the kitchen door close, then picked up the glass and bag and went to the bathroom. Instinctively she poured the smoothie down the toilet and flushed. She waited a few seconds to make sure all signs of it had disappeared. She walked out, descended the stairs, grabbed her phone from her bag and called a cab for 10 am to go to the Life clinic to see Alex, then over to the morgue to identify Patrick, as she had agreed.

Stuart flung open A wing's fire exit doors, which led out into an alleyway, where the clinic kept its skips for rubbish. The alleyway led out onto a little country lane which connected to a small road. The small road linked with a main road that led to a dual carriageway into London.

Alex said his goodbyes and made his way down the lane, which had spooky, spindly trees on either side that went on for as far as the eye could see. The road was so small it looked as though it was one-way only. Vapour puffed from his mouth and nose. In the distance he could see two red brake lights – the cab he had requested, parked to one side among the trees.

Alex approached and confirmed with the driver he was there for him. He jumped in, gave him the address and they were off.

Valda met her cab on the corner. She slid in, gave her destination and they moved off. She looked at the title of the book written in gold: *Women of Religious Texts.* She opened the book and felt as if she were opening a passage of time to Patrick's last moments. The thought threatened tears but she resisted. She went to where it looked as though he had been reading – pages 104 and 105 were folded over at the corners. She read both pages, which spoke of Mary Magdalene in the Bible, but found nothing she hadn't come across before. She went to read more pages, but found they skipped several numbers straight to 108 – pages 106 and 107 had been torn out and were missing. She looked out of the car window and one name came to her immediately: *Tricia!*

Alex approached Hammersmith Broadway, bound for home, with no plan of action, his mind ticked over trying to develop one.

Valda's cab approached Hammersmith Broadway, a branch of BBL coming up on her right. She ordered the cab to pull into the next side road to her left. She gathered her things, gave him his fare, walked to the pedestrian crossing and waited to cross over. Alex passed Valda, heading in the other direction in his cab: the pair would have seen each other if their heads hadn't been entrenched in their thoughts.

She crossed over among the crowd of Friday shoppers and walked into her shop. On sight, store workers began rushing around in a panic, like chickens in the presence of a fox. The store manager, Charley, rushed over to her, her face adorned with a prosthetic smile.

"Oh Valda, we didn't expect you in today. I hope everything's okay?"

Valda scanned the shop floor as if she were inspecting it. "Where's your office?"

She pointed towards the end of the store towards some doors that blended into the paintwork.

"Do you have internet access?" Valda asked.

"Yes, of course."

"Okay, I'm going to need that for the next ten minutes or so."

Charley nodded.

"I'm not to be disturbed."

"Got it."

"Good."

Valda walked towards the office, went through the doors, located Charley's office and sat at her PC.

Alex realised he had no cash with him, so he asked the driver to pull up on the high road at a cashpoint machine.

Valda placed the book on the desk and typed its title into Google's search bar.

Women of Religious Texts, pages 106 and 107.

An index page listing popped up. The title of 106 and 107 froze her to the core: Lilith: demon women of the night. She clicked a link and began to read.

The cashpoint made a funny noise and then swallowed his card. The message on screen said to contact his card supplier. He looked at the screen, registering his misfortune. He looked over his shoulder at the two people waiting, then over at the cabbie, who peered back at him.

With no phone, no ID and no other method of payment, Alex was up shits creek without a boat, let alone a paddle. A thin line of sweat crowned his forehead, the cabbie's stare growing ever more irritated.

"Sorry, mate, you gonna use that or not?" said the person next in line.

A modern spin on Lilith is that she is at constant war with God, an ally to Lucifer, and is trying to establish a following on Earth, made up of the wealthy, powerful and those who have influence over others. She offers the person the one thing they want the most: fame, riches, whatever else it may be, and in exchange they submit their children to her teachings for one year. This must all be done of the patron's free will, and the deal consummated by the wearing of a bracelet or piece of jewellery given at the meeting, rendering God virtually powerless to stop it. She uses her previous offspring to watch over the ones coming up; they usually come in the guise of carers or friends, and they gain trust and entry to the homes of those who have entered into a deal with Lilith, to ensure the baby is well cared for and subject to their teachings. Her other agenda to isolate these women from friends and family as their babies suck the life force from their mothers, eventually leading to their death. Lilith's ultimate goal is to destroy all Adam's sons, Eve's daughters and eventually God's earth, in revenge for her bitter demise.

Valda stood up, held her hands to her mouth.

... baby sucks her life force from her, eventually leading to her death ... She uses her previous offspring to watch over the ones coming up; they usually come in the guise of carers or friends; they gain trust and entry to homes ... their agenda to isolate the women from friends and family.

Oh God, what have I done? What am I involved in? Patrick was coming to me with this and they killed him; they got into Alex's head and made him mad ... Oh God, what have I done? What am I doing? The devil's work? No, never, I won't ... I won't do it ...

She shook the bracelet down out of her sleeve, dug her fingers under it and popped it off her wrist, the pieces spilling all over the desk like shattered glass.

She felt an unspeakable weight lift from her. She shovelled the pieces into her hand and placed them into her pocket.

Now what? What now?

Alex leaned into the passenger window, looking in on the cab driver.

"My card has just been eaten by the cashpoint," Alex explained.

"Yeah, so how you gonna pay me, mate?"

"You're not gonna believe me, but I'm extremely wealthy. My partner is Valda Payne. If you get me home, I can pay triple."

Valda's mobile rang.

Claire.

She answered it.

"Is everything okay?" Claire asked.

"Yes, why?"

"We're getting some pretty frantic calls from Hammersmith store; they're worried."

Valda laughed. If only these people knew what she was actually going through, they wouldn't be so worried about a store visit.

"They have nothing to worry about. I'm, not here for that. Anyway, I need a cab."

"Okay, where to?" Claire questioned.

"Just send it. I'll tell them when they get here."

The cab driver looked at Alex's creased clothes, his unshaved face and concluded he had wasted enough time on him.

"Yeah, mate, and I'm the prince of Persia. Cut the shit – guys like you make me sick. Now fuck off."

He pulled up the window, forcing Alex to move his head back. The cab drove away; leaving Alex stranded miles from home. He looked over his shoulder at the cashpoint queue and the people looked back with raised eyebrows and judgemental, condemning stares.

Valda prowled Charley's office, pacing up and down like a frustrated jaguar, trying to decide on her next course of action, which was near impossible; there was no handbook, blueprint or monetary solution to this.

All previous test cases – Amanda, Jane, Mariah and God knows how many others – had ended tragically. *How do you beat an angel? Fallen or not, how do you fight a force older than the sun, stars and moon?* That day Lilif had come to her room and remonstrated with that magnificent light, so bright it was hot, that had been a force of God – she was sure of that, a force of greater measure. Its only handicap was Valda, who had forsaken the light's protection by succumbing, of her own free will, to Lilif's darkness. *Those horrible visions and dreams were more like threats, but still I had free will. I made a mistake, let my desire for what I couldn't have swallow my faith and, once in, the fear kept me from repenting ... But still the light came; it wasn't too late, or was it? Is it?*

Alex had covered a mile, with several more still to go. *What on earth will I do when I get there?* He questioned himself.

There was a knock on the office door. Valda opened it, and Charley was standing there.

"There's a cab out here for you," Charley said.

"Thanks, tell him I'll be out in two."

Charley went to deliver her message. Valda gathered her things, cleared the search history and shut the PC down. In the reflective blackness of the blank screen, her face stretched and for no apparent reason her skin was suddenly covered in goosebumps and she felt she wasn't alone. She spun round quickly: no one was there. *The games have begun,* she thought.

She walked through the shop floor. Charley was standing at the entrance, meeting and greeting customers, as if she did it every day. Her computer's browser history and drawers full to the brim with celeb magazines said otherwise, but Valda wasn't there for that. Maybe if she survived the day she would address it but right now she has other whales to fry.

"Bye."

"Bye."

Valda walked out onto the road. She got into the Mercedes, sliding across the back seat. She met the driver's eyes in the mirror.

"Where to, love?"

"The Life clinic."

He frowned. "That's funny; I just came from there."

They set off.

"That's nice …" Valda replied.

"Yeah, a shabby-looking chap. Didn't want to pay; claimed to be the husband of Valda Payne, owns that shop you just come out of."

Valda blinked, looking at the back of his fat neck, his words becoming indistinct. Her heart fluttered and her breathing became arduous.

"I tell you what, you get all sorts nowadays..." the cab man continued.

They passed a road sign stating that a dual carriageway was coming up.

"Where did he say he was headed?" Valda asked.

They slowed to a red light and the driver tapped the brakes. He looked up into the rear-view mirror, his frown deepening further.

"What's it to you?" he asked.

"I'm just interested."

He paused, looked at the traffic light, then back at Valda via the mirror.

"Well, if you must know, he said he was going home."

They both fell silent.

"Okay, change of plan, I need to get to Maida Vale."

"Maida Vale … Okay, but why the change of heart?"

"I forgot something for the person I'm visiting."

"There's some roadworks down there, so it might take a bit longer than usual, but it's your money, I just do the driving. Hold on … you have got the money to pay me, don't ya?"

Valda sniggered. "More than enough."

Valda smiled with annoyance and felt a flicker of bitch returning to her; a futile attempt to hold on to a life where such petty things mattered.

One is an unfortunate accident, but three lives ruined is an act of war. I will not give Lilith my baby, she thought as they moved towards home.

She took the pieces of bracelet from her pocket and threw them out of her window. Within seconds the sun grew brighter; so bright the cab man was forced to pull down his visor, squinting. She looked up to the heavens and knew the sun shone for her, and she wasn't alone.

The Descent

Alex slowed as he reached the gates of his house. He went to the keypad and typed in the entry code; the gates opened and he walked in. He closed the gate and walked softly across the gravel driveway. He looked up at the evergreens that once stood so timeless and regal, but were now sick and defeated, their needles piled around their bases. He looked beyond them and was reminded why Valda had ordered them to be planted. Across the road, looking over into their front garden was St Thomas's Church of Maida Vale, complete with a crucifix on top, huge and imposing. Within the church were windows that, if you looked out of them, you could see right over into Valda's driveway. She had claimed that privacy was the reason for lining the driveway with prehistoric giant trees, which was mostly the truth, but a part of Alex felt it was her way of blocking out the crucifix, a representation of judgement.

When he thought about things like that, it really hit home how wretched Valda could be, and part of him felt powerless against whatever piece of karma was coming her way.

They sat in roadwork traffic, with only a few cars dribbling at a time through the temporary lights.

"Told ya it was heavy, love, every bleeding weekend they're digging up some part of Westminster, causing 'avoc," the driver commented.

She looked out of the window and wished Patrick was there; a man comfortable in both silence and conversation.

He would have helped, he would have known what to do. God knows I don't, God knows I really, really don't. Her mind ran to Alex and she hoped he was still alive.

The traffic moved on a few cars, then stopped again, and the cab man's chatter continued.

Alex passed Tricia's car parked to his far right. *She's here,* he thought, and felt cold run around his system. At that instant it became apparent that within this house was a person or a thing that had been sent there to kill him and Valda. Alex wondered if Tricia acted on her own accord, or was part of a greater network of malevolent creatures. *How come no one connected the dots? How come no one saw the unifying thread that ran through the demise of these very public, mega-famous people, Mariah, Jane and Amanda?* He thought.

If he had worked out what had happened, why hadn't the police or a member of the public done the same? *How could no one have seen that Tricia was present in all cases, always with something to say; rising from a lowly nanny to best friend within months. She must be well connected, well backed up.* The thought injected fear into him, a horrible feeling of being alone against a force much bigger than he and Valda and her bank balance; two novices against an establishment of pros. *But what did she stand to gain from it all?* To this question he had no answer.

Alex stood on the front step, softly slotted his key in the door, turned it and pushed it open.

Valda was on the move now: ten minutes until home.

Alex walked in and pushed the door shut quietly behind him. Inside no longer felt like home, more like a sinister house of evil, a place where stairs creaked with no one there, doors slammed by themselves and possessed women walked down the stairs on all fours, their backs bent, their eyes as black as coal, their teeth serrated and razor-sharp. A place children were told by their parents never to go near, a place where if you entered you may never come out – yet here he was, by himself, brought there by true love, a love he was willing to die for.

The cab drove down the Edgware Road and was met by more traffic. At one point Valda almost paid him, wanting to get out and run the rest of the way. Anxiety was eating her up, her fear for Alex so big inside her that she felt like crying, crying until she fell asleep, never to waken.

Alex panned the lower floor, then looked up in haste, having felt like he was being watched. *No one there.* He stepped forward, his every breath felt and heard in his head. He walked towards the sofa and stood by the table in front of the TV besides the chipped-faced Olympian. He stared at the front door. In its window's misted glass reflection, he could see a person standing above, on the balcony that connected the two staircases. If he could see them in the window's reflection, they could certainly see him. He almost held his breath, thinking about his next move, then she spoke.

"Why don't you come up, Alex?"

No, he thought. *No, I won't …*

He held himself in silence.

He heard her sigh then heard her move to the stairs. Alex frantically looked about the living room, one step, two steps, three steps, four … six steps left. He moved quickly towards the kitchen and through the doors. The smell he met was nothing short of cloying. It halted his movement, his eyes watering and his nose on the verge of sneezing. He clambered forward, one hand holding his nose, and went to the cutlery drawer for a knife but found nothing, not even a teaspoon. He slammed it shut with so much panicked force that it bounced right back out and stayed there.

He looked over at the glass of the kitchen door, expecting to see her, but didn't. To his right, in his peripheral vision, he saw someone standing in the conservatory behind the doors frosted glass. He looked at it and it looked at him. Alex stood frozen until his attention was drawn back to the kitchen door. A figure stood there as well. Then he looked back at the conservatory door – but the person was gone.

Suddenly he started to feel as if he didn't trust himself any more; the same feeling he had when he swore he saw Tricia at Dr Ryan's.

The figure stood behind the kitchen door and knocked on it with its knuckle.

He felt himself drifting out of himself; his stomach felt loose. He leaned off the sink and walked towards the conservatory door, needing to get out of the kitchen. He went to open the door but it was locked, and the smell of whatever had been prepared in the kitchen came again, hitting him like a tsunami. His belly gave up its contents, bringing him to one knee, violently projectile vomiting everywhere. His mind was unable to comprehend the pain his stomach and throat were feeling.

He stood and staggered along the work island, which was adorned with plates of exquisite food, cakes, roasted meats, baskets of bread, steaming rice, and salad in a bowl with croutons.

He swung his hand across the table, sweeping the food off. The plates smashed on the floor, and the bowls bounced off the cabinets and units along the sides of the kitchen. He made it to the edge of the island then threw up again but nothing came; his belly was empty. His head began to swoon, his eyes seeing double. He pushed himself to reach the kitchen door, leaned against it and fell right through, his legs in the kitchen, his torso in the living room.

Tricia was sitting on the sofa knitting, her beautiful curly hair in a ponytail. On her face was a massive smile. He looked up at her and she down at him.

"I hope you're going to clean that mess up, Alex? I went to so much trouble preparing it."

He wanted to tell her to go fuck herself, but everything faded away to black before the "Go" had made it up his throat.

~

"And I say to her, if she's got a problem with washing ma clothes on Tuesday then I want a divorce," the cab man blabbered.

"Just here please."

The cab man braked suddenly and looked to his right at her house.

"Jesus! Is this your house?"

He turned in his seat to face her, and was met by a fistful of orange notes. His eyes widened; a smile brought to his face.

"You sure?" he said.

"Yes."

"Well … if you insist."

He suppressed his childlike excitement and forced himself to be gentle in taking the notes from her hand.

"Thanks, love."

He turned back to face the front, licked his pudgy thumbs and commenced to count the crisp notes. He hadn't noticed Valda get out, close the door and go through the gates into her driveway.

Valda walked straight to the door with no plan in mind, but the sense of surprise on her side. She pushed the key in the door and walked in as if everything was normal. Tricia looked over from the medium sofa, the TV on. She placed a single finger over her lips for Valda to be quiet, and pointed at the long sofa. Valda closed the door and walked slowly towards her. She walked to the long sofa and looked over at Alex lying on it, a can of beer in his hand, his clothes rough and his face no better.

Valda walked around and went to sit next to Tricia. Tricia placed her knitting on her lap and spoke.

"He came in like a raging bull, ranting and raving, with a bag of beers. I've called Dr Ryan already and he said he's on his way," she whispered.

Valda looked to Alex for signs of life, looking for his chest to expand and deflate – anything that indicated God's breath still lived within him.

"He smashed up the kitchen and everything. All the food we were going to have tonight – ruined! Valda … V!"

Valda snapped out of her trancelike state and looked at her.

"Yeah?" Valda replied.

"Are you listening?"

Valda looked her dead in the eye.

"Yeah, just a bit shocked he's here. How'd he get out?" Valda asked.

"Well, that's what I would like to know. Aren't these places meant to have top security?"

"Obviously not," Valda replied.

Come on, show me something Alex, show me you're still here, baby ...

Tricia picked up her knitting and began to knit again quickly, the needles clicking; Valda stared at Alex, still hoping. When she looked back at Tricia, Tricia was staring at her wrist, the wrist that had once worn the bracelet. She knitted faster, harder, harder, faster, her eyes so intensely fixed upon Valda she could physically feel her gaze: she knitted even harder, faster, knitting at a speed Valda had not known was possible.

Valda stood up and Tricia stopped suddenly, as if her movement had broken her concentration. She stared at Valda and began knitting once again, but at a normal speed.

Valda walked around the sofa towards the stairs.

"Just going to check on Heaven."

"Please don't; I've just put her down."

Valda paused on the first step and looked across at Tricia who continued to knit, her back to Valda.

"Pardon?" Valda responded.

"I said, don't disturb her. I've just got her off to sleep," she said, annoyed.

"Excuse me … I think you'll find I'm her mother."

Tricia stopped knitting and turned to face Valda.

"Are you? Are you really her mother, Valda?" she said through a wicked smile.

Valda's stomach did somersaults and cartwheels, and her legs nearly gave way, but she stood firm.

They stared each other out; Tricia shook her head in disgust. Valda prayed she didn't stand and walk towards her; she didn't know what she would do. She was in the hands of fear now; fear and whatever Tricia was.

"You creatures are so predictable. You get what you want, but are not prepared to fulfil your end of the bargain. Why he made you like that I'll never know."

"What are you talking about?" Valda replied.

Tricia sighed. "Stop it … just stop it, Valda … You have forsaken your end of the deal, just like the rest of them. The funny thing is, we never have this problem with poor people; they seem to get it, but you rich ones are magnificently defiant."

Where are you, Dr Ryan? Valda thought.

The pair paused once more. Valda began to sweat as if she was already in hell. The doorbell rang. Tricia stared at Valda, frozen to the spot as if she was Valda Wright, stuck on the naughty step.

"Guess I'll get it then," Tricia said mockingly.

Tricia got up: she was in complete control here and Valda knew it. She went to the security screen, buzzed the gate open and left the door ajar, then went back to sit opposite where she had been sitting previously. She now faced Valda, sitting like Abraham Lincoln, her hands at rest on the chair's arms.

Valda looked at the door. A car pulled up on the gravel and the engine switched off. She could hear a single pair of footsteps. Dr Ryan walked through the door, slowly, with caution, and closed it behind him. He paused, looked up at Valda, then over at Tricia. Tricia smiled, then spoke.

"Your salvation, Valda." She laughed and Dr Ryan smiled.

Valda's body began to shake and she suddenly became incontinent; pee ran down her legs and into her shoes. Dr Ryan looked her up and down.

"Oh dear, one is making a mess, darling."

He looked back at Tricia and the pair laughed. Tricia stopped abruptly and cleared her throat.

"Valda, meet Dr Ryan, my brother."

Dr Ryan took a bow. "We are two of many siblings and many of more, doctors, actors, lawyers, detectives, singers, celebrities, black, white, Asian; you walk among us every day, children of darkness, slaves to our lord and saviour Satan."

Dr Ryan walked towards Valda, and she retreated a step.

"There's no use running; you're in too deep, Valda, far behind enemy lines, with no hope of rescue. You came of your own free will. He can't help you now," Dr Ryan said.

"That's right – call for him as much as you want. He knows the rules: you came to us and now you've fucked up. You are meant to wear that bracelet for a year, as agreed…" Tricia added.

Dr Ryan shook his head.

"We prefer when the parents are on board to fulfil the process; the children usually turn out better for some reason, like me and my sister here, but if not – it's no big deal, you'll pay the price."

Dr Ryan took paper and a pen from the inside of his jacket pocket and walked to the table in the middle of the living room. He placed it down, looked over at Valda and waved her over. She didn't move towards him; instead she moved up another step. The room paused. Tricia exhaled, dug beneath the sofa she was sitting on, pulled out a chopping knife, and walked over to Alex. She placed the knife behind his ear and pulled it up and down, semi-severing it from his head. He let out a muffled moan of pain.

Valda ran down the steps, her hand held out for mercy, tears erupting from her eyes.

"No, please don't! I'll do anything!" she screamed.

Tricia pointed the knife at her to halt her movement towards Alex, blood dripping from it. Alex's ear was drooping, attached by nothing but raw flesh and tendons.

"Shut the fuck up! I told you Heaven's having a rest," Tricia screamed.

Tricia's brow dipped and her teeth ground together.

"Now sit the fuck down, bitch."

Valda sat on the last unoccupied sofa. The sound of Alex in pain brought further tears; she wished she had never picked that card up, had never made that call to Lilif. She wished she had been satisfied with what she had had.

Dr Ryan pushed the table over to her, the piece of paper in front of her, the pen besides it. She read what was written:

I, Valda Payne, of sound mind, pledge that in the unfortunate event of my death, all my worldly possessions will be left solely to my daughter Heaven Payne, to be used by her carers when she is a child, and to revert exclusively to her once she reaches eighteen.

Signed______ Date____ Co Signed___ __ Date____

Valda signed. As she was about to date it, Dr Ryan stopped her.

"Make it Heaven's birth date."

She dated it and he snatched it from her.

"I'll do the rest."

Tricia smiled, and then Valda felt a sharp pain, from the left of her neck, right through her flesh to her voice box. She shot up and grabbed at the area the pain radiated from, removing a syringe, the plunger pushed to the hilt. She stumbled back, her vision becoming so fluffy and hazed she couldn't even find her feet. Like a newborn deer, she fell back into the chip-faced Olympian, and looked up at him. He blurred to white and she went to black. She could hear the sound of movement around her and could feel that she was being dragged this way and that by her arms. Sound seemed to mute, then came the sound of Heaven crying, Valda cried as well, in that darkened place, her mind without vision. She cried in her body, which was now her immobile tomb.

~

Suddenly there was a smell of burning and an immense feeling of heat washed over her body. She could hear the sound of cracking and popping material and glass all round her. At first she thought she was in hell – a horrible place where she was blind but could feel every excruciating thing being done to her for an eternity – but she wasn't. She could still feel the feet of the Olympian she had fallen beside; his toes dug into her back, which brought her back to reality. The room was beginning to fill with smoke. With no control over her limbs, she would surely die there, roasted alive. She prayed for God to take her now, to make it quick for both her and Alex.

Suddenly she felt something being pushed under her – an arm being pushed under her back, maybe? It heaved her up, and dragged her over different surfaces, and then the air became cool and cold. She could feel rain, sweet earthly rain. She could feel the gravel beneath her back, the pinpricks of each individual stone. Her face was wet. She heard a sudden sound of feet shuffling through the gravel besides her. She thought she could hear Alex murmuring. She screamed within her head: they were both out of the house, but would they ever get out of themselves?

Salvation

Valda felt a cool glass pressed against her dry lips. She slurped from it, eager to get as much as she could. She brought her hand up and held the hand that held the glass, pulling it in closer, her other arm coming up to aid it.

"Valda, can you open your eyes?" she was asked.

She thought about the request and pulled her lids apart. The light was so offensive that she closed them quickly and started again, opening them more gradually, letting smaller amounts of light in, wider and wider until they were fully open.

With her vision blurry, but growing better by the second, she looked about her surroundings. She was propped up in a bed, the room lit by what looked like a million candles. A man sat on the edge of her bed, a plump black man: he wore what looked like a monk's robe, his head balding in the middle, and with tufts of afro hair surrounding it.

She knew this man: he was Rudolph West, a famous black actor from the early 90s; one of the only black British actors of that era to make it big in Hollywood.

"Rudolph West? Aren't you d—" Valda asked.

"Dead! Hung myself apparently …"

"But …"

"They will say the same about you, Valda, and it's best that way. Trust me, I got what I wanted but not what I deserved."

Valda leaned forward, pain radiating up her back, and she let out a groan. Rudolph leaned over and eased her back to the pillows behind her. She looked around and the room looked old, with everything dark, aged, unpolished. There were wooden walls, like the pews in a church, but no shelves or light fixtures, and no windows.

"Where's Alex?"

Rudolph swallowed and shook his head.

"Sorry, they couldn't save him."

She brought her hands to her face and shook her head, tears gathering in her palms, more rolling down her cheeks.

"Where is he?"

"They left him there …"

She began to sob.

"I have nothing left. My life … My life is finished; you should have let me die."

"We can't afford to do that; we need as many people as we can get … People who have been touched by her, people who understand."

"Who is this we?"

"We are the LRAE, the Lord's Resistance Army on Earth. There is a war going on, Valda, a powerful war that we are unfortunately losing and which will soon end … I know how this may sound, but given what you have been through I know you'll comprehend."

Valda paused and tuned in.

"Since the dawn of time, the world has been run with balance: man and woman, day and night, fire and water, life and death, the way God intended it … but where there is good, there must equally be evil to balance the scale. This is to be expected, but there are entities that seek to destroy that balance, seek to plunge the world as we know it into darkness – disgruntled fallen angels, agents of the devil and Lilith. Do you follow?"

Valda nodded.

"They control almost everything. Their influence is vast – beyond your comprehension. They want people in positions of power to turn the world against God, but we must not let this happen, we can't lose or all will be lost … Anyway, I think this is all a little too heavy for you right now and enough for today. We'll get into everything at a later stage. Get more rest; you can meet everyone tomorrow. Just realise you are lucky we got to you in time."

Rudolph stood up from the bed and she saw where the rope had burned into his neck; a curling scar twisted around it. His head sat at an awkward angle from where it had been broken and not set straight.

"Wait … Will I ...Will I see my baby again?"

Rudolph shook his head.

"She belongs to them; she always has. You were just a host, a wealthy host, and your daughter was a key to that wealth and influence. She will grow, no doubt, to be one of the most powerful women on Earth, envied by all, her wicked deeds encouraged by her adopted mother and father, children of Lilith. She will be emulated by young women all over the world; more youthful souls will be lost to the other side … Look, you've got me started again. Get some rest Valda, we'll cover everything tomorrow, I promise. Get some sleep. You'll love it: in this place they can't infiltrate your dreams; this is holy ground. Good night."

Valda watched him limp out of the door; he closed it behind him. The candles reacted to it, curling every which way in unison. She raised one leg and the other. Her muscles felt filled with lactic acid. She repeated the movements over and over again until her legs felt normal. She leaned forward and pulled herself up and down, down and up, relieving her discomfort.

She turned around and placed her feet down onto the cold concrete floor, stood, wobbled and gripped the room's walls, pulling herself along until she reached the door. She opened it and eased herself out into a dark hallway. A cold breeze rolled through it; little lanterns lit room doors below them. She eased her way forward, towards the other end of the corridor. A large door stood at the top, no more than five steps from the end.

She walked to the steps and heard muffled voices talking on the other side. She placed her ear against the door but still couldn't hear what they were saying, so she cracked the door open and peeked but couldn't see a thing; a curtain hung down that rippled in the breeze. She parted the curtain. Beyond it she observed a large hall with rows upon rows of seats as far as the eye could see. There were at least five hundred people, of all nationalities and religious denominations. She saw people in hijabs, turbans, kippahs. They were all sitting facing one direction, looking at a woman standing at the far end of the hall, with several religious symbols placed behind her. Large candles burned in various spots, giving the hall an ancient, eerie look.

The woman's voice bellowed, firm and commanding, echoing throughout the hall and bouncing off the walls.

"So they have control of more money, with the capture of Heaven. We must do better, or all will be lost. This is a battle for hearts and minds – if we have to kill, we know we fight on the right side. Be afraid, let it spur you on in all your missions. We have had conquests, war, famine, and now we are in the last phase, awaiting death … the horsemen are here, and time is running out: we have less than twenty years. We must now move out of the shadows and into open warfare. As we are ready, so are our brothers and sisters all over the world."

Valda had heard enough and came away from the door, back down the steps, and walked along the corridor in tears, back to her room. She lay on the bed and let sleep take her away, back to life before she had made the mistake. Back to before, when she, along with most other people, believed they knew it all; before, when things just happened and God was a mere story, a mythological entity, and religion a means of controlling the masses; before, when money was king and she was its queen; before, when her life was an echo of a cruel upbringing. Her mind went back to the day of treats, her mother's maddening smile and the death of the devil, back to all three of her loves, Patrick, Alex and Heaven…Back to Heaven, back to Heaven, back to Heaven, back to Heaven …

The coming of the lawless one is by the activity of Satan with all power and false signs and wonders, and with all wicked deception for those who are perishing, because they refused to love the truth and so be saved.
(Thessalonians 2:9-1)

For you yourselves are fully aware that the day of the Lord will come like a thief in the night. While people are saying, "There is peace and security," then sudden destruction will come upon them as labour pains come upon a pregnant woman, and they will not escape.
(Thessalonians 5:2-3)

The End

Thank you for reading my book.
If you enjoyed it, please take a moment to leave a review at your favourite on-line retailer.

Visit my website: www.rpfalconer.com

Made in the USA
Charleston, SC
01 July 2014